COLLEGE DAZE AT PUNXIE

AN ADULT LOOK INTO THE HUMOROUS ASPECTS OF HIGHER EDUCATION

SEMINARY HALL 1866

by   BERNARD ADAMS, Ph.D.

ALLEGHENY PRESS   ELGIN PA 16413

ISBN 0910042780

Correspondence cncerning this work should be addressed to Allegheny Press   Elgin PA 16413

The words Punxsutawney State College, Punxie State and variations of these are copyrighted. Coming soon T-shirts and Sweatshirts. Write for details.

1. WELCOME TO PUNXIE

"As Provost of this institution I would like to welcome you all to Punxsutawney State College. You should all be proud to be a new member of the faculty of Punxsutawney State College. The competition for the positions you now hold, at least temporarily, was fierce and the fact that you landed the position is a credit to your experiences and your portfolio."

It was Provost Dr. Lawrence Simmons speaking to the new members of the faculty and in the presence of their mentors. Although Simmons was billed as the Provost he was actually the "acting" provost since the position was not solidified and the college was presently holding a world-wide search to fill this position. The Provost was the number two man at the college. Mentors were old members of the faculty, those who had been there at least a year. The mentors were to keep the new members informed of protocol and other facets of college life.

Introductory remarks continued. The history of Punxsutawney was reviewed. It started as a seminary for Methodist ministers in 1857. Indians lived on the grounds. An elk was killed on the very spot where they were now assembled. The seminary advanced to a two-year teacher's college. There was much time given to the curriculum of the two-year teacher's college.

The teacher's college was purchased by the State of Pennsylvania and became a four year institution, Punxsutawney State Teacher's College. Today it is known as Punxsutawney State College since it granted a liberal arts degree as well as teaching certification. Punxsutawney takes its place along with the 14 other great institutions in the State System of Higher Education. It's central location makes it an ideal setting for its mission which is to educate the children of Pennsylvania.

Punxsutawney was still relegated to state college status while the other 14 institutions had advanced to university status, even though some of them were no better than Punxsutawney.

The first of the state owned institutions to get university status was Indiana located in the town about forty miles south of Punxsutawney. The faculty members at Indiana considered themselves and their institution to be a cut above the other universities in the system.

The Provost went on. "There is a tendency for faculty members to call our renowned institution by its slang name, Punxie State. I can assure you at this time that the president of this institution frowns on such usage and we don't want to see any memos with this shortened form of recognition." As he spoke he frowned when he mentioned the forbidden shortened name.

It seemed like an eternity. The Provost went on and on, introducing various people. There were three deans, one for Humanities, another for Science and Mathematics and another for Education. Each gave a five minute description of their areas within the framework of the college. According to the Provost, having three different schools and three deans should qualify Punxsutawney for university status but the wheels of legislation turn slowly.

Perhaps this was valuable information but Jim Tailor had heard it all before in one form or another. He had been a high school teacher for six years and had landed the history job at Punxie since he was working on a doctorate at Penn State and his advisor had some influence on the department of social studies at Punxie. When Harold Gregory, the department chairman, called Penn State for a quick replacement they were immediately put in contact with Jim.

Jim found it hard to concentrate on what was being said. His mind wandered around the room to see how others were dressed. He didn't care much for formal clothes but everyone seemed to be in a dark suit with a white shirt and a red tie. His tie was blue and this he thought, might label him as a non-conformist. This was important information for his future but somehow he just couldn't get his mind to settle on what was

4

being said.

Finally. "We will be taking a twenty minute break. I hope each new faculty member will meet with his or her mentor during this break and you will get to know each other. The mentors will at least show you where the coffee and donuts are hidden."There was a slight murmur of polite laughter scattered among the fifty or so people in assembly.

Jim's legs were getting numb from sitting. He had been there for two and a half hours. He rose and flexed his leg muscles then walked out into the hallway. A clean looking young man walked up to him. "Hey, Jim Tay-lor. I'm Jerry Swartz, your mentor. I'm here to officially welcome you to old Punxie State and the Department of Social Studies."

Jim shook his extended hand. With the other he pointed to his name tag. "The name is spelled T-A-I-L-O-R and pronounced Ty-ler, like the Tai in Taiwan."

"Sorry Jim, but it looks like Tay-lor to me and probably to everyone else. It is spelled like the person who adjusts clothing you know."

"Yeah, I know, but Tyler is the way the old man pronounced it and I don't want him to be turning over in his grave."

"Well, I'll remember that and from now on you're Tyler in my book. Let's get some coffee. We're going to need it since we're in for another two or three hours. Why can't the provost just be content to pass out the information on paper. Why does he have to read it to us?"

"Beats me."

Several people introduced themselves to Jim and commented on his pronunciation of his last name. Before the break was over Jim figured he might as well be called Taylor but it was a source of irritation.

Since every new member filled out his own name tag there was some interesting variations. One man just had KREBS written on his. Another, an obvious trouble maker, had a rough

5

outline of the map of Pennsylvania on his with the words "Kiss Me" in the center. Some were written in longhand and were illegible. Jim's however, was written in bold block letters and easily read.

The crowd started shuffling back into the small auditorium. Jim was nudged along toward the assembly. He still had a half cup of coffee and half a donut as he approached the doorway. On the right was a crudely made sign NO FOOD ALLOWED IN THE AUDITORIUM. Jim wolfed down the donut and chugged the coffee and deposited the plastic cup and napkin into a container placed by the door for that purpose. There was a smattering of cups on the floor where depositors had missed the container. Coffee dripped out of some of them.

Back in the conference room, schedules were handed out as well as office assignments to those who arrived late and Jim was one of them. He had been notified of his appointment only three days earlier. He had to notify his high school principal that he was leaving but this posed no hardship since the principal's wife had teaching certification in history. This was her chance for full employment. Usually, if the history job was open in high school it went to some football or basketball coach. The school usually wanted the coach and most of them had social studies or phys-ed degrees. Later, Jim would remark that college students were ill-prepared in social studies since most of them were taught by jocks who had no interest in teaching.

The Provost turned part of the introductions over to the head librarian who related the procedures for library service. The head librarian was a woman who looked like a caricature of a librarian. Her graying hair was pulled back and held with some sort of red ribbon. She wore horn rimmed glasses and a dark blue business suit.

The librarian went into great detail of library policy toward professors. She encouraged all the new faculty to get identification cards as soon as possible and present these to the library for incorporation into the computer files. She told those assembled the location of the library as well as the hours of operation. She went into detail on how the students were ushered out at midnight but faculty members could stay on into the morning if they wished. Books could be borrowed from libraries all over the country so there was no longer any need for Punxsutawney to have every book ever printed. These were not vital items at this time but she was asked to speak and she had to say something.

The campus police chief explained parking regulations. Everyone had a generic Punxsutawney State College sticker. There were three parking lots on campus. When winter came they were only to park in the lot by Mahoning Creek. Vehicles could be moved to the other lots once they were cleared of snow. "For those of you new to this area, we had 126 inches of snow last winter."

The chief assured the new faculty that if they didn't obey the parking regulations they would be ticketed and charged a five dollar fee. If the fine went unpaid for a week the problem would be turned over to the local magistrate and this would cost the violator thirty five dollars.

The chief custodian explained locked buildings and the need for this. The librarian asked for the floor again and emphasized the fact that their phone numbers were in the student handbook recently given to each new faculty member. The chief custodian asked for faculty cooperation in keeping buildings clean and lights turned off in rooms not in use. Each room had an evacuation route posted and the faculty member using a room should become familiar with that evacuation route. "Last semester, we got a lot of bomb scare calls and the law requires us to evacuate the building. Of course we could choose to ignore these calls since they are obviously fake. But, there's always that one time when the call might be genuine."

When the Provost returned to the podium he asked an aide to hand out yet another sheet. The hand-out was handled gingerly by the Provost. "It was" he said " the most important paper you will ever receive at Punxsutawney." It had a lot of information about the health care program, pay days and locations of college administrative officers.

As the ceremonies continued Jerry Swartz nodded to Jim. Jerry was in the same row sitting six seats to Jim's right. He apparently had not sat next to Jim in order to be with a buddy of his.

Jerry had made an airplane out of the "most important piece of paper" and had written a message on it for Jim. He took careful aim and shot the airplane toward Jim.

The warm moist air in the room picked up the airplane and sent it aloft. It circled over the heads of the assembly and soon everyone's eyes were on it, including those of the Provost. The aerodynamics were spectacular as the plane sailed around and lifted to great heights. It circled over the heads of the dignitaries on stage and landed in the midst of the assembly. A thin bearded professor, with an air of disgust, promptly crumbled the plane and passed it along to be thrown in the wastebasket.

The Provost was rattled but still made a weak attempt at humor. Jerry slid further down in his seat even though it was impossible to identify him as the source of the airplane.

As the audience settled for another verbal onslaught a murmur went through the audience and all eyes shifted to the doorway. In it stood a tall man in a black suit with a white shirt and red tie. The Provost braced himself and smiling said "We are fortunate that the president of Punxsutawney State College could take some time from his busy schedule to visit us. Would you say a few words of welcome Dr. Curry?"

The man in the black suit smiled, exposing vampire pointed eye teeth. He made his way to the front of the group. He looked around the room and at those assembled. He smiled and faced the Provost.

"I guess I could say a few words, doctor Simmons."

Simmons turned to the audience. "I would like to introduce our president Dr. Harold Ignatious Curry."

Jim thought, his initials are HIC, and bet everybody referred to him as hick.

Although Provost Simmons and the other speakers felt need of the microphone Dr. Curry did not. He began by telling the audience that he was known for his loud booming voice and didn't need the microphone. If anyone couldn't hear him to speak up, he would shift to his other lung. The man sitting to Jim's left turned to him "What did he say?"

Dr. Curry went on with platitudes of welcome and how Punxsutawney State College was on the verge of greatness. The football team was looking forward to a winning season. Later on, Jim would come to know that the football fortunes of old Punxie were of special concern to the president. A winning football team meant publicity and increased enrollment. The president ended with "my door is always open to faculty members."

The glazed eyed professor to Jim's right looked at him. "Don't you believe that for one minute buddy boy. I've been here twelve years and have never been in his office."

Finally, the ceremony was winding down. Introductions of new faculty were made along with their respective departments. When it was Jim's turn he was introduced as Taylor. Jim stood up and was about to give the correct pronunciation of his name but a signal from Jerry told him to forget it. After the meeting was adjourned Jerry said "It's not worth it Jim. Just go along with Taylor and cash your checks, that's the bottom line anyway, isn't it?"

"Yeah, I guess so. By the way, where is Seminary Hall, room ninety six. That's my office. I better go check it out."

Jerry looked at him. His mouth turned upward into a grin. "Oh, you're probably in with Abdul."

"Who's Abdul?. I didn't see anyone by that name in the college catalog."

"That's a nickname someone gave him and it stuck. He teaches philosophy and other things at Punxie. Don't worry.

9

You'll be out of there by next year and have your own office when the new batch of faculty comes on line. We have some retirements coming up and you will probably come over to our building, maybe even before next year."

Jerry didn't mention that it was he who gave the man the nickname of Abdul. Jerry had a nickname for most luminaries on campus. Most of the names stuck since they matched the person's personality or habits.

Jerry put his hand to his mouth as if he was thinking. "Seminary Hall is directly ahead, out that door. You can't miss it, brick building with yellow trim, a bell tower on the top."

Jim looked into the ceiling. "I thought that was some sort of maintenance building. Well, see you around Jerry. By the way, where do I get supplies, you know, like a grade book, lots of red pencils and so forth?"

Jerry grinned. "Go easy on the red markers Jim. You can pick the stuff up from our secretary and guard Mizz Rosemary Needs. You'll have to convince her you really need the stuff though, she just doesn't give it away without justification."

"I haven't met her yet. I guess I'll get supplies later, after I check out the office. I hope the key fits."

Jerry poked Jim in the arm. "Hey Jim, if I can be of any help, be sure to let me know. It's good having someone close to my own age in the department. The rest are old geezers."

"When the committee interviewed me, I didn't think they were that old."

"Old geezer is not strictly related to age, it's more like a state of mind."

Jim walked out the door. The air smelled good. The well manicured grounds were rife with flowers. Punxie State had a pleasant campus.

The new instructor walked with a mission, he was now a college professor, well actually an instructor. His star was rising. No more dealing with children "mewing and puking in their nurse's arms."

2. JIM MEETS HIS FIRST CLASS

It was a short walk from the auditorium to the basement of Seminary Hall. This was a building used by students for study and worship back in the old days when the grounds belonged to the Methodist Church. The mortar was falling out from between many of the bricks on the face of the building and it looked like it would take heroic efforts to save the structure. The college had applied to the U. S. Government to register the building as an historic treasure. There was also an application for restoration funds. English Ivy climbed the south face and it truly gave the impression of a college building. In block letters, centered over the double doors was the inscription in stone SEMINARY HALL.

The stairs to the basement were not illuminated very well. A one bulb light in the hallway above the stairs lit the top half and a one bulb light at the bottom of the stairs lit the lower half.

Room numbering seemed to start with 91 and Jim easily found room 96. On the door, cast in metal, was the name JAMERSON. Apparently, this was Jim's office mate. It was explained that offices were in short supply since the college had recently converted some of the larger offices to conference and seminar rooms. Jim inserted the key and the door opened. A smell of perfume or maybe it was shave lotion wafted from inside. Jim fumbled for the light switch.

Inside were two desks with a chair behind each of them. There were two other chairs in the room, each positioned in front of each desk. One desk had a neat book holder, filled with books. Scattered on the desk were a stapler, a tape dispenser, a desk calendar and an in-out basket. The other desk had a pile of books on it.

Jim tried the long top drawer of the desk with the pile of books and it was open. Inside was a key. He fit the key into the hole in the middle of the drawer and a small square of metal popped up. He tried the side drawers and they were empty except for a yellow tablet in the bottom of the middle drawer. Jim assumed that this was to be his desk.

The room was lighted by a bank of fluorescent tubes embedded in the ceiling and positioned in the middle of the room. Jim noticed that he cast shadows on the wall. There was an oil painting on the wall behind the occupied desk. It featured waves on water and was a study in blue and white. There was no window to the outside world in the room. Jim muttered to himself that he would not be able to see the first robin when it arrived in spring. An air conditioner hummed noisily in the background.

The pile of books were removed from the top of the desk and Jim went about putting some of his materials on it. The first to be established was a framed photo of his wife Martha and their two children, eight year old Susan and five year old Jimmy. Jim sat back in the straight backed chair and spoke to the photo. "Well gang, it's the first day of the rest of our lives."

Jim made a mental note of things he needed - grade book, colored pens, note paper, stapler, tape and dispenser and most of all the list of students who would be in tomorrow's classes. He hoped his office would have a computer or at least a typewriter, something to make hand-out sheets and tests. There was none. At least he had his schedule. Jim thought a quick trip to Krieder Hall and the Department of Social Studies would fill his knapsack with his material needs.

There was no one around the office when he arrived. He looked for the department secretary, Ms. Rosemary Needs, but even she was no where in sight. Come to think of it, except for the people in the auditorium Jim hadn't seen very many people. Didn't anyone come to work on the day before classes started?

There was nothing to do but root around through the drawers and cabinets of the office and lift any of the needed materials that surfaced. As yet, there was no roster of students in the mail slot that had his name on a slip of paper tacked under it.

Other department members had a nice plastic name indicating that they were there for some time.

The big cabinet next to a small gray filing cabinet was open and had the supplies. Jim helped himself to a roll of Scotch Tape, a stapler, pack of staples, grade book, three red ink pens, three black ink pens and a desk calendar.

He saw reams of typing or computer paper behind the windows of another cabinet but it was locked. Little did he realize that this was a priority item in the eyes of the department secretary.

Jim briefly scanned the names under the mail slots of the department members. The only ones he recognized were Swartz whom he had just met and Gregory who was the chairman of the department and he who hired Jim.

Back at Office 96 Jim cut up a scrap of paper and carefully wrote TAILOR on it in red letters. It didn't look right so he outlined the name in black ink. He looked around for thumb tacks but there were none so he taped the name to the door under JAMERSON.

It was a lonely beginning. Jim sat at the desk with his feet propped up and looked over his notes. He had three sections of History of the United States to 1865 and one section of Economics, his specialty. There were two classes of U.S. on Monday, Wednesday and Friday and the others were scheduled for Tuesday and Thursday. This was a weekly total of twelve contact hours, a far cry from the thirty he had as a public school teacher.

A mailbox note attached to a blank schedule ordered Jim to list six office hours. He listed one office hour each day with two on Wednesday. He placed his schedule in the clear holder on the door which was obviously meant for that purpose. If Jamerson had a schedule, it was not yet posted.

When Jim returned to the office the next day to get ready to meet his classes he noticed that the photo of Martha and the kids and the rest of his desk material had been moved to one

13

side. There was a sweet smell in the air, like perfume which Jim thought might be cleaning fluid. He thought that this was the work of the cleaning person who tended to the needs of Seminary Hall.

As every professor knows, there is usually one class in a semester which stands above the others. This class has rapport and the professor likes to be there and the students also like it. They share some of the secrets of their lives and there is mutual affection. Sometimes the memories last forever. Often the memories and the academic adventures are filed away and almost forgotten as another class rises to take its place. So with this in mind we shall concentrate our story on just one of Jim's classes this semester.

The class roster had not arrived. It was Wednesday and Jim went to meet the 10 A. M. section of History of the United States to 1865. It was his first class of the day. He arrived fifteen minutes early.

Students began filing in, taking seats with some talking to each other. Jim stood behind a lectern and looked down at his papers, not really wanting to look up at the students and stare at them. The fifteen minutes seem to drag on for an hour. He thought perhaps he should make idle chatter with students as they sat in front of him but he was unable to think of anything clever to say. He had made a mistake arriving at the classroom early on this first day. It would have been better, so he thought, if he had been a few minutes late and arrived with a flourish. He would do that for the next class.

When Jim did look up he was startled to see mature people. He had been used to senior high school students and his mind could not accept the growth and difference between the people filing into the room and the students he remembered at the last high school graduation. This was the first of many shocks for Jim.

The new professor was astounded at the attractive

14

women coming into the classroom. Every one was beautiful. Had he forgotten what it was like to be nineteen and twenty years old? The thin girls, overweight girls, they were gorgeous. He began staring and finally caught himself at it and went back to his papers. He didn't notice the young men except to note that many of them were wearing baseball hats backwards and didn't remove them when they sat down.

When the big hand moved to the top of Jim's watch he looked up from the desk and cleared his throat. He looked at the class and for a moment was wondering what to say even though he had rehearsed his opening remarks for about three days. He picked up a piece of chalk and walked over to the board and wrote TAILOR on it.

"My name is Tyler and this is History of the United States to 1865, section one. If you're not signed up for this course feel free to leave now." He paused and tightened his lips.

Two goofy young men shuffled around in their seats, rose to their feet and departed the room. A few members of the class laughed. Jim walked over and closed the door after them.

Jim went from row to row counting out a one sheet syllabus which he went on to describe in detail. This included reading requirements, textbook requirement, his grading system and his office number and hours.

"Anyone have any questions about this?"

A student asked about absences and what did he consider an excused absence. Jim stated that the student handbook answered that question and students who don't know the policy should refer to the student handbook. One student wanted to know where he could get a student handbook. As it turned out, most of the students had never heard of the student handbook. Later Jim would discover no one in his department had heard of it either. Jim figured everyone received a copy when first employed and then it never surfaced again in their experiences. Maybe the handbook was a new invention and the old members just didn't get one.

15

Jim then distributed a 3 by 5 file card to each student. "I've told you about this course now you can tell me something about yourself. The class roster didn't arrive yet so I would appreciate it if you printed your name so I can read it."

Jim asked the usual things - name, campus address, major field, other history courses taken, class standing and for his own kicks, the student's hometown. Jim gathered the cards and positioned himself in front of the middle row. The students were asked to pass in the cards.

"When I call your name, would you raise your hand or make some kind of sign that will let me know it's you. If I mispronounce your name, correct me. I know how it is to have someone mispronounce a name. I always get the name Taylor when my name is Tyler."

A male student mumbled "It's Taylor, like the clothes maker. That's how it's spelled."

Jim grimaced but did not acknowledge the student. He started in on the cards and the names. Naturally, they were not in alphabetical order.

"George Persak, Pamela Clark, William Dyzniski." He could pronounce those hard names since he was cognizant of names. He stared in the faces of the student whose name he had just called.

"If I look at you kind of funny, it's not that I'm odd. It's just that I want to start linking your face up to your name. Elmer Glutz, Sarah Rice, Helga Anderson and so on."

One of the cards had the name Benjamin Franklin on it and the other data. Was this a trick? In high school he had been taken in by students who signed fake funny names like Joe Fart. He put the card back in the deck and continued to the last name.

A young man rose to his feet. "Professor, you didn't call my name."

"Oh" said Jim "What is your name?"

"Benjamin Franklin, I filled out a card."

Jim pretended to shuffle through the cards but he knew

16

the exact location of that card and finally extracted it.

"Here it is Mr. Franklin and I see you are from Philadelphia."

"Yes sir."

"Are you by any chance related to the Revolutionary Benjamin Franklin of Philadelphia?"

"I think so, but I'm still working on it. I'm left handed, just like old Ben was, so maybe there is a connection." He held up his left hand and made a mock salute.

Ben Franklin was the first male student Jim really took a good look at. The young man was shorter than most men his age. He had dark neatly cut hair, shining black eyes, pale skin and a wide grin. He was dressed in a blue work shirt and jeans. Jim looked around at the other boys. Many of them had wild hair and some of them wore earrings. Benjamin Franklin seemed to belong to an entirely different tribe than the other males.

Jim had taken a good look at all the young women. He couldn't get over their attractiveness. He mused to himself, "Is there something wrong with me?"

Ben Franklin asked "Is it doctor Tailor?"

Jim was slightly embarrassed since he wanted the students to think he had a doctorate but didn't want to admit that he didn't, at least not until they got to know each other better.

"No I don't have a doctorate. I have two more courses to finish and then I'll be A-B-D, all but the dissertation."

Ben pursued him. "Where are you doing your work and what is the nature of your thesis?"

"I'm enrolled at Penn State and the temporary title of the dissertation is The Economic Theories of James Knox Polk."

"Who is that?" asked Pamela Clark.

Jim grinned. "You'll know by the end of this semester. He was an obscure president. My advisor is working on a massive volume on the economic theories of the presidents after Jackson and before Lincoln, He has this idea that the economic structure of the country was set during that time period. So if I

17

ever want to get my Ph.D I have to go along with it. Other students are working on such guys as Van Buren, Harrison and Tyler. It's a chore. So if I get bogged down with lectures in this time period I hope you will be a little charitable towards me."

"We will if you will be charitable toward us Mr. Tailor." said George Persak.

Sarah Rice held up her hand and Jim nodded at her.

"Are you married?"

"That's getting a little personal Sarah." He remembered her name. "Yes, I'm married."

This admission sent a shuffling of feet by a couple of the women. Helga Anderson raised her right fist and brought it down as if to say "Doggone it."

A series of thoughts flashed through Jim's mind. Surely professors, he corrected himself, instructors, don't date students. He was warned about that when the department chairman told him he had the job. Chairman Gregory said that a man Jim's age should think of the female as just another student and "don't let them charm you."

Jim went on. "I have two children, a daughter in fourth grade and a son in kindergarten."

Ben Franklin asked "What did you do before you came to Punxie?"

"I was a high school teacher at Clearfield, about sixty miles northeast of here. I taught senior high social studies. I'm sure many of my former students are enrolled here at Punxie." He took a stab at humor. "Don't ask any of them about me."

Jim looked at his wrist watch. "I was going to give you a few introductory remarks concerning our subject but I see we only have fifteen more minutes left in the class. So let's call that it for today and if any of you have any questions stop by the desk."

Students rose and started filing out. Ben Franklin came to the desk and with a bright cheery grin said "I think I'm going to enjoy this class Mr. Tailor. Presidents are my favorite subject matter. Believe it or not, the presidents after Jackson are kind of a specialty of mine."

Jim had heard this move before and began to tune Ben Franklin out. He noticed Helga Anderson move up behind Ben Franklin to wait her turn to speak with the instructor. Jim didn't pay much attention to what Ben was saying. Ben rattled on and on but Jim kept glancing at Helga.

Helga had a beautiful oval shaped face. Her lips were pouty. Shoulder length strawberry colored hair hung straight. Her body appeared well proportioned and athletic even under the sweatshirt that read Punxie State.

Jim tried to determine her eye color. He wished Ben would shut up and move on so he could hear what Helga had to say.

Ben kept on talking about how he thought Polk was simply reintroducing policies that Van Buren had started and how Polk was caught up in the decision to give Vancouver to the British and to back away from the slogan "fifty four forty or fight" and settled for the 49th parallel instead. Had Jim paid attention he would have realized that Ben Franklin knew a lot about Polk, even more than he did.

Instead Jim kept thinking about Helga as she looked at her watch and heaved sighs as well as her breasts. She did some pacing in place and pouted her lips. She looked at her watch again and tightened her lips. Jim felt a sense of dejection as Helga snorted and walked off toward the door.

As Helga left a few students standing outside the door cautiously looked into the room. Two young women entered and took seats in the back of the room.

Jim turned his attention to Ben. "We better move out of here Mr. Franklin, another class is due in here soon and I have to get over to my office."

Ben beamed. "Call me Benji, please. I'm sure looking forward to this semester with you Mr. Tailor."

3. THE FACULTY LOUNGE

Getting into the routine of college teaching became somewhat of a chore to Jim. He had been there two weeks and he still hadn't met his office mate. His office in the basement of an old building made him feel that he was in some sort of medieval monastic setting. He thought that perhaps the physics and chemistry departments taught courses like "Alchemy" and "Turning Base Metals Into Gold."

At the first meeting of the Social Studies Department, Jim met most of the members he hadn't seen before. He counted thirteen members in all, along with the secretary, Ms. Needs, the guardian of supplies. Four members were absent. Jim asked Ms. Needs for a ream of typing paper and she replied that she would give him whatever paper he needed but not an entire ream unless he was going to run some lengthy manuscript on the duplicator. She would be happy to duplicate materials for him since many department members didn't know how to operate it and jammed the machine.

Dr. Harold Gregory was the chairman of the Social Studies Department. He was a thin gray haired and short bearded fellow who constantly took his glasses off and put them on during the course of the first meeting. After making some pronouncement he would ask the secretary if she "got that" and if he was moving too fast for her.

Gregory had paid his dues. He was one of the original workers who founded the union, the Association of Pennsylvania State College and University Faculties. He had been a teacher for thirty years and was one of the original professors hired when Punxie became a state related school twenty five years ago.

There were many committee assignments to be filled - evaluation, building and rooms, sabbatical leave, promotions, tenure and student liaison. It would be six years before Jim would be eligible for tenure. After looking over the choices, Jim decided to volunteer for sabbatical since he wasn't going to be eligible for a sabbatical for at least seven years and this didn't look like it would be controversial. Jerry told Jim that the fastest route to promotion was to be on one of the campus-wide committees. Jim assumed he was on the right track when he was assigned to the Dean's Council.

Dr. Gregory reminded the department that he was getting "up-in-years" and that he would be retiring soon and the department should consider his successor. Department chairman were elected by the department every three years. Harold had been chairman since elections were mandated. Until that time, department chairman were appointed by the administration. It was difficult for the appointed department chairman to represent the department and suck up to the administration at the same time. The election of chairman with the approval of the college president gave the faculty better representation.

Jim duly noted the one female member of the department. Ms. Agatha Aggasis. She appeared to be isolated from the other members. Her appearance suggested she was aloof and really didn't want to mix with the other members of the department. She had a comment for most of the dictates of the chairman.

Dr. Gregory introduced Jim as Taylor and at that point Jim decided not to fight it any longer. From that meeting onward he would accept the pronunciation of Taylor as his name. He apologized to his father who he thought was observing him from somewhere in the heavens.

Most of Jim's leisure time in those first few weeks were spent at the faculty lounge on the third floor of Recitation Hall. The lower two floors were used as classrooms. Like Seminary Hall, Recitation Hall was one of the original buildings on campus. It was constructed in 1882 and that year was displayed in a concrete block just to the right of the main entrance. This building was also in need of repair and attempts to get it listed as a national landmark were in progress.

The faculty lounge consisted of two sections. The first section was a dining room with linoleum floor and hard chairs and tables. A small kitchen served short-orders and specialized in hot sausage hoagies and acid rock coffee. It featured Mike on the grill and Serena on the counter and cash register. Serena took no guff from professors and required them to put their used dishes and utensils in the proper bin and their napkins into the wastebasket. When there were a crowd of professors she insisted on lining them up in single file and having them approach the counter one at a time.

The other section was the lounge which featured a rug, easy chairs, a large sofa, a magazine reading rack and several floor lamps. A sign, NO FOOD PLEASE, graced the entrance. However, everyone felt free to bring coffee into the room. Serena did not object to that. Another sign which stated NO SMOKING was ignored by many of the faculty and several arguments broke out over this violation. Faculty referred to the lounge as the "clubhouse."

Jim would eat lunch at the clubhouse since Martha was busy in the mornings getting the children off to school and he felt it was an extra burden to expect her to also pack him a lunch. Besides, eating lunch there gave him a chance to get a feel for the college and meet some members of other departments, maybe even have some intellectual stimulation. He learned very quickly that the featured food, the deadly hot sausage hoagie, was not something he could eat on a daily basis.

Whenever he would mention his department and his office, the response would more than likely be "Isn't that where Abdul has his office?" Jim would explain that he was office mates with someone named Jamerson but he hadn't met him yet. Often as not, the claimant would say "Yeah, that's his name."

Two of the regulars at the lounge were Bill Barr and Henry Blackenshep of the math department. Blackenshep was a talking mannequin who had an opinion on everything. After all he was a college professor and insisted underlings call him Dr.

Blackenshep. It was Mr. Barr and once when Mike the grill master asked "Mr. Blackenshep if Dr. Barr was coming in for lunch" he was corrected with great gusto and malice.

Blackenshep did have some interesting things to say even if he leaned toward pomposity. However, after he would deliver a tirade and it was the listener's turn to speak Blackenshep would look at his wrist watch as if he had some important place to go and the speaker had better cut it short. This unnerved Jim and he decided it would be best for him to listen and not try to make comments. Sometimes when Blackenshep looked at his watch Jim would ask him what time it was but the professor never got the hint and in all seriousness he would tell the time.

Barr had been at Punxie for six years and was up for tenure. Blackenshep was on the college- wide tenure committee and always made Barr uncomfortable about it. Not that Blackenshep could block anyone's quest for tenure but he let Barr know that he had a vote in the matter. He would often say "Those who deserve tenure, don't need it, and those who need it, don't deserve it." However, he was able to express his opinions about the administration and other matters freely since he did have tenure.

Chairman Gregory of Social Studies told Jim what it was like teaching at the college level without tenure. You could be dumped at any moment without an explanation. Jim was aware of the pitfalls of not having tenure since it was also a factor in high school teaching.

The great savior of the state college and university teaching profession was the union APSCUF, the Association of Pennsylvania State College and University Faculties. Most faculty members referred to it as a professional organization rather than a union. Harold Gregory made no bones about his efforts to help organize APSCUF in the early days. He had slept in his car in Harrisburg in order to save money for the fledgling organization.

College faculty hated to adopt union tactics since it made

23

the "profession" look "sleazy." Gregory argued that they were not members of a profession since they didn't set their own salaries, own their own buildings, and had no control over their customer base. Most faculty in his early teaching career belonged to the Pennsylvania State Education Association and the National Education Association. It was a requirement at Punxie before someone challenged it in court.

The challenger didn't have tenure so he was ousted as soon as it was decreed that the faculty were not required to join the PSEA and NEA.

President Curry told the challenger that he wouldn't be around long if he kept up this type of agitation. To which the challenger replied "At least I'll go out of here on my legs and not on my knees." The challenger, whose name Jim never learned , ended up professoring at California University of Pennsylvania, one of the fourteen state universities and a leader in the union movement. Gregory lamented the fact that he had put in all those years for APSCUF but was never sufficiently rewarded.

In one personal discussion Barr told Jim that he, Barr, was a tough teacher. He said "You can ask any of my former students. They will tell you that I'm tough, but fair."

Jim wondered. "Why is he telling me that? Is it some badge of accomplishment? He is trying to project some image, but why?" It was beyond Jim's imagination and there was little time to reflect on it.

Barr went on to say that in his Basic Algebra class he had flunked 22 out of 31 students. "They just weren't prepared. I don't know what they're teaching in high school these days. Punxie keeps letting in these students with low S-A-T scores. It's like they take a street sweeper and gather up the dregs of Philadelphia."

Jim mused to himself that if he had more than half of his class flunking he would wonder what it was he was doing wrong, not what someone else, in this case high school teachers, had done wrong. After all, these were high school graduates who had satisfied many requirements before being accepted at Punxie. Out of 154 students the only one from Philadelphia was Benjamin Franklin and Jim wondered what Barr meant by that.

After Barr reiterated his flunk percentage Jim offered "Isn't it your job to teach them, pick them up from wherever they are?"

Barr countered "That's true and I do that but our students have such low SAT scores they just can't comprehend something simple like basic algebra."

"Well some people just can't hack it. I barely passed algebra in college. Perhaps we should revise our requirements and not make algebra a required course. Maybe give the students a choice in the matter of math and science, have them take a math course but make it an elective."

Barr went on "We discussed that in our department a couple of years ago and the bottom line was that if we gave students a chance to not take algebra we wouldn't have anyone to teach but the math and physics majors. This would reduce our student-faculty numbers and eventually we would have to eliminate some math positions. It's the old protect your turf philosophy. I say, we shouldn't have such an open admissions policy. Look what happened, I had to flunk 22 out of 31 students."

Jim figured it would be better to let the matter pass and accept the premise that Bill Barr was a "tough but fair" teacher. In his first semester at Punxie, Jim was able to meet several other "tough" teachers. He also noted that Barr was the only professor who taught Algebra I and every student who had to take the course had to pass through Bill Barr.

Another lounge lizard was assistant professor Manfred Kelley of the English Department, a foul mouthed individual. Streams of profanity poured from his lips. Usually he was accompanied to the clubhouse by Henry Broadcast also of English.

Jim didn't like them very much and preferred not to be in

25

their presence. In one of the early discussions Manfred stated that he said the word "fuck" in class. He added "It's no big deal."

Jim never used the term himself and neither did almost everyone with whom he associated. When Manfred proudly mentioned this, Henry Broadcast stated that Manfred must think it significant or he wouldn't have mentioned it to him and Jim. Manfred stated that he just wanted to let them know that he wasn't going to let modern prudery influence his behavior. It was a matter of free speech and he would take any stifling of his free speech to the highest courts of the state and the country.

Not only did Manfred speak the part of a maverick he dressed the part. Most of his attire consisted of off-colored T shirts and blue jeans. He wore cowboy boots and on some occasions a cowboy hat. Broadcast told Jim that Manfred kept pistols and holsters in the trunk of his car and often practiced fast draws. Jim felt that Manfred was someone to avoid but when Manfred spotted Jim in the lounge he would sit in his circle.

The semester had barely progressed into the fifth week when Manfred told Broadcast and Jim that he had accepted a position at West Chester University of Pennsylvania starting in January. He said that when he leaves Punxie he leaves behind a lot of good will.

When asked what he meant by a lot of "good will" he said that the president and provost of Punxie thought very highly of him. Later Broadcast told Jim that the provost had met with the chairman of the English Department to discuss some way of getting rid of Manfred. The provost and the president had formulated a plan and enlisted the chairman's help. The chairman was more than willing to get rid of Manfred Kelley and replace him with someone less strident. He of course, gave an excellent recommendation to West Chester. Oh, to see ourselves as others see us.

Not many women faculty members hung out at the clubhouse. Perhaps this was because there weren't many women professors employed at Punxie. Two that did come over for coffee and some discussion were Phyllis Sanderly and Bertha Crenshaw of elementary education. They were faculty members who taught in the campus elementary school which was created to give students their student-teacher experiences. When they talked to Jim and the other lounge lizards they seemed to be on stage most of the time. They were actors or in this case, actresses. They noticed everyone coming and going. Phyllis would stare at some male sitting at another table. She was a wide-eyed pleasant looking young woman and more often than not, the person she had been staring at would come over and join their table. Perhaps they thought there might be some opportunity there that had previously gone untapped. They were usually disappointed.

Bertha was said to have taken senior college students back to her apartment from time to time. There were no rumors of sexual conduct or misconduct associated with these events. However, Jerry Swartz later speculated that Bertha would seduce only senior men since they were soon leaving the institution.

Once when Jim and Bill Barr were joined by the two women, Phyllis commandeered the conversation with a discussion of her troubles ordering a shrimp dinner from the local Chinese restaurant the night before. It took twenty minutes for her to get through the story. Jim couldn't take it any longer and said he had to leave. Bill Barr said he would walk with Jim to his office. When the two got outside they looked at each other with grinning amazement. They didn't have to speak, each knew what the other was thinking.

In the initial meeting with Bertha she remarked that Jim had gotten Kelsey's job. Jim said he didn't know anything about Kelsey and actually had never heard of him. It seems Kelsey was scheduled to teach summer classes when he received a notice that he had been accepted into an Educational Scholarship Program which took him and other professors to Central

27

America. Chairman Gregory and the acting provost had discussed getting rid of Kelsey somehow but didn't know how to do it. Since Kelsey had violated a signed contract and left the department in the lurch this was reason enough to dismiss him. No member of the department seemed to miss Kelsey and considered him a non-person, so much of a non-person they never mentioned him to Jim. There was no shortage of Social Studies professors willing to take over Kelsey's six hour summer teaching load. Some hard feeling were generated when Gregory took the assignment himself and later complained about it. It was most colleague's opinion that Gregory should have passed this plum around since he was already drawing a professor's salary and had no children to support. He did have grown children.

The Social Studies Department had a work room which passed for a lounge and department members often sat around having coffee and heating a sandwich in the microwave oven. However, Jim thought it would be to his advantage to hang around the campus faculty lounge instead of the department lounge. Here he could meet other profs and who knows, some of them might be on the promotion committee.

On some days Jim's trips to the campus lounge proved to be more aggravation than pleasure. The insights he gained by observing and listening to the entrenched faulty would prove to be an asset to his future ambitions. Some of the discussions actually gave him food-for-thought, grist for his mental mill.

Mark and Henry

Mark turned to Jim and Henry Broadcast of the English Department and laughed. "You guys hear about Gabriel Yanko of physical science?"

Neither Henry nor Jim could answer in the affirmative.

Mark illuminated. "Gabe had his name listed in the phone directory as Dr. Gabriel Yanko. He has been getting all kinds of phone calls from sick people asking for emergency treatment. He finally asked the phone company to remove the doctor label from the listing. But now, he's still has to live with it until the new phone books come out. Imagine, being that egotistical, to put doctor in the phone book."

Neither Henry nor Jim were able to come up with an appropriate response. Finally Henry said "I guess he should have listed his name as Gabriel Yanko, P-H-D."

Mark snorted "Naw, that's like putting doctor or PHD on your checks."

Henry straightened up. "What's wrong with that?"

"You can bet profs who put doctor on their checks and checking accounts are usually second-rate profs who graduated from second-rate institutions."

Henry assumed a serious expression. "I have doctor on my checks. You should see the extra service I get at the super market and shoe store, not to mention the automobile dealer."

"That proves my point about second-rate" said Mark seriously. Then he caught himself "Just kidding of course."

Henry pointed to Mark. "What difference does it make to you whether or not I have doctor on my checks or sign my name on letters with PHD after it?"

"It's kind of an assumed tackiness. It's like you're shouting hey, everybody, look I have a PHD."

"So. It took me four years of graduate school to get a PHD and students call me doctor. Hell, they're even calling chiropractors doctor these days."

Mark was no longer laughing. "Most professors look upon putting doctor in front of your name as cheapening the degree. And it is a sign of a second-rate professor who probably obtained his degree from a second-rate institution."

"Maybe so, but I'm doctor Broadcast. I earned the degree and I feel free to put it on all my academic and financial transactions. I don't use it socially, except when I'm giving talks to the Rotary Club or being quoted in the newspaper. As to second-rate, let's face it, if we are teaching at Punxie we're third-rate. Penn State's first, Indiana and Bloomsburg are second and we're lucky to be third."

"Oh" Mark paused " I wouldn't say third-rate. There's a lot of high class academic work going on here."

" Give me a for instance. I think you're an elitist and living in some sort of dream world."

"There's a lot of good research going on here, like the guy in Jim's department. What's his name. He got a grant to continue research on the Civil War and there's that guy in biology researching oysters."

Henry laughed. "Yeah, and they will get published in some very very obscure journal and nobody will read it. As to biologist Oliver Holmes how do you study oysters at an inland institution?

That's been a laugh from day one. He did oysters for his doctorate at Miami and has been toying with them ever since. He has gotten a lot of mileage out of those oysters. Maybe there's oysters in Mahoning Creek and we don't know about them."

Mark bristled "But that's still good research."

"You and I know most of those journals were created to give profs a leg-up on publish-or-perish. Most of them will charge you to publish your research. It's all a lot of nonsense and a con game that everyone knows."

"That's your opinion."

"No, not my opinion, research on research journals indicate that less than five percent of the recipients of the journals even look at the table of contents. We're talking about second-rate here, remember. Somehow you get the impression that you're first rate because you don't put doctor on your checks. You don't want to admit that you are at a third-rate institution."

Mark began to lighten up. "Okay, okay. Let me put it this way. I consider myself a first-rate professor teaching at a third-rate institution. Does that satisfy you?"

"No that doesn't satisfy me. You go around with

smugness and a feeling of self-importance and refuse to admit you haven't climbed very far on the academic ladder of success. This is something I'm willing to face concerning myself."

Mark turned to Jim. "What do you think Jim? Are you at a second or third rate institution?"

A smile came across Jim's lips. "Whatever the rate is at Punxie I'm glad to have a well paying job at a state tax supported institution. That's real security. I hope to be at Punxie a long time. Knock on wood."

Henry arched his eyebrows. "Are you going to put doctor on your checks next year?"

"I won't have to do that. If I get the degree, my wife will walk ahead of me and broadcast it to the universe. She's already getting a line on Christmas cards which will say doctor and Mrs. Tailor."

Henry pointed to Mark. "Well Jim, Mark here will consider you second-rate."

Jim grimaced. "Gimmee the degree and the promotions that go with it and Mark can consider me anything he wants."

Mark assumed a humorous air of indignation. "I am shocked, shocked. I tell you. You'll be cheapening the profession for all of us."

the economic impact survey

Jim and Harold trudged over to the faculty lounge. There they sat with Bill Billings of philosophy and Knute Rowlands of biology. Bill welcomed them warmly and asked Knute if he knew them. Knute said he did and extended warm greetings.

Bill turned to Harold. "I just got your packet here." He held up a few sheets of paper and waved them at Harold. "So you're our liaison with the State System of Higher Education on the important project that will turn our lives around."

Harold seemed embarrassed. "Yes I am and when the project is complete the state legislature will be sending us barrels of money and we will all be whistling Dixie."

31

Bill turned to Knute. "Did you get your mail today?"

"No, I didn't."

"Well, there's an interesting questionnaire from the S-S-H-E and you can ask Harold about it. The state is doing an economic impact study concerning our fourteen universities and Punxie. You tell them how much money you spent, where you spent it and they will compile it all and tell the people of Pennsylvania how much of an economic impact the state owned universities have on their lives."

Knute looked serious. "Sounds like a good idea. We need to get out the message that we're as important as Penn State to the economy. All together we have more students than Penn State but that goes unnoticed in the legislature. We need to get out the message."

Bill handed the document to Knute who glanced at it and handed it to Jim who handed it back to Bill. It asked personal expenditures on housing, food, transportation, entertainment, clothing and "all other spending." There were questions concerning employment, head of household, work and children. There were also questions about relatives attending various state institutions.

Bill turned to Harold. "Who designed this anyway?"

"I think it was somebody at Penn State."

"Don't we have anyone in the state system of higher education who can design this kind of crap?"

"Of course we do but Penn State already did a similar project and we just borrowed their document and didn't have to pay out big bucks."

"Big bucks for a questionnaire."

Knute got into the fray. "Most of our legislators think that Penn State is a state owned institution. They haven't the slightest idea that it's a private school just like Pitt, Penn and Temple. When you consider the amount of money they give Penn State, Pitt and Temple and compare it with us it's disgusting."

"And so it goes" said Harold "Penn State has a well paid public relations program and the state legislators have no idea of its true nature. The Penn State football team wins bowl games and the legislature doubles its contributions. Nobody checks on the teaching load of a Penn State prof. My daughter went to Penn State and majored in biology. Her advisor was off in Peru for two years and his classes were covered by a graduate assistant. When he did get back he was so busy giving speeches he sure didn't have time to help my daughter. She would have been much better off going to Millersville, Lock Haven or Kutztown."

Bill said he was going to throw the whole thing in the circular file but Harold assured him that would be a mistake. If the document was to have some impact then at least sixty percent of the faculty would have to participate. He was the only one who took the questionnaire seriously. After all, they were working for the state and had job security. Acquiring funding for the state system was not someone else's responsibility.

Soon Jim would discover that questionnaires, surveys and seemingly innocuous forms to fill out was a part of the job. Somewhere, it is assumed, there is a person diligently compiling the information and selecting data from it to bolster some cause.

Several professors working on degrees in education sent out questionnaires concerning the status of teachers at Punxie. One had an elaborate questioning concerning the feeling of parents about the local school busing program. About half of the professors participated in these. The education professors all participated since they relied on this type of information in their own careers.

The library sent a questionnaire on faculty use of the library. They used yellow paper in order to quickly separate this data from other questionnaires they had color coded. When Jim picked up his mail he noticed five or six yellow sheets in the office waste basket.

4. JIM HIRES BENJI

Three weeks had passed before Jim met his office mate. It was near the end of September when a somewhat rotund man with straight black hair walked into the office and over to Jim with an outstretched hand. "Hi, I'm your office buddy Tony Jamerson."

"Yeah" said Jim "I was hoping to meet you before the end of the semester."

Tony moved to his desk and started pulling papers from a briefcase and piling them on the desk. He looked at Jim. "I'm working on getting my own office and I'm close to success, so you might lose me before the end of the semester. But don't worry, they'll just move someone else in with you, at least for this semester."

Tony said most of his classes met clear across campus and he stayed over there most of the time. He taught philosophy and was a member of the Fine Arts Department. He was one of two who were teaching philosophy and the college didn't want to make them a two man department.

By now Jim had learned that Tony was called Abdul since it was rumored that he had a harem of women and that was a synonym for an Arab potentate. Jim couldn't believe this portly, short man could be such a womanizer. He stood beside Tony to see how tall he really was. Jim was one inch short of six feet. To Jim's surprise Tony was about the same height. What could woman possible see in this fellow. Maybe there were a lot of desperate women in the world. He just looked short and ordinary. Jim couldn't wait to tell Martha about the meeting with a legend.

Tony stopped shuffling papers. "Hey, Jim, I hope you don't mind but I've been using your desk from time to time since mine is so crowded and yours is so neat. There's more room to spread things out on your desk. I tried to put everything back in its right place, sometimes I can't remember where everything belongs."

"Yeah, I did notice some of my stuff moved around. That's okay, as long as you don't break my family portrait."

"Fine, I appreciate it Jim."

Tony gathered a few sheaves of paper, pushed them into his briefcase and walked toward the door. He gave the thumbs up sign as he left the room. Jim wouldn't see him again for another three weeks. Tony did have a night class and Jim did not.

Jim settled down into a routine. He found college teaching to be pretty much the same as high school but he still couldn't adjust to mature young men and women and the fact that he was dealing with adults. He had to remind himself that he couldn't give orders to these students in the manner that he did with the high school students. He had to adjust his thinking from one of giving orders to one of asking for cooperation.

Students would be friendly with Jim and he responded in kind. He made some notations on his class cards concerning the personal life of individuals. A few were married and some of these had children. He would take that into consideration when he gave final grades. He realized that this was not a good idea and it put the traditional students at a disadvantage.

Jim was able to separate "apple polishing" from genuine friendship in most cases. Why not, he was an expert at the trade and it takes one to know one. There are some times when even the experts can't tell the difference between buttering up and friendship..

Benji was his favorite student. There was no doubt about that. He really liked the kid. Benji discussed President Polk and much of U.S. history with an expertise that impressed Jim. He knew Benji had more knowledge of history than he did. History was Jim's second subject, his first interest and area in which he invested his future was the dismal science of economics. Unfortunately for him, the college was too small to offer more than one section of economics. Since U.S. History I and II were required of all students these became the bread and butter courses for the Department of Social Studies. Jerry Swartz carried the sections of U.S. History II which was U.S. History after 1865.

In their discussions, Benji and Jim traded, not only information, but affection. Finally, Jim knew that Benji was something special. He asked Benji if he would do research for him and Jim would pay him by the hour. Benji said he didn't want any money but Jim said he would use the research for his doctoral disseration and if Benji didn't do it, he Jim, would have to spend long hours in research. When Jim got the doctorate his salary would increase dramatically and he would get his money back many times over on his investment in Benji.

Jim assured Benji that he, Jim, didn't have many hours available for research. Most people took a year off when they reached the dissertation stage but with a family, Jim could not afford such a luxury. Benji said he would do it, he could use the money.

Benji's parents lived on a farm just outside of Knox, a town southwest of Punxsutawney. They would gladly pay for Benjamin's education but he wanted to earn his own way. It was a game to him and he was winning. When Benji recorded Philadelphia as his home town, it was more of a joke with him. However, he did live in Phillie for a year and worked in one of the city's libraries.

Last year, Benji worked for the Department of Social Studies. This year he had a part-time job with the administration and with the library. He said he could do a lot of research in the library. Jim really didn't know his way around a library very well and he appreciated the fact that Benji knew the ins and outs of the system.

Jim and Benji would go to Rudys Bar and Sandwich Shop from time to time and get a beer and a pizza while they discussed life and Benji's progress in gathering ideas and data. Rudys was a place frequented by many students and faculty who mixed freely. Punxie was an informal college where rapport between faculty and students was the norm. Of course, there were faculty who were appalled at the mix of students and professors. Henry Blackenshep said "We have to maintain that separation for the good of the institution." He also criticized professors who didn't wear a tie to class.

Female students soon found out that they could get just about any assignment or grade commitment they wanted from Jim. He was putty in their hands and they knew how to mold him. His demeanor was halfway between awe and academia when it came to female students. Many times, he caught himself getting too personal and had to back off and assume his professorial stance, even though he was a lowly instructor. It would be at least another year before he began to look upon the young women only as students. He had the archaic notion that women were still dependent on men for their emotional sustenance even though his wife was strong and Jim relied more on her for support than she did on him.

One female in particular caught Jim by surprise. It was the beautiful Helga Anderson. Her body was stupefying. Jim couldn't believe that such a beautiful women could also be intelligent. He should have realized that a girl with her intelligence didn't need any extra help or tutoring. She used this as an excuse to come to Jim's office and talk to him.

Often Helga would come in with some problem concerning the reading assignment. After a brief discussion, she would turn the conversation around to Jim's personal life and throw in bits of her own. Jim was fascinated and he often spent an entire office hour with her while other students were waiting in the hall.

Helga had shoulder length hair with a light strawberry colored tint. She often dressed in jeans and loose sweaters. When she stretched, which was often, her breasts moved up and down in the sweater. Jim was embarrassed but he liked that an awful lot. Sometimes when she was talking Jim didn't hear a word she said, his mind was busy absorbing her beauty.

On one occasion, Helga invited herself to join Benji and Jim on their trip to Rudys. She drank beer along with the guys. They liked her and she liked them. She had been a friend of Benji's before Jim came on the scene. The previous semester, she like Benji, worked for the Department of Social Studies so they were well known to the rest of the department members who always gave her a warm greeting when they came upon her.

When Jim referred to her as Helga, she put her face close to his and whispered "Please call me Hellie." It wasn't long before she was referring to him as Jim. She did this in front of Chairman Gregory who let her know that he didn't consider it proper.

The smell of Helgo brought back old instincts in Jim. He remembered the first intimacies he had with Martha, back at Bloomsburg University of Pennsylvania. It was a reincarnation of spirit. But, this was a student and he was an instructor and close association would violate every commandment of teaching. He rationalized, "If I can be friendly with Benji then I can be friendly with Hellie. I certainly wouldn't violate my marriage vows with Martha under any circumstances." But, alas, Hellie had other ideas on this subject.

In one office discussion, she looked Jim in the face. "You know I am in love with you."

Jim offered, "We have a nice relationship but don't mistake it for love Hellie. I'm very fond of you but I have certain obligations to my job and to my family so we have to keep our relationship on a friendly but not intimate basis."

Hellie heaved her breasts. "I'll accept that but don't turn me away. I'll keep my distance and my schoolgirl crush will go away and life will be normal for us both once again. I guess life is normal for you but right now it's not normal for me. The first day I saw you I prayed you weren't married. But why would a handsome accomplished man your age not be married."

"Well Hellie, that's the breaks of life."

She leaned back in the office chair. "I had a boy friend last year but it didn't work out. He wanted sex but I wasn't ready for him at that time and it broke us up. He eventually started dating another girl and believe it or not, in less than a year they were engaged to be married. Maybe she's pregnant. I'm not sure but both of them graduated last year and I lost track of them."

Hellie tried to delve into Jim's sex life and his past sex life. She wanted to know how many trophies he had in his display case but Jim was too much of a hick to know what she was angling about. When Jim finally figured out what Helga was driving at he admitted to himself that he only had one trophy in his display case and as far as he knew Hellie didn't have any.

The moment of truth came on a Thursday. Jim and Benji usually went to Rudys after the three o'clock class. It was this ritual which was joined by Hellie from time to time. On this particular Thursday Benji didn't show. Hellie arrived to join them but it was just her and Jim, one on one, so to speak.

Jim thought it would be okay for him and Hellie to get a beer and a pizza but he felt uncomfortable. They got in Jim's car and drove slowly to Rudys and parked in the parking lot. Jim breathed deeply and stared at the windshield.

Hellie realized that he was stalling. "Well, are we going in?" Her voice was forceful and demanding.

"I don't know Hellie, it might not look right for you and me to go in together under these circumstances."

"I don't see why not. We are not doing anything out of the ordinary. It's not like we're going to make love in there. Well Jim, make up your mind, are we going in or aren't we?"

She had him trapped. If he really cared for her he wouldn't mind going in to get a beer and pizza. Then again she thought that if he was hesitant to go in with her then he must have some feeling for her since he would go in if she didn't matter to him. She would have to sort these events out at a later time. At this moment she wanted to go in and this act would indicate some sort of declaration toward the future.

Jim offered "I'm sorry Hellie, but I just can't do it like this. It might not look right. "

Hellie muttered something under her breath. She opened the passenger door, got out, slammed the door and walked into Rudys. Jim grimaced, started the car and headed back toward Clearfield and home.

The Strategic Initiatives Committee

Chairman Harold Gregory approached Jim. There was an air of caution about him and Jim's intuition told him that something was afoot and he wasn't going to like it. The tip-off came with slow and methodical body movement and deep breaths by the chairman.

Gregory explained that the college was organizing a strategic initiatives committee and the purpose of it was to get the college more value for the money spent. President Curry wanted two members from each department to serve on this committee and considered it the most important committee on campus.

The chairman explained his philosophy on the subject and it was that the department should send an old experienced member and a new member. The old experienced member could look for flaws in academic thinking and the new member could protect his own future by monitoring and contributing to the dialogue. Since Jim was the only new member he was the only possible selection.

Jim countered that he didn't have tenure and besides he was working on his dissertation but Gregory reminded him that he would be at Punxie a long long time and it was in his best interests to participate on the committee. Gregory put the message gently that he was chairman of the department and Jim had no choice but to be on the committee. Jim would just have to adjust this into his already busy schedule.

The old member would be Paul Bossert whom Jim considered as "sour" Paul who seemed to disagree with anyone and anything. Paul had been one of the founding members of APSCUF the Association of Pennsylvania School College and University Faculties. Even though there were No Smoking signs posted everywhere and every building was a non-smoking area Paul continued to smoke in his office and when his door was opened a blue haze rolled out like some monster from a science fiction movie. It was also rumored that Paul drank too much and that he kept a bottle of whiskey in his file cabinet. Paul referred to himself as a "designated smoking area."

During the first meeting Jim was amazed that the members of the committee were taking their mandate seriously. For some reason he believed that there was no dedication of the faculty and that everyone was trying to get by with as little energy expended as possible. He was particularly impressed with Paul's contribution to the meeting. Paul seemed to know exactly what the problems were and had some plans for their solution. He particularly emphasized that the college should move quickly from the proposal stage to the initiative stage.

Paul proposed that the resources of the institution should be committed to upgrade the student record system and change the advisement, registration and degree audits in the next two years. He said that courses should be developed that provide more interdisciplinary study and greater coherence in education.

A short stocky professor with a thick head of black hair said that the college was already doing that but Paul countered him with a statistical analysis he had made of students majoring in social studies education in the department. He pointed to a weakness in science and math. "Indeed", he stated "many students get into social studies education to avoid math and science. This certainly is not what we want in a liberal education."

Jim sat in awe of the cigaret smoking and whiskey swilling junkie. He came to realize that he had a lot to learn from

41

the older members of the department. Their years of experience had given them insight that no new member could possibly have.

The portly black haired professor turned out to be Mike Castro who taught physics in the Department of Physical Sciences. His thrust was to get an integrated computer information system and related hardware firmly established even if it meant "getting rid of football and basketball." Castro was often seen wearing a T-shirt that said "Physics Majors Do It At The Speed of Light."

A prof who taught foreign languages in the Fine Arts Department said that they were instituting a program that would send honors students to study in England, China, Russia and Canada. The reference to Canada was some sort of inside joke and it brought a loud chuckle from a small group of the committee.

Acting Provost Lawrence Simmons said the college was going to implement two new programs, one in Women's Studies and one in African Studies. A thickly bespectacled black professor said that California University of Pennsylvania and Edinboro University both had black studies programs and they were discontinued for lack of interest. He also said that follow-up of Women's Studies programs indicated that this also was not successful at Indiana and Kutztown. Paul looked ahead but leaned over toward Jim and said that the black professor was named Rupert and he was in charge of the affirmative action program at Punxie.

Another member brought up the fact that the library has not purchased a new book in five years even though his department submits a book-want list every year. A defender of the library said that their budget was consumed by unnecessary expenditures for academic and professional journals which were all over-priced. He said that a data study showed that nobody uses these journals but the departments keep insisting that they be purchased. Besides the Punxie library was a part of Inter-Library Loan and you could get just about any book you wanted with it. Apparently this was going to be a time consuming topic and the chairman of the meeting said that they would table that for some time in the future.

As to the library, the committee chairman stated that a half million dollars has been committed to increasing computer lab facilities in the library. Books would soon be obsolete and faculty had better get used to the idea. Castro, the physicist, remarked that he doesn't like sitting up in bed while reading a laptop computer screen.

When the meeting was adjourned Jim was glad that he was a member. During the meeting he was able to see a lot of campus personalities that normally did not cross his path. He met professors he didn't know existed. Although it would cut into his precious time he would be in on the ground floor of changes at Punxie and he would be in a good position for advancement, at least in the eyes of the institution.

During the second meeting which was held two months later the real business of Punxie came to the forefront. It was the retention of students and ways of increasing enrollment at Punxie as well as the 14 related state universities. A dean from Edinboro and an enrollment and registration official from Mansfield gave a brief discussion of their attempts to increase enrollments by off-campus facilities, distance learning and giving older students up to 30 credits for life-experiences.

Questions posed to these individuals were succinct and there were no attempts to pad out discussions with unnecessary discussion. Paul wanted to know what strategies to protect professor jobs would be in place if distance learning became the norm. The Edinboro dean said that they had a television studio where classroom programs were broadcast to campuses in Warren and Sharon. Students at these locations were free to ask questions to the TV screen. A person was assigned to each of these off-campus facilities to give tests and transport materials to and from these classrooms. Paul said that perhaps this was good for the institution budget but he hated to see professors being eliminated.

Paul turned to Jim and said that Jim should be concerned about enrollment. Students were being accepted for college now that can barely read and write. The recruiting officer must go through the towns and villages of Pennsylvania with a drag net and Punxie would take anybody. Jim said that he thought his students were pretty good and he could make no disparaging remarks about them.

When the retention and recruitment of student discussion seemed to run its course the committee chairman asked the secretary to read the list of proposals concerning this topic.

Professor Pinkerski rose and said it was a pretty long list of proposals and if members would bear with him he would move slowly through the list. He said he would prepare a final copy for each member of the committee as well as a copy of the minutes of the meeting.

There would be construction of a Student Services Center which would handle all problems related to students. This would be a combination of financial aid, records and registration, enrollment management and scheduling. Paul remarked to Jim that there were more than enough non-teaching faculty around to handle this load. He said that Punxie was over-managed.

The feasibility of establishing a student access information program would be investigated. This would permit Punxie administration to schedule, bill, send transcripts and accumulate address data on-line and at the convenience of students.

A candle-lighting service, similar to those Christmas services held in churches, would be held for incoming students. It will be a pageant and ritual that will make the student feel a part of some higher spiritual organization and perhaps give a closer family feeling to the individual. To Jim's surprise, Paul said that he thought this was a good idea even though he would never be there to witness it.

An inter-university committee consisting of members of

44

Punxie, Indiana, Clarion and branch campuses of the University of Pittsburgh and Penn State would consider the possibility of offering combined courses that would be acceptable at each institution. For instance, a course in Computer Science could be taught at one location and students in that area could get credit at one of the five institutions.

Perhaps it would be feasible to give honor roll students at local high schools a five hundred dollar reduction in tuition. When this proposal was introduced Castro said that it would discriminate against students of meager financial means since their poor scores might be the result of having to grub for money with part-time jobs and the like. It was his experience that better students came from more affluent families. Costs at the state related institutions were already lower than at other similar places. He said that the cost to students at Punxie was only one fifth that of Grove City or Thiel. This he said was in spite of the fact that the state salaries were almost double those of Grove City or Thiel.

Punxie should give college credit for local high school students enrolled and successfully completing honors English courses in local high schools. Many of the other state institutions have already implemented that program. The idea behind this was to suggest that if students already had college credit at Punxie they might go there with the idea of saving a few hundred bucks. Anyway, it would be a good deal for students already planning on going to Punxie.

The college will nominate a faculty member for the "Award for Innovative Teaching" and that nominated member will be sent, at college expense, to the International Conference on College Teaching and Learning. There should also be a program where students can nominate Teacher of the Year. When this was proposed someone said "Why not teachers of the year, why stop at only one teacher. This was not quite settled and Pinkerski asked for a show of hands and everyone seemed to want teachers instead of teacher. Paul opined that at least more

45

teachers would get to put that on their resume and who knows they might even get their pictures in the Woodchuck News. After two meetings it looked like the committee had done its job and there would be no need to continue meetings but one more would be held just to tidy up loose ends. At the third meeting programs were discussed which would attract adult learners. There would be an adult information night to be held in various area communities. Perhaps more courses could be offered in the evening and on Saturdays.

Paul wondered who would be asked to teach Saturdays. He had taught Saturday classes and night classes during the same semester years ago when he first entered the profession. Back then there was no limit on the number of semester hours one would be assigned to teach. Paul had twenty one contact hours even though the semester hours were set at fifteen. The chairman had designed "lab" courses in social studies. Not only that, Paul traveled to an off-campus location two nights a week. He told Jim that's when he decided to get active in forming the union.

Paul again warned Jim about suspecting any innovation in college teaching. He figured that the administration's main goal was to get as many students into a classroom or course situation and hiring as few professors to handle them as possible. He had been burned too many times by promises of lower class loads that never materialized.

During this third and final meeting of the year there was an announcement that Punxie would be teaching a distance-learning class in Brookville during the fall semester. Punxie representatives were busy setting up the program. There was some objection from Clarion University since they considered Brookville to be in their sphere of influence but President Curry had some political clout here and the Clarion objections were not given serious consideration. The following summer a huge billboard advertising Clarion University appeared along the major roads leading into and out of Punxsutawney.

5. JERRY SWARTZ, FOOTBALL AND HOMECOMING

A special relationship developed between Jim and Jerry Swartz. They shared confidences to the degree that involved their spouses and past history. It was like finding a long lost soul mate. Each told anecdotes from the past and the present which cemented the relationship. Jim was certain that he could trust Jerry to look after his interests and he would be willing to put his reputation on the line for Jerry.

Jerry was one of the few Punxie professors who didn't graduate from one of the other 14 state institutions. He had a bachelors and masters degree from Columbia University and was in the last stages of a doctorate there. The administration at Punxie was more than happy to get an Ivy League graduate on the faculty and into the college catalog. However, when Jim once talked about buying property in Punxsutawney, Jerry remarked "You aren't planning to stay here are you?"

Since Jim came from a small rural town and was now on the staff of a college he thought he had progressed to a pinnacle beyond his imagination. Jerry further disturbed Jim when he stated that Indiana University was the asshole of Pennsylvania and Punxie was 40 miles up the gut.

Jerry often talked about his mutual fund and stock investments. He subscribed to the *Wall Street Journal* in order to follow the rise and fall of the stock market. Often he would engage Jim in conversation about the stock market. Jim didn't have any money to invest so these discussions were wasted on him as it went into one ear and became quickly neutralized by other thoughts. When Jim mentioned Jerry's stock analysis to Martha she thought it might be a good idea to get Jerry's advice and put some money into stocks. Jim pointed out that they were barely able to meet required expenses and he was an instructor and Jerry was an associate professor.

There was an incident with a paycheck. When the paychecks arrived, Jerry said his was short fourteen cents. Jim didn't know if his was short or not. He was content with the ballpark figure.

Jerry stewed about the fourteen cents all morning and into the afternoon. By two o'clock he couldn't contain himself and called the payroll division in Harrisburg. He was informed that the fourteen cent shortage did indeed occur but that it was an adjustment of two cents a pay for payments to the retirement fund. Jerry spent the next hour trying to explain the shortage and adjustment to Jim. This was not a high priority on Jim's agenda. However, it was somewhat of a compulsion to Jerry. Before Jim left for home Jerry took another shot at him on the fourteen cents.

In another instance, Jim and Jerry drove to Harrisburg for a meeting with their state representative concerning his appearance to speak at their Social Studies Club meeting. They traveled a small portion of the Pennsylvania Turnpike. The turnpike fee was $1.05. After Jim paid the money but Jerry asked for a receipt. He explained that they could also deduct the mileage for the trip from their income tax even though they were driving a state car. Jim said he didn't make enough money to pay income tax. This was an exaggeration but it reflected Jim's thinking.

One day when Jerry showed up at the parking lot with a new car, a Lincoln, he was greeted with catcalls and jostling by other faculty members. Almost apologetic, he told Jim about his old car, about how it was about to fall apart and how he needed something dependable. He wanted something less ostentatious but his wife insisted on the Lincoln since they often took hectic trips to New York City.

"That is one great car" enthused Jim. "What did it cost?"

Jerry gasped and was silent for a moment. His face had a look of bewilderment. "More than it should have." he answered.

Jim was taken aback. He couldn't believe it. Was the price one paid for a car a forbidden topic? It wasn't like they were nomads in Mongolia and he was asking the number of sheep in the flock of his colleague. This was taboo in Mongolia and apparently the price one paid for a car was taboo in America. Since the price could be ascertained by simply calling the Lincoln dealer it didn't matter and Jim really didn't care about the price anyway, he was making conversation. He laughed to Jerry "I'll have to trade in my yak any day now."

After reflecting on this incident Jim figured Jerry was too proud of his financial abilities to have them tarnished in any manner. Perhaps he didn't want to be accused of being "taken" by the dealer. He spent a lot of time talking about insurance policies and did a lot of shopping around. Jim noticed that Jerry's new car had New York license plates. Jerry's explanation was that he didn't want to go through the mandatory inspections of Pennsylvania. Jim didn't buy that explanation since New York also had car inspections as well as emission inspections. Jim chalked it up to a quirk.

Jerry was an "insider." He knew the scuttlebutt of the campus and most of it on other campuses. He was the first to report that a member of the state legislature proposed closing Mansfield and Cheyney Universities since the enrollment of both places was low and their students could go to the other institutions. He wondered why Punxie wasn't mentioned but concluded that the legislator probably didn't know Punxie's status as a state institution. The legislator also erroneously thought that Penn State was a member of the state university system.

Another rumor Jerry had gathered was that there would be a large retrenchment of faculty at Punxie. In serious tones he mentioned it to other members of the department. He treated this rumor as fact which upset several people, especially faculty spouses. Jerry was usually right on the money in predicting the future of Punxie and so the retrenchment rumor was especially debilitating.

These speculations of Jerry never accomplished anything

49

except to disturb others. The retrenchment rumor was outside the realm of possibility. This was part of Jerry's psyche and it seemed to contrast his easy going confidential manner.

Most everybody liked Jerry. He went out of his way to cultivate the favor of administrators. They often made humorous remarks about him during meetings. This was a clue to participants that the meeting was informal. It was also a clue to others that Jerry was someone special in the eyes of administrators.

When October rolled around, Pennsylvania was a panorama of color as the leaves turned to golden, red, brown, yellow and orange. It was a ritual for Jim and Martha to take a day off and drive through the splendid foliage. On this particular October the leaves were early in changing color and the forecast of rain promised to down most of the leaves.

Jim asked Jerry if he would cover his two classes on Wednesday in order for him and Martha to take in the leaves. Jerry asked Jim why he didn't take a personal day and Jim's reply was that they were only going to be gone a half day and he didn't want to use up a day. Besides he was willing to do this for Jerry at any time.

Jerry worried that the administration would get wind of it but he would do it. Jim assured Jerry that "Pratt was asleep at the switch" and there would be little possibility of discovery. The caper went off without a hitch.

When Saturday arrived, it was time for football. Since Jim lived in Clearfield, about fifty miles away, he never bothered to go to the games. However, Jerry went to all the home games and sat down and in front of President Curry's reserved seats. Jerry often rose and walked to the refreshment stand and rest rooms. This was a ploy to get Curry and wife to wave to him as he returned to his seat. Jerry wanted the administration to know that he was a regular guy and attended college functions. He knew that Curry was a football fanatic and this was a way to cash in on that knowledge.

50

Football at Punxie could best be described as second rate even though President Curry put a lot of effort into it. The team was not of the same caliber as the other 14 state owned institutions. Indiana, Edinboro and West Chester regularly were ranked among the best in the country in their division. They often sent players to the pros. Any of them would have killed little Punxie.

Punxie's football challenges came from colleges such as Moravian, Waynesburg, Thiel, Grove City, Elizabethtown, Susquehanna and Gettysburg. It was difficult to create interest in football since Punxie did not belong to a conference.

President Curry spent a lot of time with Coach Phillips and his assistants. He authorized without question, scouting and recruiting travel. This irritated many professors who were turned down in their request for travel reimbursement to conferences.

Punxie was not high on the desirable list of high school football players. The team consisted mostly of players from local high schools. The few exceptions came from the Pittsburgh area.

The star of the team was Ernie Ploget, a black bolt of lightning from Carnegie in Allegheny County. In Jim's first year at work Punxie had one hundred and thirty two black students in a student body of 1,628. Of the 67 black male students, 43 were on athletic teams with scholarships.

Ernie Ploget was everyone's hero. He scored at least two touchdowns a game. Rumor had it that he was turned down by Penn State because of low SAT scores but was accepted at Notre Dame. He turned down Notre Dame since they had at least thirty running backs, all probably bigger than 180 pound Ernie. At Notre Dame he would not make the first team but at Punxie he could be a star.

Ernie had a lot of academic problems and Coach Phillips hired a tutor exclusively for him. With this intensive tutoring and letters from the coach to Ernie's instructors the star was able to maintain a solid C average.

Martha wanted to see at least one football game and it

51

was decided the family would go to the homecoming game. It was on a bright clear cool Saturday at the end of October. Someone had figured out that it rained a lot at the beginning of October and if they held homecoming at the end of the month it was usually dry and clear. Proposals by Professor George Grecco of the Faculty Senate to do away with homecoming were always met with jeers. Grecco was noted for this proposal which he introduced each year and another one which would select a new "short" name for Punxsutawney State College. He said the name was too long to be comfortable.

So Jim, Martha and children arrived at the stadium which was the former stadium of the Punxsutawney High School. When the town built a new stadium for the high school the old one was given to the college. It was refurbished into a pretty good stadium with plenty of seating for the usual small crowds at the games.

Admission was free to faculty members and the family headed for the bleachers with the band, figuring that was the Punxie side. A small but enthusiastic crowd dotted the bleachers on the other side. A large banner "Go Eagles" was strung between two poles. Today's game was with the Juniata Golden Eagles of Huntingdon. Of course Punxie's mascot was the groundhog. Cheerleaders were already whipping up the crowd with chants of "Go Hogs."

As the entourage reached the bleachers a voice called out "Jim, up here." It was Jerry so Jim and family went up to the middle of the bleachers in full view of the president's reserved section. It didn't matter from an "apple polishing" angle since President Curry had no idea who Jim was or what he was.

The band was surprisingly good for such a small group. Excitement mounted as the team broke through the large paper poster held by two of the cheerleaders. The team was surprisingly large for such a small college and the team booster's coffee was hot.

It looked like a wipeout for Punxie when Ernie Ploget

took the opening kickoff back for a touchdown. However, the run back was a fluke as the Golden Eagle defense tightened and their offense was a good match for Punxie. The score was 20 to 14 at the half in Punxie's favor.

Jerry left his seat several times. Once he came back with soft drinks for everybody. Martha and Sandra, Jerry's wife, were eyeball to eyeball discussing everything imaginable about the college. Martha said she was out of it, living so far away. Sandra said they usually held a party in their home before the end of the semester and she definitely would see that the Tailors were invited. The two of them seemed to be soul mates, similar to Jim and Jerry.

Midway through the second quarter a man appeared on the cinder runway. He was surrounded by six children all under the age of ten. They seemed to be stuck together and clinging to each other and the man who was holding a baby in his arms. They moved down the cinder track which circled the field and the man appeared to be looking into the stands as if someone was waiting for him.

Jerry said "Here comes Murphy."

Martha asked "Who's Murphy?"

Jerry went on to explain that Murphy was a teacher of ethics at Punxie and he apparently was trying to prove something by having all these kids. During every home football game he and his kids show up just before the half and he parades them down the sidelines. There didn't seem to be any reason for this but it happened every home game. Jerry referred to them as the Murphy Clump. He had a way of description that reached the core of things.

He went on to say that Murphy was working on an evening law degree at Duquesne University in Pittsburgh and he commuted there on a daily basis. Of course, Mrs. Murphy had the seven dwarfs to contend with.

During the half, a red and black uniformed band member carrying a clarinet approached the stands and made its way up

53

the steps. "Hi Mr. Tailor" it called.

The band member turned out to be Benji and Jim was happy to see him. He practically embraced Benji. It was a happy round of introductions. Martha knew that Benji was someone special in Jim's life and was happy to meet him. She immediately felt motherly toward Benji and invited him over for dinner "some evening."

Jim was a popular teacher. His easy going manner attracted students and invited them to more intimacy than perhaps an instructor should have with his students. Many students who recognized Jim in the stands would call out "Hey Mr. Tailor". Jerry made some remark about payoff time when grades came out. None of the passing students hollered "Hey Mr. Swartz."

In the short time Jim had known Jerry he had yet to hear Jerry give a compliment to a student, colleague or administrator or for that matter, to anyone. Perhaps the opportunity for compliments had never been presented.

Coming out of the corner of the stands, Jim could see Hellie and two other girls sauntering toward the center of the walk below. He knew the other two girls were also in his class but couldn't remember their names. To himself he thought "Don't come up here, don't come up here." He didn't think it was a good idea for Martha to actually see the beauty of the girls but it was unavoidable.

Hellie and the girls marched right up to the center of the stands and made comments to Jim and Jerry. "We think your husbands are the two best teachers in the college" said the brunette with large silver earrings."

"That's great" said Sandra. She sensed some sort of threat. "We think they are also great husbands too."

Hellie looked at Jim and with great care examined Susan and Jimmy. She didn't want to stare at Martha but she could do that from the side if they paused on the steps.

The trio of girls left with a lot of giggles and small

waving. Hellie stopped to tighten her shoe laces and took a good look at Martha who was laughing in Jim's face. The children seemed uncomfortable.

Jerry mused " See what we have to put up with."

Martha laughed "I thought they were kind of cute. I didn't realize that college students were so young." Jim breathed easier after that statement.

Jim offered "Well, they are only a year or two out of high school."

Half-time gave Jim a chance to examine the program. He was interested in seeing if he had any football players in his classes. Pictures and names of the cheerleaders were also in the program. Jim did have a football player, Bill Hockberry a wiry defensive back, in his economics class. Hockberry seemed to be a good student. Jim winced when a pass went over Hockberry's head for a touchdown. Later the defensive back vindicated himself by intercepting a pass and running it back to the opponent's forty yard line. Jim made a note to compliment him on that.

The most interesting part of the game came when the Eagles had the ball. Their highly touted quarterback, Bart Zimmer, threw a pass to the end zone. It hit the tight end right in the chest and bounced off. On the next play, Zimmer's pass was again perfect and again to the tight end who again missed it. When the end came back to the huddle he was carrying his helmet. Quarterback Zimmer pulled back a fist and hit the end in the jaw sending him sprawling.

The referees didn't know what to do. They could penalize such an act between teams but not when it happened within a team. After a ten minute discussion they penalized the Eagles five yards for delay of game.

Punxie went on to win the game by a score of 31 to 24. Ernie Ploget made three touchdowns. On the way home Susan waved her Punxie banner in the car and Jimmy clutched his Punxie groundhog with the big letter P on its stomach.

6. HELLIE MAKES A MOVE

Jim was amazed at the variety of excuses students used when they cut classes. He was vulnerable to the excused absence ploy for field trip and college activities. Since he didn't know most of the professors he had to take the student at face value as well as the official looking form they placed before him. When Jim mentioned excused absences and questioned field trip absences to Mark he was met with a grin. Mark, Jim and Homer were at the club house relaxing and Jim stated that already the student field trips for science majors and conferences for education majors were having an effect on his classes. Homer said that this was a bone of contention between many of the disciplines on campus.

According to Homer, there were many ingenious students at Punxie who seemed to delight in outwitting professors. If they spent half as much time on their studies they would graduate with honors. Too many are content to squeak through.

Homer related a story from the vast files of his past. It was his first year of teaching at Punxie and he, like Jim, was vulnerable to student pranks as he called them.

Homer said his best student in History of Europe was one Mike McElhenny. He aced every test and ended up with almost a perfect score in this class. Since this was his first year of teaching and he was protective of the security of his tests Mike McElhenny was indeed an exceptional student. The next highest grade was a low A, followed by a smattering of Bs.

"Well" said Homer " I found out later the guy in my class was not Mike McElhenny, it was some guy named Shawn who pretended to be Mike and take the class for him. He had the course before and was really a good student. Like everyone else I don't ask for identification so I just assumed it was Mike McElhenny. The laugh was really on me."

Jim was uneasy. "What did you do about it?"

56

"There wasn't much I could do but accept it. I didn't find out about the scam until the end of my second year when another student related the facts to me. He said McElhenny paid Shawn to do this for him. The student also said that Shawn went to Pittsburgh on different occasions and took the Graduate Record Exam for a couple of graduating seniors.

Mark said " I have another story you'll both get a kick out of. "

He said he lived next to one of Koski's rental units and there were four male students living in the unit. He used to sit on his porch and watch the guys out in the street throwing football in the fall and catching softball in the spring. He got to know the guys quite well. One guy in particular whose name was Eddie Gist was always out there. Mark said he knew the other three from his classes and seeing them on campus but he had never seen Eddie on campus.

The four rental students seemed to be decent guys. They didn't hold wild parties and they would have girls over once in a while. He never noticed any of the girls staying overnight.

Mark went on. "One day when Eddie was throwing softball with another guy just before noon I asked him why he wasn't in class and when do you ever study? Just about everybody connected with the college has classes in the morning. If they don't have classes then they are off studying somewhere."

Eddie said that he didn't have to study much since he had a photographic memory. He could look at a page, skim it, and the information would be locked in his mind. Since he enrolled at Punxie has always been an honors student."

Since he didn't know Eddie academically this made Mark curious. So when he got the opportunity he punched out the name Edward Gist on the college computer information system which was accessible only to department chairman and profs like Mark who knew the code.

It turned out there was no Edward Gist registered and one never was registered at Punxie. Now Mark was really

57

curious and anxious to ask Eddie about it..

He approached Eddie who swore Mark to reluctant secrecy. He admitted he had never registered for college but was telling his parents he was a student at Punxie. They would send him money for tuition, books and living expenses. Eddie would pay his rent and convince his parents he was doing honor roll work at Punxie. He even took them around the campus when they visited. He didn't think his house mates were aware of his scam. Since we no longer send grades to parents they never found out about it.

When Mark asked Eddie about graduation Eddie remarked that he would tell his parents he graduated with honors but he would have to skip the commencement exercises because he had a lead on a really good job in Florida. He would need a little seed money to get down there for the interview.

After that story Jim would always reserve a little skepticism in his dealings with students. Again he marveled at the ingenuity and guts of the college age group.

Homer had another story of interest to Jim. He said he went on the annual field trip to a meeting of the state history teaching organization. This is a trip shared by students and professors alike.

He was sitting with Ralph Green a student they all knew. The trip was long and they had a lot of time to talk. Jokingly Homer said that everyone needed a little deviousness in his life. Ralph said he had deviousness in his life and it bothered him.

Homer didn't want to pry but his curiosity was now up and he asked Ralph to elaborate. Ralph said that his books last semester cost two hundred and twenty five dollars but when he told his parents about it he said he had spent three hundred and fifty dollars on books. His parents trusted him and sent him the amount he stated. He said this was bothering his conscience so much he would never do that again. However, he kept this source of income in reserve in case he ever needed money.

There were occasions when Jim had to stay into the evening at the college. These involved such things as department meetings, college programs, the Social Studies Club and preparation for the next day.

Usually meeting time and dates were known in advance and Jim was able to tell Martha. When this happened, Martha and the children would go to a fast food place and gorge. Most often it was out for pizza. The children preferred this and Martha liked the break from her kitchen.

On these occasions Jim would eat at the local dinor or the Italian or Chinese restaurants. He preferred the dinor since it reminded him of his Bloomsburg college days when he worked in a dinor as a short order cook. His shift was nine in the evening until two a.m. and he did it for four years. Needless to say, he didn't have much of an evening social life.

The Punxie Faculty Senate met in the evenings since an hour or two during the day was not enough time for their important debates and work. The fact that they had no power to pass any binding legislation didn't seem to phase them. It was a group which took its work seriously. They considered themselves an important advisory group to the working of the college. The president and the rest of the administration considered them a nuisance.

Jerry was on the Faculty Senate since it was a quick step to promotion. Since Jim had asked Jerry to cover for him while he and Martha went leaf viewing, Jerry felt no hesitation in asking Jim to cover for him at the November meeting of the Faculty Senate. Jerry was always quick to cash in on his vouchers.

Jim found the Senate to be a nightmare of meeting decorum. Points of order were challenged and arguments over the minutes of the last meeting took an hour to resolve. He tried to follow the discussion and listen to those who had the floor but his mind kept wandering in and out of the droning. It was as if he was hypnotized and could not listen.

59

In reference to some serious point, Bill Grecco said that "As Charlie Brown stated, we have met the enemy and they are us."

Henry Broadcast of the English Department rose immediately. "Mr. Chairman, I would like to correct my learned colleague. It was not Charlie Brown but Pogo who said we have met the enemy and he is us."

Jim wondered "What in the hell is going on here?"

A few minutes later Grecco made reference to college professors as being call girls, prostituting themselves for money. He never quite explained what his point was but he was satisfied with the splattering of giggles he received. He also used clichés such as "Let's run it up the flag pole and see if anyone salutes it."

Boris Sullivan of the Threatre Department insisted on smoking cigars and stinking up the room. Jim thought he would gag. John Freemont rose to point out the NO SMOKING IN THIS ROOM sign. This prompted others to light up with loud ha ha ha. Blue smoke filled the room and John Freemont uttered something and left the room. The chairman of the meeting didn't have any control over this situation and chose to ignore it.

Basically the only item on the agenda that was settled was the parking sticker issue. From now on, if the president agreed, the faculty would have their own parking lot and would not have to park in with the students. Students would get an S sticker, faculty an F sticker and service employees an E sticker. Students would be assessed a forty-five dollar parking fee. Faculty would park free of charge. When this proposal reached President Curry he decided that everyone would pay an annual fifty dollar parking fee since it would help to pay for the enormous cost of blacktop for the new lot. Parking and parking regulations were the prerogative of the college and the state had nothing to say about it.

Jim made a mental note never to be on the Faculty Senate. Perhaps the senate members realized that they had no power to make any changes and it was just a forum to express their individual personalities.

Jim had heard rumors about the Dean's Council and this seemed more of a horror. He thought he was on his Dean's Council but he wasn't sure about that. He would simply have to get on one of the campus-wide committees where he could bury himself and never surface. However, he knew the Senate and the Councils were the routes to promotion and he was a lowly instructor. He was at the bottom of the totem pole. A professor at Clarion University referred to that institution as "second rate" in an article published in the *Chronicle of Higher Education*. If Clarion was second-rate, where did that leave Punxie?

Another occasion to stay into the evening almost caused Jim's downfall. It was a meeting of the Social Studies Club. The chairman of the department, Harold Gregory, hinted that he would like Jim to take over the club next semester since the present advisor, Earl Gratis, was not very enthusiastic about it. Jim would soon learn that those who goofed up an assignment were usually relieved of assignments and those who were dependable usually had to do them. The doers also got the assignments of the goof-ups who didn't seem to be accountable for their goofing-up.

The meeting of the Social Studies Club consisted of the minutes of the last meeting, the state of the treasury and suggestions for the upcoming field trip and the next meeting. The club received one hundred dollars from the student activity fund which would be used toward the field trip.

The featured speaker for the meeting was the local state representative, Phillip French, who spoke on the need to increase taxes and get out the vote. By increasing taxes, more money could be shifted to Punxie.

French encouraged students to register to vote and chided them for their parent's failure to vote when they were students. At one time, the legal voting age in Pennsylvania was twenty-one and college students rallied to get the vote at eighteen. If you were old enough to fight and drink beer, you were old enough to vote. When the vote was finally given to eighteen year olds, less than ten percent of those between eighteen and twenty-one voted. The percentage at present was twelve percent. If college students never voted what are the chances that someone flipping hamburgers in a fast food restaurant would get out and vote.

Congressman French figured that if he could get the college student vote he would never be defeated.

Most faculty members at Punxie never bothered to vote. The Social Studies Department was an exception to this even though members such as Earl Gratis thought that not voting was a badge of honor.

There were heated discussions between big city Jerry and rural Harold Gregory. Punxie was in the middle of Republican conservatism. Most of the rural people of Central Pennsylvania voted a straight Republican ticket. Phillip French's position was assured in the regular elections. It was an unexpected challenge in the primaries that worried him.

After the meeting, Hellie approached Benji and asked him to ask Jim if they could go out for beer and pizza, to which Jim agreed. They went to Rudys as usual and were joined by other attendees of the club meeting. It was a nice time and the students appreciated Jim's presence. Harold Gregory appeared briefly, had a piece of pizza but drank a ginger ale. He bid everyone good night and made some remarks about the police and underage drinking. Gregory knew college life well and accepted beer drinking as a part of it. There was no need for him to get preachy.

It was near ten o'clock and Jim decided it was time to leave. Hellie asked for a lift back to her dormitory. Benji decided to stay and quaff a few more beers. He and a few friends were enthusiastically debating the latest college football rankings.

On the way to the dorm Hellie asked Jim to park and help her solve a social problem involving her room mate. Jim was unaware that the old room mate ploy was rampant on campuses. Students couldn't get their work done because they were up all night keeping their room mate from committing suicide or keeping their room mate from dying from some unknown disease contracted only before exams by college students.

While sitting in the car Hellie leaned on Jim and positioned herself to be kissed by him. He didn't take the hint and continued babbling in a pedantic manner. Finally, Hellie grabbed him and kissed him on the lips.

Jim stiffened "You shouldn't have done that Hellie, I'm a married man."

"You might be married Jim but you're not dead. I really love you Jim and I wish you would respond to me. I would do most anything for you."

Jim held her close. He felt warm and content. "No Hellie, I just can't let myself go. I love my wife and my children and wouldn't want anything to come between us."

She whispered "I would never come between you. It's possible to love more than one person. Don't you find me attractive and desirable?"

Jim gulped. He found her all of that and more. He held her closer. Jim could never accept the fact that this beautiful intelligent creature was in love with him and willing to do "most anything for him."

Hellie whispered "Just talk to me."

Jim didn't know what to say after this but Hellie did. "We could have a close relationship and when I graduate next year it will all be over. You will go on with being a professor and I'll go on with whatever life has in store for me I've just got to be with you, I can't think of anything else. I figure if you give me some response I can work on getting you out of my mind. You know how it is, romance dies down after a while."

Jim put his hands on her cheeks and pulled her head to his. He kissed her on the mouth. "I want to do that Hellie, but I really don't want to get involved. I won't be kissing you again."

Jim didn't want to get involved but now he was involved. They talked for an hour about nothing and the time went by quickly. Hellie became upset. "Oh, my God, look at the time, its eleven fifteen."

"What's wrong with that. I'll take you back now."

"You can't take me back now, the dorm is locked after eleven o'clock. I won't be able to get in."

"Can't you go to the window and yell for someone to come and let you in?"

"No, if I do that, the dorm mother will know I'm late and write a letter to my parents and I'll be put on probation."

Jim asked "What kind of place is this? At Bloomsburg, the girls could stay out all night if they wanted to and that was fifteen years ago."

"Well Jim, this ain't Bloomsburg and I don't know what to do. Don't leave me off somewhere and abandon me."

Jim thought about it for a minute. "I know, I'll take you up to DuBois and get a motel room for you. In the morning when I come back to Punxie I'll swing by DuBois and pick you up."

Hellie liked that idea. She could envision Jim coming into the room with her to see if everything was in order and she could take it from there. Yes, that was an excellent idea, a great idea.

It would mean an hour out of his way but it would be worth it to Jim to settle the problem since Hellie seemed to be thinking that Jim should spend the night with her somewhere and that was out of the realm of possibility. Oh what a tangled web we weave.

Hellie again said "Don't leave me in the motel room right away, make sure it's safe."

Jim looked at his watch. Time was fast a flying. He tried to think ahead.. "I better call my wife and tell her I'll be late."

A pay telephone was found and Jim made a call. He came to the car and said that everything was under control. He took several deep breaths and rubbed his face and said that before they headed for DuBois, they better check the campus and the dormitory.

When they got to the dormitory, female students were standing on the lawn. Most of them were in sleeping clothes. Lights were on in every window.

Campus police cars were in evidence and a town emergency vehicle was standing by. A man in a yellow fireman's coat stood in the middle of the street and Jim couldn't get through. Jim backed up and swung around the block to the rear of the building where several students had gathered.

Jim pulled up to a few students standing near the road. Two girls came over to the car.

"What's going on?" he asked.

One girl said "Oh, it's one of those damn bomb scares. There's no bomb but they made us get out here in the cold anyway. We've been out here for ten minutes now and it's disgusting."

A girl in curlers and white face makeup said "Every time there's a crowd at Rudys someone gets drunk and makes trouble."

Jim looked at Hellie. "You're problem is solved. Just get in with the crowd and go in the dorm with them. Nobody will realize that you weren't there to begin with."

"Don't you want to go to DuBois with me?"

"No that wouldn't be wise, it's not necessary now, besides I should be getting home."

Hellie narrowed her eyes at Jim. "I hope you called home and not a bomb scare to the dorm."

"What kind of guy do you think I am?" he laughed."

A handsome, intelligent one" she whispered and kissed him on the cheek " and also devious." She slammed the car door extra hard.

65

7. THE NOT SO SECRET LIFE OF TONY

It was the second week in November and Jim had stayed over supper in order to work on his evaluation package. Tenure was not granted to instructors and professors until six years of satisfactory evaluation had elapsed. There were many requirements that had to be met and a formula was given for submission of the total document. He had to demonstrate continuing scholarly growth, contributions to the college, contributions to the community, satisfactory student and peer evaluation. It was a problem to determine which of his experiences were relevant to these criteria.

After supper Jim worked at the department office computer setting up his data and creating a rough draft of his presentation. He didn't have a computer in his office since he was assured his present office was a temporary assignment. Only four of the department members had personal computers so Jim's hopes of getting one were not high. Nine members were ahead of Jim in the quest for a computer. The other members didn't want one.

There was a letter in the mailbox from the Sigma Sigma Sigma sorority asking him if he would be interested in being their advisor. He considered it but right now he was too involved with the dissertation and getting used to his new role of college teacher. It was signed by Pamela Clark, a student in one of Jim's classes. He couldn't remember which one but he did remember Pamela Clark. Then it came to him, this was the sorority called Tri-Sig back at Bloomsburg. He laughed at himself for not having made the connection before.

Another social invitation was offered by Phi Kappa Theta which Jim assumed to have a biology connection since it was for lunch in the biology student work room.

Fraternities and sororities at the state owned institutions never had the same drawing power that they did at private institutions. At the bigger private schools they had house managers, cooks and cleaning personnel. It's nice to have money.

Time was beginning to pass too quickly and Jim started yawning. It was only eight o'clock but he decided to call it quits, return to put the papers in his office and head home to Clearfield. There was the matter of locking the department and turning off the switches to the duplicator, the computer and the coffee pot. He slowly made his way from Krieder Hall to Seminary Hall and his office.

When Jim reached the basement office door, he paused to admire his new plastic name plate. At last he looked like a recognized member of the faculty. To him it was the difference between eating out of a brown bag or at the dining table. The posted schedule of Professor Jamerson indicated that he had a night class which ended at nine.

Jim opened the door and stepped in. The lights were on and Jim's mouth dropped open at the sight before him. Leaning over his desk was a blonde woman with her dress draped over her back and Tony Jamerson was shoving a dick into her. His shorts and pants were down at his ankles. Jim had little time to think and make a move. He was frozen in place.

Tony turned to Jim. "Jimbo, close the door, we don't want strangers walking in here."

Jim tried to be cool and collected. "I'm sorry, I thought you were in class." He bumbled around for a few seconds then backed out and closed the door, remembering to push in the center locking device.

Standing in shock outside the door, Jim tried to collect his thoughts. He looked for a place to sit down but there was none. He sat on the steps. Eventually a half grin came over his face.

Where had he seen that woman before? What a body, what a well shaped ass. He saw her somewhere. Was she a student in Tony's class? He didn't know Tony's class so it couldn't have been there. Just before his exit the blonde looked back and Jim had a good look at her. Those closely wound curls covering her ears looked like ear-muffs. He had seen her somewhere. What a scene. What an experience for an inexperienced lout like Jim.

The next day Tony appeared during Jim's office hour. He began shuffling papers, emptying his briefcase, reloading it. "Hey Jimboy I hope we didn't give you a heart attack last night."

Jim gave a half laugh." Well, I must say I was shocked. Do you do that often?"

"Every chance I get."

"I guess that explains why the stuff on my desk is moved around and the sweet smell of success hangs over it."

Tony grinned. "No, usually when I move your stuff I'm doing it from the front. If you notice, your desk is about two inches lower than mine. This is just the right height for me to shove it in and still be comfortable and get some leverage with my legs."

"I hope you're not shooting gism over my desk."

"Oh no, nothing like that. Your desk is really comfortable though. You ought to try that with some of those girls that come in to see you all the time, especially that red head."

Jim looked amused. "No, I couldn't do that. Couldn't you be fired for doing something like that with students."

"Hell no Jim, a lot of professors are doing it. I believe you could be fired at the University of Virginia since they made that a policy. Somebody is challenging the rule there and it will probably be overturned. Anyway Jimboy, you won't have to put up with me much longer. At the end of the semester I'm getting my own office and you will get a new office mate. By next year you should be getting your own office."

Jim wanted to pry into Tony's private life but didn't know how to do it. He offered " I guess you're not married."

"Why do you think that. I'm happily married and have three children. My wife and I have a good sex life. It's just I can't

68

see passing up these opportunities. Life is short and old age will come galloping in on me. I still have some red blood left and I want to use it while it's still there."

"Are you a sex addict?"

"Naw, I just like it and so do the women I make love to."

"Is it love, or just sex. I believe there's a difference."

"Maybe it's just sex, but it's love to me. I don't make any promises and the woman I mess with know that I'll quit them sooner or later and they are free to quit me any time they choose with no strings attached. Unfortunately, some of them do get attached and that presents a big problem. Especially when they start following me around."

So that is why Tony had the nickname of Abdul. Jim had to admit he was fascinated by the adventures of the man, not that he himself wanted to duplicate them. He would have liked to discuss Tony with Jerry or Martha but he didn't dare since it might reflect on him and Martha might think there was too much temptation. There was temptation and there was opportunity and Jim promised to discipline himself.

Tony began to confide his adventures to Jim. What good are adventures if there is no one to share them with. One day he stated "Yesterday I screwed four different women. Boy was that an adventure in juggling. One at breakfast, one at lunch, one at supper and then my wife in the evening. Four women in a twenty four hour period, more like a sixteen hour period. What a day. A day to remember. And I'm only 42 years old. Imagine what I'll be doing when I'm fifty."

Jim peered at him. "You'll probably be dead."

"Maybe you're right Jimboy, maybe you're right. But I'll meet the grim reaper with a smile on my face."

"Aren't you afraid of catching some disease?" asked Jim.

"No, not here in the boondocks. Maybe in some sophisticated location like West Chester or Penn State. These are rural women who don't get around much. I would never do this at the University of Pittsburgh."

Jim went back to his papers. He lifted his head and stared at Tony. "You know if some woman had told me she screwed four different guys yesterday, I would have thought she was a whore or some real low-life. But when you tell me you screwed four different woman yesterday it looks like a badge of merit, some accomplishment. I'll have to think about that. There must be something wrong with my way of thinking. Perhaps it's our male dominated society."

"I could argue with you about male dominated society Jimbo. That's my field, philosophy. Women really want to castrate men and I want to get to them before they succeed. Women are not the minority they claim to be. "

It was such statements that made Jim wonder if Tony really liked women. Perhaps his sexual escapades were an attack on women and not as romantic as Tony thought. He had read somewhere that womanizing men really feel inferior and inadequate but Tony certainly did not give an impression of insecurity.

Tony had a lot of advice on how to make-out for Jim. He said that a married woman in her late twenties with two kids was the easiest to seduce. They were desperate to know that they were still attractive. Next, he said, were 39 year old woman, married or unmarried. They were approaching the magic age of forty and were vulnerable. He said he usually "gave counseling to the women along with his dick."

Once near late November when Jim answered the phone he shared with Tony a voice on the other end said "You better quit hanging around my wife or you'll be six feet under."

Jim blundered " I'm not hanging around with anyone's wife. You must have me mixed up with someone else."

"No" said the voice " I know it's you and if you keep this up I'm going to get you." Then the phone went dead.

Jim worried about the call. He could handle most situations but a sudden panic came over him. The anonymous caller, a voice with no face, was having an effect. Maybe someone would plant a bomb in the office and he would be killed instead of Tony. He mentioned the call to Tony who shrugged it off by saying "You better stop messing around with that guy's wife Jimboy."

As luck would have it, in the very next hour the caller repeated the message and Tony was there to field it. He went to hang up the phone but changed his mind.

In a serious tone he offered. "Look man, I don't know who you are but if you tell me which one of my women is your wife I'll leave her alone. I don't want to give up all my women just because there's a disgruntled husband out there. Who are you?"

Jim gulped in disbelief. Wow, was Tony asking for it.

"You better quit messing around with my wife and stop being cute about it."

Tony blurted in "I'm not the one you should be discussing this with. Talk it over with your wife. If it's not me having sex with her then it will be someone else. Can't you understand that dummy?"

Wow, thought Jim, what a philosopher. You have to admire a forthright man like that, a foolish but forthright man.

In another incident a man followed Tony's car onto the parking lot and when Tony got out, the man came over to him and challenged him to a fight. Tony asked the man who he was and what this was all about. The man answered that Tony was getting involved with his fiancee and the man wanted to have it out. Tony again used his standard ploy that the man should take up the matter with his fiancee and leave him out of it. He ended the confrontation by saying "No woman is worth fighting over."

Jerry would often scare Jim by telling him that someday a strange man might walk into his office and start punching him thinking that he was Tony. Or perhaps some disgruntled woman who thought Tony was cheating on her would plant a bomb in the office and blow them both up. Jim laughed off those suggestions but they remained in the back of his mind most every time he entered the office.

Tony had a lot of opinions on morality. After all, he was a professor of philosophy and taught Ethics to prospective teachers. He probably developed many of his opinions in order to justify his actions. He was a proponent of Utilitarianism, a philosophy articulated by John Stuart Mill who expanded on views of earlier philosophers.

Tony reasoned that while many things were good as a means to an end, there is only one intrinsic good and that was the pursuit of pleasure which results in happiness. The opposite state was pain.

Since many acts bring pleasure for some and pain for others we should try to acquire the most pleasure against the least pain, which is utility. So what is morally right should not be thought of as identical with whatever maximizes utility. Tony reasoned that he received pleasure in greater amounts than the pain received by others affected by his actions. He also gave many others pleasure by his association.

Tony further claimed there was no such thing as good and evil in the world. There were just events. The ideas of good and evil were perceived by individuals from a point of relativity. The world didn't care that the Nazis annihilated about twelve million people. We have replaced them fifty times over since World War II.

There was another office incident but Tony was not there. On one occasion at the first week of December a tall comely reddish faced girl with brown reddish hair, dressed in light brown suede entered the office and asked Jim if he knew when Professor Jamerson would be back. Jim answered that he thought Jamerson would be back in a few minutes and the girl could wait in the office if she wanted to.

She took the seat next to Jim's desk. Efforts to strike up a conversation with the young woman were futile. She seemed nervous and constantly glanced around the office and out the door. Her mouth was grim. She held her hands on her lap and exposed white knuckles.

After about ten minutes another woman hurriedly entered the office, looked around and then at Jim. "When's Tony coming back?"

Jim said he wasn't sure.

"I haven't met you before, have I?" said the lady. "I'm Tony's wife Wanda."

"I'm Jim Tailor."

"Well" said Wanda "I'm not going to wait for him. Just tell him I was here and I'll see him in DuBois this evening." She gave a small wave and left.

Jim looked at the red brown girl in his guest chair. She had wilted almost into tears. It appeared that she was on the verge of collapse.

"Looks like a lot of people want to see Professor Jamerson"

The girl held a hand over her mouth. "I think I'm going to faint"

Jim said " I'll get you a glass of water, don't faint. Shall I call the college nurse?"

"I'll be okay" said the nervous girl "Just let me close my eyes a minute."

She closed her eyes and stretched out on the chair. Her body remained relaxed for what seemed a long while. Jim wondered if she had really fainted. He was tempted to go over and shake her.

Eventually the girl opened her eyes. "I guess I better leave and go back to the dorm and lie down. My allergies are acting up in this dusty basement. I'll see the professor in class tonight and I can get some answers then. This has been a bad day for me all around."

She slowly left the room. Jim wondered if Tony was having an affair with this gazelle. She certainly was attractive, but spooky. Jim muttered to himself "Next semester can't come too soon."

8. THE PARTY

The semester was closing fast. Some genius schedule maker had figured out how to get fifteen week semesters to end in the middle of December. If a week of final exams was added, then the genius of the schedule maker would certainly be taxed to the limit. The middle of December gave students and faculty a chance to celebrate Christmas and New Years in their own way. There would be a month off between semesters.

Two weeks before the end of the semester found Jim up to his elbows in making tests and calculation of grades. Unfortunately, Jim had assigned term papers in his U.S. History classes and had sixty eight of them to read. Since it was his first semester he worked diligently on them. It would be another year before he stopped assigning term papers altogether.

Jim wished there were more weeks in the semester. He had just started the events leading up to the Civil War and he could never get to 1865 by the end of the semester. This upset him.

The Faculty Senate was debating whether or not to add an extra week for final exams, an idea supported by President Curry. Since the faculty were already accustomed to fifteen weeks, it seemed unlikely they would be willing to add two weeks a year to their work schedules. Adding an extra week would mean the end of the long break between semesters and it would bring the closing of the first semester right up to a day or two before Christmas.

Jim had supper in the China Restaurant then settled in his office. He methodically started taking a paper from a left stack, reading it, marking comments and corrections, recording a score, then putting it on a pile to the right. It was a dull task but he wanted to get them back to students before his final exams on the last day of classes.

A low knock came from the framework of the open door. Hellie poked her head around the frame. "Can I disturb you for a few moments?"

Jim looked up. "You're not disturbing me. I need a break anyway."

"Did you read my paper yet?"

"Yes I did. You do excellent work. I checked yours and Benji's right away. His is like a master's thesis. I wish I could say the same for the rest of them. A lot of students can't do a paper. Many of them simply copy material. Since I have spent most of my life reading articles on history I recognize much of this copying."

Hellie beamed. "You should have had us all do a paper on James Knox Polk. Then you could have combined them for your doctorate. You could have it done by now."

"Things are progressing pretty good on that score. I have four more resident credits to pick up this summer, then it's a straight shot to the P-H-D. I'm beginning to get giddy. Do you want a cup of tea or coffee? I have instant and hot water."

"No my dear professor. I just want to drink you in with my eyes - you know, Elizabeth Barrett Browning. She sings " Drink to me only with thine eyes and I will pledge with mine."

Jim sings back lowly "Or leave a kiss but in the cup and I'll not ask for wine."

"I know all the words" boasted Hellie. "I guess you do too."

Jim smiled "I used to be hung up on poetry. In fact, I've written several hundred poems, none of them worth a farthing."

"I'ld like to read them sometimes."

"Actually, I burned them all and that got it out of my system. I hate to be rude Hellie, but I still have a stack of papers to read and I have to get them done."

"Say no more, say no more, I'm on my way out, but first a surprise."

She went to the doorway and reached around the frame. Her hand came back with a large flat package which she handed to Jim. "Merry Christmas mon cheri."

75

Jim was embarrassed. "I don't know what to say. You shouldn't have."

"It's nothing. Open it up."

Using his clumsiest fingers, Jim unwrapped the package. It was a large framed photo of Hellie. It looked like an enlarged version of a yearbook picture.

"I wanted to give you something to remember me by over the semester break. I sure don't want you to forget me since I won't be in your class next semester. Maybe I'll sign up for economics even though I don't need any more courses or extra credits."

Jim's mind raced. What to say. What in hell would he do with a large framed picture of Hellie. He couldn't put it up in his office and sure in hell he couldn't take it home. Was this some kind of test of his affections? He dismissed the ulterior motive theory and just assumed she was still a school girl with a desire to give him something that he would value. He finally said. "You shouldn't have " and meant it.

"Well that's it. I guess I'll be leaving." She headed for the door.

"I'll walk you to the stairs."

At the stairs there was a stumbling conversation and some kicking of the first step. Hellie put her arms around Jim and he responded by kissing her on the mouth. It was special. Who wouldn't want to kiss the beautiful Helga.

"Remember Hellie, just friends."

"Just friends, I can live with that."

She floated up the stairs and Jim returned to the office. He put the wrapping paper back on the picture with the plain side out, then taped it on all seams and edges. Before going home he returned to the department office store room and placed the portrait in a locking map file. He locked it in and put the key in his pocket. Somehow, he would solve the portrait dilemma. If he couldn't come up with any ideas he would have to throw it away.

As promised, Sandra Swartz held her semester's end party. The entire department and spouses were invited as well as the Dean of Humanities. Jerry had told Jim that "fuzz nuts" would be invited. Jim had never heard the nickname before and Jerry had to admit he didn't know what it meant when he used it but it was a name that stuck and was widely used by faculty members in the School of Humanities.

Drinks were given to guests as they arrived. Martha drank a small glass of white wine and took another. Jim decided he would drink his martini slowly. He didn't want to get loose mouthed. Neither he nor Martha were drinkers. They kept a bottle of red wine at home in case special visitors came. None had come since the wine was purchased three years ago. They almost drank it when Jim was notified of his appointment to Punxie. However, they hired a baby sitter and went out to dinner instead.

The Swartz couple were excellent hosts. After all, they were from the New York area where parties were a specialty. A buffet table groaned with food and snacks. They had a gallon mix of martinis and another of manhattans. With thirty two people in attendance these were dwindling fast.

Dr. Charles Gordon Pratt, Dean of Humanities, entered and dutifully went around talking to everyone. He was accepted by the faculty and no one spoke disrespectful of his abilities but they did snicker at some of his foibles. His wife was friendly and down to earth. She wore a tight form fitting knee length dress which exposed her attributes admirably. She was about forty five years old and in excellent form. She knew it and dressed for maximum attention.

Jim tried to decipher the nickname "fuzz nuts." The dean was pleasant enough. When he stood still, it looked like he was still moving. Maybe it was the martini catching up with Jim. The dean's brown hair stuck out and was obviously unmanageable. Perhaps it was his hair which could be described as fuzzy.

The party was going well with plenty of booze and

snacks. Martha was drinking too much and Jim reminded her to cut down which she did. Others were starting to feel the effects of the martinis and manhattans. Agatha Aggasis said she never touched the stuff but rumor was that she went bananas after one drink and so she resisted drink when she was in a social situation. She stayed about an hour, then left.

As usual at such affairs the men began to cluster in the kitchen while the women were trapped in the living room along with the dean and Elwood Liston, assistant professor of medieval history. The women discussed the local school system, their children and some television programs.

The dean didn't know how to extract himself from a testy situation. He had Elwood at his left side on the sofa. Elwood's legs were feeling numb and the feeling obviously was edging toward his brain. He told the dean a few off-color jokes which was embarrassing to everyone within ear shot. People who were standing nearby began to ooze to other parts of the room.

Elwood kept repeating " Jerry and Sandra sure knew how to throw a party. It's the big city influence, yes sir, it's the big city influence."

The dean turned from Elwood and spoke to Edna Felderberg seated at his right. Edna was a serious woman who worked as a legal secretary in Indiana, a town forty miles south of Punxsutawney and home to a state university. She reminded everyone of Emily Dickinson. It was not her intellect but the way she dressed and wore her hair.

Edna was a fragile woman who worried about her husband and his future. Sitting next to the dean couldn't hurt but perhaps enhance the future. Her conversational abilities were wanting and the best she could do was the weather. However, she struck a chord when she asked the dean about his new projects. The dean spent some time explaining how he planned to move departments and offices around.

Elwood's wife, Ginger, spoke in startling terms. In reference to the background music, she made remarks such as "tango music makes me want to have sex."

After about a half hour of all women talk, Ginger wiggled into the kitchen and declared that she was tired talking to women and needed to "hear some he-man voices." Chairman Gregory blurted out "There's no he-men in here, we're all history teachers."

Ginger snapped "I thought all history teachers were jocks."

The chair replied "Your husband is a history teacher, he's not a jock."

"Oh" said Ginger pursing her lips "he made the football team at Lock Haven." Then she laughed "and so did I."

The men were taken aback at the joke but were pleased to have a change of pace from the protective trivia of cars, academic subjects and football. The basketball season was starting and it was slowly replacing football in trivial conversation. Jim figured he would have to start memorizing team names, cities and maybe watch a game on TV if he was ever going to fit in.

Earl Gratis didn't know much about basketball or football for that matter. He tried to shift the conversation to the most significant event of the twentieth century. He had taken in Paul Bossert who thought it was the collapse of the Soviet Union. When Earl said something about the Lindbergh trial Paul staggered away from him and filled his glass with another manhattan mix.

In a corner of the living room Earl's wife Rachel was telling everyone about her membership in a great books reading club. They had shifted to modern novels in the last couple of months.

Rosemary Needs was a member of the reading club and said she was only interested in Hollywood personalities. She wanted to read biographies of movie stars but the group kept insisting on these social problem novels. She invited Martha to join them at their regular monthly meetings.

Over by the sink Clyde and Homer were engaged in serious discussions about best and worst presidents. They seemed agreed that Truman was the best president we ever had but were divided on the worst. Clyde was holding out for Reagan and Homer was nominating Coolidge. When Jim diluted his martini with water he had to step between them.

Jim injected "My favorite president is James Knox Polk. He did more for the country than anyone except Washington." Clyde and Homer were happy for the diversion and eagerly sought to include Jim in their discussion. They both agreed that Polk had a lot going for him but he wasn't listed by anyone as being "great."

Jim said he was sure Benjamin Franklin endorsed Polk as a great president. In fact he had just read a paper to that effect. Clyde offered "But Polk was president at least fifty years after Franklin died."

It was Jim' private joke. He backed off saying "Maybe I'm drinking too much and my time line is shifting on me." With that he went back to the football group and avoided Jerry and his automobile discussions. The new Lincoln was still rearing its ugly head. Jerry knew all about camshafts, horsepower and car models.

Eventually women started communicating to their husbands that they had better come back to the living room and mix a little. Clyde's wife asked him to come in to the living room and explain Punxsutawney property values to Martha who stated that she and Jim were considering moving there. Clyde had a small real estate business on the side.

The real estate agent started by saying they should wait until Jim had tenure and reiterated the rumor about impending retrenchment. This sent Martha to panic. Her fears were somewhat minimized later when the dean stated that President Curry had authorized a full time position and a temporary position for the Social Studies Department. A search committee would be organized next semester. A temporary replacement will be hired next semester for Homer who would be on sabbatical leave and doing "research" in the archives of the Library of Congress.

Martha thought that a new faculty member would be an insurance policy for Jim. If faculty retrenchment took place it would have to be on the last hired-first fired basis. But then, they might fire two from each department. She took another glass of wine and told Clyde that when she was ready to purchase a home he would be notified.

The dean was still flanked by Edna and Elwood who was one of the few still drinking. It was near midnight and people were leaving. The living room and kitchen populations were dwindling fast. One of the Swartz girls came downstairs in her pajamas and asked her mother to come upstairs to see what one of the other children did. The Swartz dog which had been relegated to the basement began barking. Jerry took the dog for a short walk and made some scatological remarks when he came back.

Martha said to Jim "We better get home and get to bed and get some sleep. We have a big day tomorrow." Jim wasn't sure what the big day tomorrow was but he was willing to call it quits and head for home.

With that statement, Elwood leaned across the dean and reached a hand toward Edna. "If I go to bed tonight, it will be with Edna."

Everyone stopped. Edna's expression turned to wide-eyed horror. Elwood leaned back and took up his drink. Ginger broke in "Don't worry Edna, all he does is sleep."

That didn't help Edna any. She had little sophistication and couldn't recover. Others started conversing and working their way to the door. Martha promised to have the Swartz family over some Sunday afternoon. They could all go roller skating which was the rage in Clearfield.

Alas, the party was over but the aftershocks continued. At the next department meeting Henry Felderberg said that he

81

would like to make a statement. He was given the chance.

Henry looked down at the floor. "There is a man in this department that I no longer want to associate with. He insulted my wife. She was ill and vomiting for three days. My life has been a nightmare. I don't want to be in a social situation with this man. I don't want this man in my house. However, I will continue to work in the department with him since it is my duty."

Chairman Gregory adjourned the meeting. There was no need for him or anyone else to make a comment. As a long-time chairman, he was familiar with the foibles of college professors and he knew that the situation would work itself out in time. He told Ms. Needs to not put those last statements into her minutes. She said she never bothered to copy them down.

Later in the day, Jim and Jerry were having coffee at the clubhouse when Elwood came in. He ordered coffee and sat with them. Jerry laughed to Elwood. "I guess Henry was upset with you."

Elwood looked seriously at Jerry. "Me, I thought he was talking about you."

When Jim related the events of the meeting to Martha she had an opinion. "You mean to tell me a fifty year old woman has never had a man make an unwanted statement to her. It wasn't like Elwood was serious. What cocoon did she crawl out of? To me, she's more sickening than Elwood."

Martha said she considered joining the reading book club but on second thought she wouldn't jump into it until she had a better chance to assess the situation. She was going to squeeze it in somehow despite her exhausting schedule. She didn't know where she would be able to get an hour of reading time anyway. Besides, she was a very slow reader and doubted if she could read a book in one month. She also sympathized with Rosemary and wanted more light reading, maybe some kind of castle intrigues of the British royal family.

Jim gave her a friendly touch. "We better not have a get together until after I have tenure."

9. END OF THE FIRST SEMESTER

E-mail

Ms. Rosemary Needs informed Jim that he should check his E -mail since he did have an account number. Jim said he didn't have a personal computer in his office and therefore he didn't get involved in E-mail. Ms. Needs said that everyone on campus had E-mail and that was the main method of communication between the president and the faculty. This was also the main method of communication with many of the vice presidents.

Jim wondered how he had an E-mail address when he hadn't authorized anybody to make one up for him. Ms. Needs said she took the liberty of putting in a code-word or key for Jim. She used his daughter's name and opened the account with the password SUSANT since her name was Susan and T was the first letter of her last name.

Ms. Needs said that most faculty used the names of their children and had to adjust the name to six digits since that was how the campus computer system worked. She made some remark about Jim being egotistical and giving his son the same name as him. Jim thought Ms. Needs was out-of-line and said so but she didn't flinch. According to Ms. Needs every child should have a name of his own that is his very own and giving a child your own name was the height of egoism. Jim said that he was James A. and Jimmy was James B. and thus they had different names. Ms. Needs said "and I suppose Jimmy's child will be named James C. and when the alphabet is used up the family would have to go to numbers or begin to use the Cyrillic alphabet."

Jim tried to laugh but couldn't. He wanted to get on with the E-mail. From this moment on he always had the impression that Ms. Needs would be smirking at him and he wondered if maybe she had a point. Before the conversation ended Ms. Needs said that she hoped cloning wouldn't be perfected because then we would have a world full of egotistical nerds.

Jim asked for instruction on how to retrieve his E-mail and Ms. Needs wrote down the steps and told him he could use the office computer or one of the computers of the more fortunate members of the faculty. However, she warned that they considered their department computers as their personal property and to ask them would be considered some sort of affront to them. She told Jim that she would print out all his E-mail and have it in his box by the end of the day. She wanted to know when Jim considered his day ended since many faculty members departed as soon as their last class was over.

When Jim received the print-out of his E-mail he was shocked to see that he had 84 entries. Since it hadn't affected his daily academic life he assumed they were not of any importance but began to wade through them as he sipped coffee in what passed for the department lounge.

Most of the mail seemed to generate from the Fine Arts end of the campus. There was a LeRoy Tyrone Art Studio somewhere on campus and they had what appeared to be twice-monthly exhibitions.

Several of the mailings wanted immediate answers to certain questions about campus operations. Of course, Jim never gave the immediate answers and he asked Clyde what the outcome of his neglect would be. Clyde assured him there were many organizations on campus that were created to give people an opportunity to expand their credential file and these really were of no consequence. They didn't care whether you answered or not as long as "hick" knew that the organization existed. They were sure he knew because these organizations sent him a copy of their minutes and activities at every turn. If Jim thought his mail was stuffed with nonsense he should go over and check president Curry's.

There was a notice that student withdrawals and notifications of absences would no longer be handled in the College Center but the operation was moved to the Student

Union, second floor. This was sent by William Stem, PhD. who was listed as the "Special Assistant to the President for Communications, Institutional Planning and Campus Improvement." Jim wondered if he would ever get a title with twelve words in it. There was another message from the "Senior Executive Associate to the Vice President for Student Affairs and Student Success."

Jim asked Clyde about the number of Vice Presidents at Punxie. Clyde thought there were six at last count but wasn't sure. He offered that there were as many support staff as there were faculty members and a large number of them were drawing higher salaries than full professors at Punxie.

There was a notice that any faculty member or student who wished to use one of the four college vans would have to pay a ten dollar approval fee. It was explained that the fee was to cover the cost of insurance since this was out of the realm of the college budget. The method of payment of this fee had to accompany the application. Payment may be cash or a check made out payable to the Student Activities Fund.

There was a notice from Phyllis Sanderly of elementary education listing the members of the campus research committee. Jim wanted to ask Clyde about that one but Clyde had left the room. Jim noted that Glenn Thomas of his department was one of the members. All research proposals had to pass through this committee. Jim would have to find out if this included all research or just research having to do with Punxie or those research projects desiring Punxie money.

Bill Billings, teacher of philosophy, was trying to get a group together to visit China in the summer. His glowing proposal indicated that they could visit the Great Wall and the birthplace of Confucius. Now that we were the best customer of China they welcomed Americans with open arms. The plane would depart from Pittsburgh's International Airport.

Some apple-polisher had put excerpts of the last speech of President Curry on three pages of E-mail. He had been the speaker at the Rotary Club. His topic was the expanding influence of Punxsutawney State College on the region. He had taken maps of the campus with him and had penciled in red the potential expansion projects. He reminded them that the college was the biggest employer in the town.

Clyde returned for another cup of coffee and Jim asked if he had seen the E-mail on the search for the new provost. The message stated that there were three finalists for the position. These were Lawrence Simmons who was now the Acting Provost, a male PhD who was an administrator at Albertson College in Idaho and female D-E-D who was an administrator at Hayward California. The college and the committee were flying the two strangers to Pittsburgh where they would be picked up and driven to Punxie for their interviews. Faculty members who would like to meet these people were invited to one of the many interviews set up for the two different days. Naturally, there were no interviews for Simmons.

Clyde said that he never worried about things like that since Simmons had the job sewed up and the "worldwide" search was just a farce. Everybody knew it. The big job of the committee was to figure out how to get around the female applicant and not suffer the outrages of affirmative action. He started into affirmative action opinions but caught himself and said "ah, no sense in going into that, you know all about it." He filled his cup and departed.

Jim thought he should check his E-mail more often since there were some items of interest among them. He thought perhaps when he applied for promotion he would blast messages into everyone's mail. As some movie star once said "I don't care what they say about me as long as they spell my name correctly."

End of semester chores

It was a week before the end of the semester and Jim began thinking about Christmas presents for Martha and the kids. Buying presents was not one of Jim's strong points. It was on his mind from time to time but he drew a blank each time and put it off until the next time, whenever that would be. Finally, it came to him. He would get them all sweatshirts with the Punxie logo. The bookstore was in the basement of an old house that had been incorporated into the original campus. It went by the name of Student Union Building.

The first floor was a snack bar where burgers and soft drinks occupied the menu. The second floor consisted of two large rooms with television. A matron kept check on the rooms as well as the snack bar. Not many students used the facilities. They preferred the snack shops in the town and all had television in their apartments and dorm rooms. A survey indicated the average student spent more time watching television than studying. Another national survey indicated students spent more money on beer than on books.

When Jim walked down the stairs to the basement bookstore he felt right at home, it reminded him of his office. He was at a loss in the dimly lit corner of the bookstore which held the sweatshirts and other articles of clothing. He was taken aback by the prices. Finally he settled for PUNXSUTAWNEY STATE COLLEGE for Martha and PUNXIE STATE for Susan and Jimmy. Perhaps the full name of the college was too large for children's garments.

There was no one around and Jim made noises to attract attention. Finally, a blonde lady came out from behind stacks of cartons and said "Can I help you sir?"

Jim was always taken off guard by the term "sir". He didn't feel old enough to justify that title. He pointed to his stack of sweatshirts on the counter. "I want to buy these."

The lady came over to the counter, slowly checked each label and punched them in on a computer. She drummed her fingers on the counter. Some distance away, a printing machine cranked out the results. Jim and the lady waited for the written verdict.

Jim felt he knew the clerk. Where had he seen her

before? The tight blonde curls around the ears seemed familiar. Finally, it came to him. She was the one in the office with Tony. In fact she was wearing the same dress on that night, the dress that was folded up on her back.

With this revelation Jim shifted nervously. Did the woman recognize him? If she did, she didn't let on. Maybe that night when she looked back as she bent over the desk she didn't really see Jim. There was no reason to be nervous but Jim was in a mild state of embarrassment.

Jim thought about the great body and muscular legs beneath the tan pleats of the dress. He thought of a ball room dancer with her pleated skirt swirling as she twirled. He could see those legs before him. He wanted to say something friendly, such as "Why would a nice person like you get involved with the sordid likes of Tony Jamerson?"

However, he just imagined things. The bill was tendered. Jim paid it and departed for his office to await the bell for his next class. As MacBeth said "It is a knell that summons thee to heaven or to hell".

Waiting for Jim at his office was a skinny young man. He knew the fellow was in one of his classes but couldn't come up with the class or the guy's name.

The student mumbled "Mr. Tailor, can I talk to you?" He looked pathetic, like he might have been nursing a cold. He hunched his shoulders and looked down at the floor.

"Come in" invited Jim. He wished he could remember the lad's name but he couldn't. When Jim taught high school he would learn every student's name by the second week of classes. He couldn't seem to do this with the college crowd. He thought perhaps he could bluff it until the student gave him some clue as to his identity. Why couldn't the student just say "I'm Joe Blow and I'm in your second period class" or something like that. Jim hated himself for being so prissy about admitting he didn't know the student's name. Why didn't he just say "Who are you?"

Finally, Jim said "You're in the morning class, aren't

88

you?"

"Yes, the economics class".

"O.K. economics" thought Jim, but who the hell is he? Jim was too embarrassed to ask. He laid the grade book on the desk. "What's your total points" asked Jim. "I can't read it in this poor light."

You might as well have asked the student about the last moon landing. He was totally confused. Jim finally told him to go down the list of names in the grade book and find his and then read the last pencil number on the end of the grades. Jim put the final tallies in pencil in order to correct errors without messing up the grade book.

The student went down the list of names and found his, then said "136".

Jim picked up the book and glanced down the list to find 136, the lowest score in the class. "That's out of 200 points George." The quick scan indicated the student was George Pitlak. Jim continued "That would be 67 percent, a D".

George Pitlak assumed a most pitiful expression. "Can I do something for extra credit Mr. Tailor, like write a paper, make out a map or something, anything?"

"No" said Jim "that would not be fair to the other students. You're only six points from a C. If you get a 76 on the final you'll make a C."

"But" said student George Pitlak " I really need a B in this course. I need to bring up my QP in order to stay in college. I'm already on probation."

Jim had heard a lot of excuses and requests from his high school students but he was not ready for the appeals and devious appeals of older students, more experienced in the ways of begging and mooching. George had four years of high school to practice his skills on teachers. Add to this his two years of college and his skills were honed to perfection.

The implication in George's case was his entire college career rested on Jim's shoulders. The ruse was working. Jim never questioned the lad about his first two years and his academic probation. The gist was in bold letters - if Jim didn't give him a B his college career was over and it was Jim's doing. Jerry had warned Jim about the begging students. He related an instance where a male student told Jerry he was transferring to Kutztown and needed a higher grade in order to be accepted there. Jerry fudged the grade to a B. In the next semester the student passed Jerry on the sidewalk and waved "Hi Mr. Swartz." Jerry said he knew he had been taken and didn't question the student. He vowed- never again.

Finally Jim said "Well George, the best you can hope for is a C and if you don't get at least a 76 on the final you won't get that." It was not in Jim's nature to be stern and he held his breath while he waited for the student's reaction.

George Pitlak wasn't about to go down without a fight. "Could I borrow your notes for last week Mr. Tailor. I missed last week because I was sick. I can bring you my doctor's excuse."

"I don't give my notes out George. Besides, you couldn't read what I write anyway. I use a shorthand technique and it's my own system. Sometimes I can't even read what I write. Just ask someone in the class to duplicate theirs."

George looked pathetic. "I don't know anyone in the class. The semester went so fast I didn't have time to meet anyone."

"Well then George, read the assigned chapters and the references in the sheet I gave you on the first day and you should have all the material you need to take the final."

"I don't know Mr. Tailor. I don't know if I have time to do all that. I have a lot of work in other classes to catch up on. It's going to be rough on me. I really would like to do extra credit work. I need the B."

"Look George, you're going to have to study for the final anyway and so you're too busy to do extra work. If you don't mind now, I have to go to my class. By the way, I have you down for eleven absences this semester. I thought you dropped the course but here you are."

George wasn't a quitter. "Could you give me a copy of that first day hand-out. Somehow I lost mine." Jim fished out an extra copy from his desk and handed it to George. He was certain George would never consult the references. If George did poorly instead of better on the final, Jim was set to flunk him.

In those final two weeks Jim was approached by students with an array of reasons why they were doing poor work and why they should have a higher grade than that earned.

When Jim brought up the subject of grade moochers at the faculty lounge Bill Barr went into his usual tirade about the poor caliber of students. He actually didn't want to win converts to his way of thinking, he just wanted to express his frustration.

Bill was not an effective teacher and was not able to put his knowledge into the heads of students. Those that did succeed in algebra did so by the power of their own abilities. There are students that effectively teach themselves. For them, the instructor's experiences can show them different approaches to learning. Instructor's may point out facets of their subject that the student didn't know existed.

Jim could not join in the discussion of poor students. At no time did he consider himself superior to the students. He realized that they were intelligent and the differences was not intellect but rather experiences. There was no doubt that Benji knew more about history than he. Not only that, but Benji was able to relate historical events to the cultural attitudes of the time, an extremely difficult concept to grasp. When Jonesey suggested Jim do that, it was up to Benji to do it for Jim. No, Jim didn't consider himself superior to the students, he was one of them, but in a different manner.

Of the old timers who hung around the clubhouse Chauncy was one of the more interesting. Jim didn't know if it was his last name or first name and was too embarrassed to ask.

Chauncy said "When you get frustrated Jim, look at it this way. All you have to do is appear busy for a few years, keep out of trouble and you will have a job for the rest of your life. You can't beat this job for security."

He went on " When I first started teaching college we were at the mercy of the administration. When you started making a decent salary you were furloughed, fired. Actually there was no such thing as a decent salary. We were all low paid. I was teaching at Shippensburg as an assistant professor thirty years ago. My salary was sixty eight hundred dollars. The same rank at Harvard in that year only brought in seventy six hundred dollars. All the great universities in this country exist today because professors subsidized the institution by accepting low salaries. We don't accept low salaries today and the burden of running colleges like Punxie falls on the taxpayers. Well anyway just give the appearance of professoring and you'll be guaranteed a job for life."

Another of Chauncy's pet topics was the waste of time created by professional journals. It was his opinion that most professional journals were publications to give professors an extra line on a resume. "Nobody reads them" he would say. "They go on a shelf somewhere and disappear into oblivion."

Elwood happened to be there and challenged Chauncy's statement. "I'm a member of the American Historical Society and I read their journal. They have good stuff in there."

Chancy smiled "Naturally, I'm a member of various societies also. Tell me the title of one article in last months journal. If you don't know the title, tell me the gist of one article."

Elwood backed off. "I didn't' get a chance to look at last months, but I do read it."

Chauncy went on. "Get off it Elwood, you couldn't tell me the title of an article for the last year. My journals are stacked in my basement. They're useless. Mostly discussions from graduate research papers. Go to the storage room of the library and you'll find hundreds of journals donated to the library by professors who had no use for them. The library doesn't know what to do with them either."

Elwood said "Well I had some papers published in the journal and I received some letters from other professors about them. Even if the journals are useless, they got me promoted."

Chauncy went on, "The real test of writing is will someone dish out money for it. Will someone buy it and actually read it. I never write anything unless there's money in it for me."

"Money's not the only yardstick we should use to measure a thing's value" wailed Elwood. "There are other values, like scholarship."

Jim liked these discussions between two old pros. He liked their divergence of opinion which stimulated each of them. He was learning about college teaching, but in ways he never thought possible. There was a lot to learn about nuances and how a simple bibliographic reference might be the item that gets the promotion.

In reference to Elwood's money versus scholarship statement Chauncy replied "It's the only measure we have. Does it play in Peoria? Does someone pay to see the play Maybe I see it differently since they changed the rules on me. It used to be, you advanced in the profession with publications. I wrote over a hundred articles for journals, magazines, newspapers. No one applauded. Now you get promoted for bringing high school chemistry students to Punxie for science day. I'm lucky I got full professor when I did, when doctorates were scarce. I don't have the stomach for what you have to do today."

Jim grinned at the old timer. "What do you have to do today to get promoted?"

Chauncy grinned back. "You have to suck up to promotion committee members. Find out who they are and hang around places that they frequent. It's not what you know, it's whom you know and in your case it better be the people on the promotion committee."

10. THE NEW SEMESTER AND GROUNDHOG DAY

When Jim went to his office a few days before the start of the new semester to check his supplies he noticed the metal plate which bore the name JAMERSON was removed. He had mixed emotions about this. Tony was interesting and gave Jim vicarious adventures but he did cut into Jim's time and one never quite knew what the next day or the next hour would bring with Tony. Perhaps he would never run into Tony again.

The new semester started with a coed waiting to see Jim. She wanted to know why she received a C when she had expected a B. Jim removed his grade book from his locked desk and carefully explained his grading procedure. She was sure she had a B when Jim went over the grades before last semester's final. Jim assured her that there was some mistake and she was lucky to get a C. The girl asked Jim if he could change the grade to a B and Jim assured her he couldn't or wouldn't do that.

Jim thought about a story that Elwood Liston related in the club house. He said a female student came up to him and was concerned about her poor grade in his medieval history class. To many students learning the terms used in this class was like learning a foreign language.

Anyway, this girl comes in and seemed to be propositioning Elwood for a grade. According to Elwood she said she would do just about anything to improve her grade.

Elwood said "that's interesting, are you busy Friday evening?" The girl answered "No, I'm free on Fridays."

Then according to Elwood he said "Then you should have time to study for the test I'm giving next Tuesday."

A male student was close on her heels and he wanted to know if Jim could see his way to giving him a B instead of a C. He brought his grade report with him and showed Jim that his grades were all A except for the C in Jim's class. Jim wondered to himself how this student did it, since Jim had considered him to be a borderline student. This attempt to make Jim feel inadequate as a teacher did not meet with success either.

Jim surely didn't want to change a grade. Not that grades were carved in granite but he didn't want anyone in records or administration to have the least doubt about his grading integrity. Grades were the coin of his realm. They were certification of his integrity. Later, he did discover a mistake in calculation and raised a student's grade from D to C.

As the male student was leaving a man about forty walked in and extended his hand to Jim. "I'm Bruce Evans and will be replacing your colleague Homer who is on sabbatical this semester. My office is two doors down. I wanted to use Homer's office but he wouldn't let me."

The usual pleasantries were exchanged with Jim offering to help Bruce in any manner that he could. Bruce explained that this was his third semester as a temporary employee and he had applied for the position that Jim landed. He wondered why Jim got the full time job and not him. After discussion it was determined that Jim's being A-B-D, all but the dissertation, had something to do with it. Jim hated to admit it but the fact that Jonesey knew chairman Gregory also had influenced the decision.

Bruce was a journeyman teacher. Since his graduation from Millersville University twenty years ago, he taught at many institutions. When he received his masters degree he was kept on at Millersville for a year as an instructor. Union agreements prevented him from continuing as a temporary employee so he was not rehired at his alma mater. The agreement states that if a temporary employee works two years for a university they have to make the position permanent. Millersville was not in a position to do this at that time.

Since the Millersville stint, Bruce worked at California University of PA, Kutztown University of PA, Frostburg University in Maryland, Slippery Rock and Edinboro, also in Pennsylvania. Now he was putting in his second semester at Punxie.

Bruce was one of the best read persons at the college, if not in the entire world. When he was employed at the various colleges he would ask the librarian to save the *New York Times* and *Wall Street Journal* for him. He would read these from cover to cover. When Bruce taught history he knew it all. Bruce never subscribed to these publications with his own money. When faculty members needed some information they could save themselves a trip to the library or poking around on the computer by simply asking Bruce. More often than not he could help them.

Bruce was also a fanatic about recycling. He constantly searched the wastebaskets for aluminum soda cans and plastic bottles. He recycled the newspapers and the waste typing papers of the department. He had an interesting comment about Edinboro. He said that when he worked at Edinboro it was on a full year contract. He kept every notice and bulletin that was sent to him or the professor he was replacing. At the end of the year the stack of paper was 23 inches high. "Can you believe, almost two feet of paper for every one of the six hundred faculty members?"

When Jim asked Bruce where he was living, Bruce had given him a vague answer. Later Jim would discover that Bruce was living in his office, sleeping at night in a sleeping bag, showering in the gym and eating in the student dining hall. No need for Bruce to settle down in housing for a one semester job. Bruce's parsimony made Jerry Swartz look like a big spender.

The proximity of their offices put Jim and Bruce together often and they became reliable friends. Bruce would take over Jim's classes when Jim and Martha wanted a respite and Jim helped Bruce in other ways. They often ate dinner together at the Chinese restaurant.

Jim apparently had a new office mate whom he had never met. He wondered how Bruce was able to get an office to himself while he, with one semester of seniority, had to still share an office. Jim noticed a box of tissues on Tony's old desk.

This was the only indication that someone was about to move in.

Three days into the new semester a square looking lady with short brownish hair and dressed in a business suit came in and placed a briefcase on the other desk. She took off a large floppy hat and turned to Jim. " I'm Hazel Short." To Jim she appeared to be a member of the White House security force.

Jim answered "I'm James Tailor. Welcome to our humble office."

Hazel sized him up and looked right at him. In a stern voice she dictated "I want to tell you right now, up front, so there will be no problem. I'm a virgin and I intend to stay that way."

Jim's mind raced. What to say. Why was she sharing this information with him? How do you respond to that? Was this lady crazy or something? He tried to control his mouth which usually twisted into strange contortions in these situations. He tried to stay calm as he thought of the coming semester and sharing an office with this woman.

Finally he said "I'll keep that in mind. I'm sure you'll be happy down here in the dungeons of Seminary Hall. Absolutely nobody bothers you down here."

Hazel was not exactly an inviting woman. Her face was pleasant enough but there was something odd about her waist. It was as if there was extra padding there. The business suit didn't help to increase her femininity. It was a masculine cut. Her glasses were horn rimmed and businesslike. Except for the padded waist she was a well proportioned woman, not overweight and a couple inches shorter than Jim.

About a week later Hazel apologized to Jim about her virgin remark. She said she was upset and had Jim confused with someone else. In Jim's mind he knew that she was aware of the reputation of Tony and probably thought along those lines. He said that he understood and assured Hazel that their relationship would be professional.

A few days later, Hellie came in the office and Hazel was

there. Hellie had brought Jim a candy bar. She sat in the guest chair and chatted merrily. Hazel was obviously taken back. Perhaps, in her mind, she spoke too soon, apologizing to Jim. What a brazen young woman to be on such a personal level with a professor. To herself she muttered "all men are alike."

She was embarrassed by Hellie's friendliness to a professor. There were certain unwritten rules for academia and one of them was that professors and students should not associate on a personal basis. It was fortunate for many professors that this rule was unwritten.

Hazel was also embarrassed by the way Hellie's body seemed exposed even though she was fully clothed in her sweatshirt and tight jeans. There was something about her that just made it look like she was "asking for it." Then she caught herself and figured that this was the defense used by most rapists and muggers.

Hazel went to her bookcase and removed a book. She turned to Jim and said that she would be over at the library getting her book renewed and if anyone asked for her she would be back in about an hour. Perhaps this was a way of telling Jim that he had an hour of privacy. Hellie left shortly and Hazel returned in about an hour as promised.

In those first few weeks, Bruce and Jim both agreed that there was something about Hazel that didn't add up. Jim figured it was her position in the physical science department, a department and field dominated by men. Bruce said that it was something about the way she carried herself. Anyway they both agreed that there was something about her that was defensive.

The last week of January was set aside for the Snowflake Festival. In their desperation to give students a range of activities someone came up with this "snow week." It was actually a five day affair with students encouraged to enter the various snow activities.

Fraternities and sororities were competing for the big cup which is given for the best snow sculpture. The nice trophy was kept in the winner's residence and surrendered to the next years winner. Several students told Jim that they couldn't get their outside assignment completed because they had to put the finishing touches on their snow scuplture. The event had become one of the more interesting competitions on the campus. After all, Punxsutawney did get a lot of snow.

The evening of sled riding was another of the successful events of the Snowflake Festival. A hill on the edge of the campus had been cleared of brush each summer in anticipation of the event. The sledding path was lined with empty oil drums filled with burning scrap wood and cardboard. These were kept burning by the sledders climbing back up the hill.

Every once in a while someone representing the student dining hall would come over to the sled path and retrieve the aluminum trays that students had purloined after they had dinner. Even though the college provided toboggans the elongated dish trays were the favored means of transportation.

Agatha had agreed to be one of the judges of the snow sculpture contest. Even though the contestants put a lot of work into the contest most of the scuplptures were glorified renditions of snowmen or sloppily constructed groundhogs. The winners usually had several sculptures in an area. The winner this year had a snowman professor lecturing to a class of snowmen. When Clyde asked Agatha about the sculptures she said they all looked like George Washington on Mount Rushmore to her.

It was the last week of January when Jerry approached Jim. "Hey Jim, our department is on groundhog patrol this year. I'm the coordinator so I'm asking you to accompany me. It's a lot of fun."

"What's this all about?"

Jerry explained that each year on the second of February, the town of Punxsutawney had a groundhog ritual. Jim said he knew that. Jerry went on to say that the college felt it necessary to participate in this ritual to keep relations between the town and the college going smoothly. The town had slightly less than seven thousand people and the college slightly more than two thousand. When the college was in session it represented a quarter of the town's population. Most of the traffic violations and minor crimes of the town were committed by college students and the college administration wanted the town to know that it too was a citizen of the community. They had the biggest payroll in town now that the railroad had pulled out and the gas company had down-sized.

Jim agreed to do it and asked Bruce Evans to go along. Bruce seeking for something to do agreed and said it would be exciting. Bruce Evans told Jim that there were two grocery stores in Punxie, one on each end of town. He had tried to get a birthday card to send to a friend but all the stores had was cards with references to groundhogs on them. An entire wall in one store was devoted to groundhog paraphernalia.

The townspeople referred to February 1 as Groundhog Eve and there were many parties around town. Punxie students and the Culinary Arts students of Indiana University of Pennsylvania looked upon this as a chance to party. Bruce Evans was invited to a party by a couple of culinary arts students he had met when he was shopping for bananas which he kept in a file cabinet in his office.

The parties went on until daylight and Bruce wondered if he was up to going to the festivities the following day. He had met a lot of interesting people that evening and had a lot of stories and was eager to share them with Jerry and Jim.

At daybreak on February 2, the trio met at the dinor for a hot cup of coffee. They winced as the snowflakes kept falling outside. Jerry pointed to the clock on the wall. "It's almost eight, we better get moving."

The festivities were on a slight hill called Gobbler's Knob. The ritual had been going on for over a hundred years. Jerry was given a place of honor among the dignitaries and Jim and Bruce took a place in front of the small crowd. Television crews from the Penn State University station and Pittsburgh were there to record the historic event.

A red faced man with a microphone told the crowd he appreciated their presence even though it was snowing. He and the other town dignitaries were dressed in tuxedos. The red faced man wore a silk top hat when he started his harangue but by the time he finished it had fallen into the snow.

After several speeches about tradition and how the groundhog was never wrong the red faced man took back the mike. "Are there any questions before we get to the program? We have to nudge old Punxsutawney Phil's den and see if he's awake."

Bruce held up his hand and hollered "Why do you call it a groundhog instead of a woodchuck?"

The man seemed puzzled.

"Back home, we call it a whistle pig" said Bruce.

The red faced man thought about it awhile. "I guess it's just tradition. That's what the pioneers who settled this region called it and by gum that's what we're a calling it today. If you want to think of our forecaster as a woodchuck or whistle pig you can."

He went on. "You people up here, step aside. Our bank president will check to see if the groundhog can see his shadow."

With that the snow seemed to come down harder. The bank president, dressed in a tuxedo complete with tails, stepped forward. He waved a path through the crowd and proceeded to a small pen designed to look like rock. He opened the gate and extracted a sleepy groundhog. Perhaps it was drugged or perhaps it actually was hibernating.

The bank president held the animal over his head and brought it down to his chest. "I proclaim that on this day the groundhog, Punxsutawney Phil, did not see his shadow."

A round of applause broke out as the TV cameras cranked on. Jim and Bruce tried to hook up with Jerry but the crowd was dissipating and seemed to have no direction in mind

101

. Finally they met at the foot of Gobbler's Knob and worked their way toward Jim's van. Jerry didn't want to take his new Lincoln out in the snow.

There was a man dressed in a large groundhog costume. As he wandered through the crowd the college and high school boys would punch him in the arms or on the back. With his poor visibility from inside the costume he was not able to identify his attackers. Finally, he was knocked to the ground and a couple of high school age boys jumped on him and started pummeling him. The man rolled around and got one of the boys in a headlock and hollered "Call the police."

The police were in attendance and by the time they got there the boy had managed to escape from the headlock and run away. The man explained to cameras that the groundhog costume had cost him four thousand dollars and he thought it would be a nice addition to the ceremonies. He was proud of the the fact that the outfit was made from real fur. No one came forward to identify the assailants.

Back at the dinor and a plate of sausage and eggs Jim asked Jerry "If the groundhog didn't see his shadow does that mean six more weeks of winter or does it mean an early spring."

"Beats me" said Jerry "I've been here for five years now and still don't know."

Bruce was certain that it meant an early spring since when the groundhog sees his shadow he panics and runs back in the den or so the legend goes.

Bruce said that last night while he was partying in this home a man wandered into the living room. Nobody called him by name or seemed to recognize him and finally one of the girls there asked him who he was. He gave a name and when questioned admitted he didn't know anyone there. He appeared to be in his mid-twenties and said that he was from New Britain Connecticut and had heard of the wild celebrations the night before groundhog day and wanted to get in on them.

The party crasher said that he was going from street to

street, house to house, and whenever he saw a party going on he would simply walk in without knocking which seemed to be the thing to do. He said he was always welcomed. He also said he came there with three other college students from Central Connecticut State University. He didn't know where the others were but he figured he would join up with them sometime the next day and they would drive back to New Britain.

Bruce also related some sexually explicit scenes he had witnessed among the rooms of his party house. And there were several students puking from too much celebration. He saw the local police take a man from the street who was shouting obscenities and claiming in a loud voice that he loved Bunnic.

.   Before departing for their respective abodes, Jerry had an Elwood Liston story for Jim and Bruce. It happened at a party in the home of one of the fine arts professors. Jerry, Elwood, Clyde and their wives were often invited to homes of faculty of other departments. Jerry mentioned the names of the participants but the names had no meaning for Jim.

It seems the hostess was bragging to the point of nausea about the sheer beauty of her child, a daughter. In the bragging she referred to the children of other people in attendance in uncomplimentary terms. She talked of the dance lessons and how Shirley moved like a misty dream on stage. Truth was that Shirley was always in a line with other dance class children when she was on stage. Her mother didn't mean to be rude, it just came off that way.

One of the things she said to Elwood's wife Ginger was that they should enroll their daughter into the same dancing class as Shirley. Ginger explained that she worked many evenings for her father who owned a small plaza outside of DuBois. She was the main bookkeeper and the job involved many after-hours work. This left Elwood in charge of their two children and with his duties at the college he didn't have time to be taking a three year old to dance classes. She took care of the kids during the day and Elwood took care of them in the evening.

Whatever topic surfaced at the get together, it was temporary, and the hostess brought the conversation back to her Shirley and her accomplishments and the compliments from "even" strangers in the supermarket.

Shirley, the child beauty, was flitting in and out of the rooms. She had dolls and doll clothes of various sorts which she put on and took off the dolls. Shirley would parade her dolls after every outfit change. The mother ranted on in the girl's presence. She should have put Shirley to bed but let her stay up for this "special" occasion.

Shirley would go to each attendee and show off her doll's latest change of clothes. Once she stopped in front of Elwood and as she was about to leave Elwood said "Wait a minute, I want to look at you."

The mother was pleased and encouraged the child to stand still. Elwood looked deep into Shirley's face and said "Thank you Shirley." Shirley went back to her dolls and carried them to another room.

Elwood turned to the mother and said "You know they can correct that with surgery."

The mother was startled. "Correct what with surgery?"

Elwood looked toward the girl who had come back into the room. He squinted. "Naw, I thought I saw something out of whack. It must have been the lighting. It looks perfect from here. That is one beautiful child."

The woman was wrecked for the rest of the evening. She didn't enter into the conversations. She kept shooting glances at Shirley and finally took the daughter upstairs to bed. She didn't return for almost an hour.

Jerry said later in the evening he leaned over to Elwood and whispered "You bastard." Elwood whispered back, "Sometimes you have to be one."

104

11. THE ADVENTURES OF HAZEL SHORT

But First Glenn Thomas

The Department of Social Studies had a small work room attached to the department office. The room had two flat tables with chairs. An elevated light table occupied one corner of the room. Two bar stools fit under it. There was a microwave oven and a coffee maker set up on a wide bookcase which was pushed up against a wall. A television set and a VCR were on a movable stand next to the book case..

Jim, Mark and Glenn Thomas were in the room. Mark and Jim were having coffee while Glenn was busy coloring maps. Glenn was thirty years old and had finished a PhD at Akron University three years earlier. His wife worked in one of Akron's offices and literally put Glenn through graduate school. Despite his wife's efforts and generous contributions from his wealthy parents Glenn considered himself a self-made man.

Jim was never able to talk to Glenn since Glenn was always coloring maps, mostly in his office. Today he was in the lounge using the light table. He was not able to get a light table for his office even though he put in for one last year.

Glenn's map project dealt with the Civil War which he considered his specialty. He made the maps for use with the overhead projector. Most of his lectures consisted of flashing maps on the screen and discussing them. Today he was coloring in location maps of the armies of North and South at the battle near Petersburg. This involved much reading, putting in dots and then finally coloring. The Pennsylvania Historical and War Society had given him a four hundred dollar grant to assist him in the expenses of the project. At a department meeting Glenn stated that more department members should aggressively go for grants "as he had".

Glenn spent a lot of time in his office and at the department light table. Sometimes he would be in his office at 4 a.m. His wife didn't seem to mind this absence from home since it was part of his career and they both felt advancement in the career was of paramount importance.

The grant was of particular importance to Glenn's personality. He managed to get notice of the grant published in the local newspapers, the campus newspaper and the President's Newsletter which was circulated among the college "family" as the president called it. The ever-important Newsletter of the State System of Higher Education had not published the notice yet but Glenn assured the department that it was accepted for publication and would be in a forthcoming issue. As he said "this gives the department a lot of publicity and it shows other institutions in the system that we are at the forefront of social studies." Glenn considered himself a celebrity.

Most days, Glenn would arrive at the campus around 6 a.m. even though his first class didn't begin until 10 a.m. on Monday, Wednesday, Friday and 9:30 a.m. on Tuesday, Thursday. He would make the coffee in the office lounge and retire to his office where he could be seen checking slides or coloring in maps.

Even though Glenn made the coffee he didn't drink it. He always drank warm water. He would often smack his lips as he drank it. He assured everyone that warm water was the most healthy fluid one could put into the body.

After his last classes Glenn would presumably go home to his wife Francis and son Glenn, Jr. He usually returned at 6:30 p.m. every evening, do his thing, which was coloring in maps, then leave about 9 p.m. When asked about his evening hours, Glenn said that he didn't want to interfere with his wife's getting Junior ready for bed.

Mike and Mark often and openly discussed Glenn and his mania. They were in agreement that something was not right at Glenn's house. Mark would say "Why would any man spend so much time on such trivia when he had this beautiful pleasant wife at home. Mike would answer "To get out of the house." They couldn't understand the desire to be away. Mark later remarked that the four hundred dollar grant only helped to certify the nutty hobby.

Glenn was six feet tall and had a muscular frame. He was

into weight lifting and wore clothes that emphasized his magnificent chest. Mark remarked that this was an attempt to convince everyone of his masculinity and when someone does that it raises some question about masculinity.

Most colleagues accepted Glenn but kept him out of their lives. They didn't like him, nor did they dislike him. He was just not on anyone's social agenda. Once when the chairman had to list the members of the department he could only think of 18 names although he knew there were 19 members at that time. He could not come up with Glenn's name and had to check a roster to see who was missing from his list.

Mark was reading the *Chronicle of Higher Education* and said to Jim "Get this ad." He squared the Chronicle in front of Jim and read "We have an opening in Economics at the instructor level. Duties include teaching three introductory courses in basic economics and one second level course . Three years teaching experience and PhD required. This is a non-tenured position."

Mark went on "PhD required. Wow. To teach introductory level economics. The system has gone crazy."

Jim arched his brow. "There's a glut of PhDs in the world right now. I read where the biggest employer of PhDs in English and social studies was a taxi cab company in New York City. "

Mark responded "That's what's called an urban legend, something that sounds dramatic but isn't true."

Glenn decided to add his two cents worth. "I think we as a profession should strive for the highest standards of scholarship and a PhD should be required."

Mark laughed back "How about the three years teaching experience."

"That too" answered Glenn.

"Well Jim, if we stuck to the three years teaching experience old Glenn boy wouldn't be here since we had to accept his job as a teaching assistant as part of his three years teaching experience. We fudged the data."

In a low measured voice Glenn rebutted "That was teaching

since I had the classes all to myself. I made up my own lesson plans and tests and administrered them."

Mark laughed again "Just goes to show, no good deed goes unpunished."

He went on "We barely need a masters degree to teach freshman economics. What we need are good teachers and there's no correlation between PhDs and good teaching. There are too many ivory tower people who know their subject but can't teach it. Too many pompous asses that work their way into the system. We need people who have rapport with students. If we had PhD required we wouldn't have been able to hire Jim here and everyone knows he is the best teacher we have right now."

Glenn swallowed "I thought I was the best teacher here." Then he grinned "Just joking of course. Jim is good but we have to define what's best. Our duties here are not just teaching, we have other responsibilities like committee work and improving the general academic and campus climate."

"As a matter of fact" said Glenn with an air of accomplishment " I wrote to President Curry about this very topic. I told him we should tighten up on our hiring. No offense Jim, but I feel the PhD should be in hand before anyone is hired."

Mark pretended to be surprised. "You wrote to the college president. What kind of an ass-kisser are you?"

Then Mark turned to Jim. "Well Jim, let this be a lesson to you. The president probably knows Glenn's name and he's been here two years and he doesn't know mine and I've been here nine years."

Jim tried to get laughter in his voice. " Remember, Mark, as you go through life, it's not who you know, it's whom you know."

" Or whom you blow." When the temporary dean was appointed Glenn sent him a welcoming note and followed up with a personal visit to the dean's office."

Jim turned to Glenn. "Did it pay off?"

"That wasn't the purpose " said Glenn "I'm interested in the welfare of the college and I just wanted him to know there was someone here to help him get acclimated and tell him about the college. I know how it was when I first arrived here I didn't know anything about the place. I would have appreciated it if someone would have told me a few things. Paul was my mentor and the only thing he told me was the loction of the rest room. He said that was all that was important in our department. "

Mark grinned. "Jim boy, did you get a welcome note from Glenn and an offer to help get you acclimated?" He stressed acclimated and drew it out.

Jim started to feel embarrassed. "The dean probably needed more help than I do. If I don't succeed its of little importance but if a dean doesn't succeed it can have far reaching consequences."

" Yeah, and since Glenn had been here a year he has a lot of experience to answer the dean's questions."

"Glenn pouted "You're just jealous because I'm outgoing and the dean knows me."

Mark's eyes widened "you outgoing, where, with whom, not around here."

Mark sniffed. "Our job here is teaching, it says so on our paychecks. It says right on it -we exist to educate students."

"Education doesn't necessarily mean classroom instruction.'

"That's what it means" said Mark as he took the last mouth of coffee. He left and Jim followed.

Jim went to the computer in the department office and tried to call up the roster of his classes. He thought he would put the rosters on a disk and then use the computer for grading. This would also give him some computer practice.

As he began to click and move the mouse Mark came in to get his mail. Out of the corner of his eye Jim saw a male figure heading for the office lounge where Glenn was still doing his maps. He could hear the man helloing and Glenn answering with enthusiasm.

Mark sat down to sort through his mail. He seldom checked his mail box and it was usually crammed with advertisements and campus notices. He figured the notices were common knowledge and of little importance. He positioned himself on a chair and drew the wastebasket up to him. He would glance at the pieces, one by one, and toss them into the wastebasket, piece by piece. He made grunting noises with each discard. Jim tried to ignore him and continued punching out his rosters.

There was a shuffle from the lounge and Glenn appeared in the doorway with an older male student. "Hey Jim, this is Blair Willis, he has a project for individual study in mind. It sounds like something you would be interested in." Then he turned to Blair "Tell Mr. Tailor about your project." Glenn turned and left.

Blair started "I would like to do an individual study project on the influence of Lincoln's wife on Abe during his presidential years and I need an advisor in order to run it through the works and get approval. I thought that Dr. Thomas was an authority on the Civil War and would be interested in it." He motioned backwards with his thumb when he mentioned Dr. Thomas. "The Punxie Beaver Notes said he was our leading authority on the Civil War."

Jim was generous and grimaced "Go over to my office and check my office hours and then see me. I'll see what I can do for you. I'm over in the basement of Seminary Hall, room 96."

Blair left after thanking Jim for his interest. Jim went back to the computer.

Mark laughed. "You just got snookered Jim boy. As you and I well know, Glenn's time is more valuable than yours. He couldn't be bothered with an ordinary student. That's why we need PhDs to teach introductory courses."

Jim opened his eyes wide, tightened his lips and jerked his head toward the lounge door as if to indicate that Glenn might hear them.

"Don't worry about that Jim, we all know what just happened here and you're too nice a guy to protest."

Jim lowered his voice. "I don't have tenure."

"Neither does he" said Mark pointing toward the lounge. "However, he has something you don't have, a lot of gall and a feeling of self-importance. Being a nice guy is going to get you a lo of assignments you don't necessarily want. Don't worry though Jim

110

boy, if any assignment can lead to promotion or more money someone else will relieve you of that responsibility. If that guy's project had some significance to advancement you would never have seen him. He wouldn't be foisted off like some hot potato."

Hazel Short

The spring semester was moving along smoothly. Jim had exactly the same schedule as the fall semester so it was just a matter of tightening up his notes and his lectures. His office was organized and he knew where everything was on campus. He was beginning to meet people and he seemed to be accepted by them. His department colleague Clyde said that a professor does his best work the first time he teaches a course, it's all down hill from then on. He never achieves the excitement and enthusiasm of that first semester.

Jim was to discover some of Clyde's observations were true. During the first semester he had a panel discussion and it went very well. The class was actively involved. The students were enthusiastic and they formed into congenial groups. Presentations were excellent. When he tried the same thing at the beginning of the second semester it was dead. The two weeks set aside for the project were wasted. Students hated it and so did Jim. It was one of those experiments that Jim would never try again. Perhaps he could come up with some other gimmick next year.

It was in March when the Clearfield Elementary School had an in-service day for teachers. This meant the children would have a free day. Rather than have them spend the day looking for activities Jim brought Martha and the children to Punxie. The snow had melted and the day was warm.

Martha and the children sat in Jim's office as he watched the clock for his first class to begin. There was still a half hour to go and time was dragging. Martha told Jim they might go to the bookstore and then walk downtown and be back in time for two o'clock when Jim's last class ended. Susan said she didn't want to go to the bookstore. Jimmy, the copycat, said he didn't want to go to the bookstore either. Jim told Martha to let the children stay in the office while she went to the bookstore. It would be okay.

Hazel Short entered and introductions followed. She beamed at Susan and Jimmy. Two pieces of candy were extracted from her briefcase and presented to the children. She then gave the children a pack of colored pencils and a couple of sheets of blank paper. "Just leave the pencils on my desk when you're through." she chirped. After a flurry of paper shuffling Hazel left the room.

In a few minutes Hellie stopped by and introductions were again initiated. The last thing she wanted to do was meet Jim's family. It brought home the fact that he was married and few things are more disturbing than reality. Hellie covered up the true intention of her visit by asking Jim some questions about the economics class. She and Benji had signed up for economics even though neither of them needed the course for their major. Hellie didn't want to miss an opportunity to be with Jim even though it was a wasted three credit hours. Benji also thought it would be nice to be with Jim for another term.

Martha looked at Hellie and said "I know you."

Hellie was startled. "How do you know me?"

"You were one of the girls who came up to us at the football game."

"Oh" said Hellie, that's right." She paused. "Mrs. Tailor, would you like me to stay with the children while you do some shopping or something? I'm majoring in elementary education and it would be a good opportunity for me too."

Martha considered the offer and was tempted to take Hellie up on it. She decided against it. "No. Thanks. We have today's schedule worked out. But thank you for asking."

"Well" said Hellie "it's nice meeting you. I've got to get to the library sometime soon and I may as well do it now." She smiled and departed.

Martha looked at Jim. "What a nice young lady. You sure are lucky to be working with all these beautiful, intelligent, clean looking people."

Jim agreed "This is a great job, no doubt about it."

112

Time for class was getting short. Martha looked at Jim. "You know how you described Hazel to me about her square shape and how hard her body was when you bumped into her?"

"Yeah, what about it?"

"Well you might be surprised to know she wears a corset."

"What's that?"

"It's like a girdle around the waist but it comes up higher and goes down lower. It has bones or pieces of plastic, like ribs, in it which gives it the shape." All of this was said with many hand movements.

Jim picked up his materials and departed for class. Martha turned to the kids. "You guys can keep coloring. If you get tired of that you can walk in the hall but don't leave this basement. I'm going to the bookstore." With that said she picked up her purse and went singing up the stairs.

Susan immediately rose and started searching the office. She sat in daddy's chair. Jimmy watched as if something was about to happen. Jim had a new swivel chair on casters. It was a gift from the custodian. Jim learned a long time ago to be on good terms with secretaries and custodians. Even though a collection was taken for gifts before Christmas Jim always liked the touch of a personal gift. He had given the custodian a pair of fleece lined leather gloves. So it was that Gus the custodian procured a new swivel chair to replace Jim's straight backed no-wheeled chair.

When Susan discovered the wheels she asked Jimmy to push her. This was fun. They pushed each other around the room. Eventually they moved to the long hallway and concentrated on speed. They were interrupted by Bruce Evans who lectured them on safety. However, before he left he made some suggestions about locking the wheels which would get them up to higher speeds and cause them to go straight.

Martha returned to squelch the race just when Susan was getting Jimmy up to warp speed. She feigned disgust but was rather pleased with their inventiveness. She gathered them up. They walked downtown, had pizza, walked to Mahoning Creek, hung

113

around the park and returned by two o'clock to meet Jim. Since the weather was nice and winter was put on hold they took the long way home by driving to Brookville and to supper at DuBois before getting on the interstate to Clearfield. They sang and laughed all the way home. It certainly was a pleasant day for all concerned.

In the next few days Jim would examine Hazel thoroughly. She lived alone and outside of a few colleagues and students she had little interaction with people. She was happy to talk to Jim and meeting the family was a good lead in. She liked the idea of Jim being a family man.

As days passed their conversation became more personal. Hazel admitted she would like to date someone but at her age there weren't many opportunities and she didn't know how to do it anyway. She tried going to church functions and singles meetings but to no avail. She never had visitors to her apartment and she seldom visited others.

Jim flattered her by saying she was certainly attractive and in careful language and intellectual jargon said she was sexually attractive. It was a shame that such an attractive, intelligent woman wasn't active socially. This was too much for Hazel. She said if Jim had any ideas on how she could meet someone "in her league" she would appreciate hearing them.

Jim sympathized with Hazel and enlisted Martha to the scheme. To Jim it was a problem, to Martha a challenge she could not ignore. Since they had lived at Clearfield for ten years she knew many bachelors from the church, the YMCA, the school personnel and the social clubs. She discussed them with Jim and with her good buddy Paula. Jim was trying to get into the spirit of things but he wished he hadn't started the whole thing.

Paula suggested her brother Ansel. He was divorced but he was a hard working, moderate drinking man. He lived by himself on the outskirts of Clearfield. He must be about the same age as Hazel and he earned a bachelors degree from Clarion University of Pennsylvania.

114

Ansel worked for the National Gas Company as a foreman of construction. His crew laid pipelines throughout the area. Paula said it was his job and the long hours that broke up the marriage. The fact that his ex-wife wanted to travel also contributed something to the boiling pot of their marriage. She had moved out several times and the last time she asked for a divorce.

So Jim approached Hazel with the proposal. He was apologetic but Hazel snapped up the opportunity. It was just a matter of getting them together. Martha had a plan. Jim and Martha would bring Ansel to the Oasis Restaurant in DuBois and Hazel who lived in DuBois could meet them there. Hazel agreed and the date and time were set.

Jim said in a confidential tone. "You know Hazel, you have a very nice body build."

Hazel didn't know what to say. Was Jim hitting on her? This statement is too intimate even for Jim. She smiled "No one has ever said that to me before. Thank you for saying it, even if it's not true."

Jim went on. " It is true. I can't believe no one has ever said that before. You know, it would be better if you didn't wear that thing around your waist."

"You mean this thing." said Hazel banging on her waist with her flat hand. "I was thinking of ditching it. I guess this would be as good a time as any to do it. But without it I feel vulnerable."

Jim winked at her "That's the idea."

"Oh, oh" she said wagging a finger at him.

The dinner and meeting went off fine. Hazel didn't wear her corset and she and Ansel agreed to meet again and again.

The weeks went by quickly and by the end of April Hazel came into the office and said to Jim. "I guess Ansel told you."

Jim looked puzzled. "Told me what. I never see Ansel so he can't tell me anything. I never go anywhere but here to work."

She almost blushed. "Remember the first day I met you I said I was a virgin and planned to stay that way."

"Yeah, I remember. It confused me."

"Well, that statement wouldn't be true today."

Jim wanted to laugh or at least rise and shake Hazel's hand or even embrace her but he kept his composure and reserve. He offered "I hope you and Ansel continue to have a good relationship. I've never heard anything bad about him, or you for that matter." She beamed "We are going to Pittsburgh for the weekend. I can't wait. I'm just like a foolish school girl I guess. There's a lot to do in Pittsburgh, symphonies, ball games, museum, zoo, art museum, great restaurants, lots of cultural activities. "

"Great" said Jim while thinking to himself that he didn't want to know too much. He would have to report this finding to Martha who would pass it on to Paula. He tried to keep the information he gave Martha to a minimum but Martha always figured out ways to get all the information. He hoped Hazel would not divulge any more but he knew she lived alone, had few friends and had to talk to someone.

"You know Jim, when I first met you and watched your activities I was going to report your association with that redhead to your Dean of Humanities."

Jim was aghast. Boy that's all he needed. It wouldn't be illegal for him to take up with a student but it wouldn't look good to the dean. "I'm glad you didn't since there is no more personal relationship there than with my other students. She just happens to come in here when you're here. A lot of different students come in when you're in class."

"Well, you talk about personal things with her and I thought your relationship was a lot more than teacher to student. She brings you candy."

"That's my technique. I get personal with students. I talk to them about their accomplishments, their problems, their home life, the whole gamut. It lets me know what they're thinking and it gives me more ideas on how to be a more effective teacher."

Hazel smiled. "And when I met your two beautiful children I was heart sick. I imagined you and the redhead running off and you abandoning those children."

Jim thought to himself "This woman is whacko or

116

something." He better get his relationship with Hazel back to less intimacy. He offered "Maybe Ansel wouldn't like you telling me the details of your relationship, not that I would pass on any information."

"Anyway" she blustered on "I know now you would never leave or jeopardize your beautiful family. Don't tell Ansel I told you anything."

Jim would keep quiet but he knew Paula would pump her brother for information. Ansel wouldn't mention the sex parts but the fact of the Pittsburgh trip would make things evident. It would come back to him from Paula to Martha. It was just a matter of time. He didn't mind the gossip coming to him but he vowed never to let it emanate from him.

Sometime later Jim learned that a woman majoring in English had taken up with an English professor. When the relationship turned sour she went to the Provost who said that they were adults and it was between them and not his concern. It seems she didn't want the man dismissed but somehow wanted the Provost to intervene and get the professor to honor his promise of marriage to her.

There were several publicized romances between students and faculty and this was accepted in the Punxie academic community. Administrators simply looked the other way or felt it was an agreement between adults. Some of these ended in marriage.

There were also some less publicized relationships between married students and married professors. On one occasion a male "education" prof attended a conference in San Francisco. The meeting was also attended by a married female student, mother of two. Rumor had it they "flew together" in every sense and meaning of that term. It was alleged that they frequently had sex on the floor of his office. They were often seen together on rural roads surrounding Punxsutawney. Rumor also had it that the behavior of the profs of education at conferences was the stuff lawsuits were made of.

12. AROUND THE LEAGUE

Bruce Evans had a lot of interesting experiences in his twenty years of teaching assignments around the circuit. When asked which college or university had the best students he said that they were all about the same intellectually but there were slight differences culturally between campuses. Indiana faculty assumed they were a cut above the rest of the state universities and they were always complaining about Penn State getting the lions share of state funds and research grants. Indiana usually had a third more students than the second place West Chester University in the state system.

Bruce was teaching at California in southwestern Pennsylvania when a black social studies teacher was employed by two other institutions. The man had a full time teaching position at California, Buffalo State College and a college in New York City. He was able to get to the different jobs by juggling an intricate flight schedule, canceling classes and other techniques. When *Time Magazine* publicized the situation the two New York colleges immediately terminated his employment. Even though many complaints had been filed against the professor, California kept him on the faculty. Bruce thought it had something to do with affirmative action statistics.

Some years later, on Bruce's second appointment at California, a black student shot the quarterback of the football team as well as another student. The shooter ended up with a prison sentence of five and a half to eleven years. He didn't have a license to carry the weapon but those charges were dropped.

As if things weren't' bad enough at California another student was shot and killed in his dormitory room. The shooter in this case was a former student and the fracas was believed to be over drugs.

Perhaps turmoil followed Bruce around. A year after his California stint he was hired by Slippery Rock. During his time there, two white students murdered another white student over alleged money owed. This crime was a beating in an alley. Bruce thought that drinking and partying were out of control at Slippery Rock.

At most of the universities there was a constant problem with false fire and bomb alarms. These were so prevalent at Edinboro the police decided to stop evacuating buildings after a bomb threat. After this decision was made the bomb threats decreased. However, the FBI was called in and they did apprehend one caller and severe punishment was promised. Whatever happened to the caller, a student, was never made public.

Bruce believed there were good students and poor students at every campus. He often went to campus parties and regularly attended favorite student hangouts. At Slippery Rock many students went to a dive called the Magic Twanger in Ohio since Pennsylvania cops couldn't touch them there. It was about an hour's drive from the Slippery Rock campus.

On one occasion Bruce went to the Magic Twanger and had taken several coeds with him. Before the evening was out two envious male students challenged him to a fight. Bruce talked to the management and they threw the students out. The students were waiting for Bruce in the parking lot. But they were so drunk they no longer wanted to fight. They were busy hanging onto their car, puking and cursing him. Several days later the students were drunk again and went to Bruce's apartment and harassed him with hollering and challenging him to come out and fight. Bruce thought this behavior inappropriate between students and instructor.

After the Slippery Rock incidents Bruce stopped going to taverns with students. However, he did join Jim, Benji and Hellie at Rudys. These were mild affairs which consisted of polite conversation and some intellectual discussion and opinion. There were no scenes or confrontations at Rudys. On one occasion Rudy had rented his place out to a fraternity. They were having a beach party and brought in ten tons of sand. When

Rudy found out it was too late, the sand was on the floor in one room. He let the show continue but had the fraternity boys working throughout the next day cleaning out the sand.

A notice had been circulated among the Punxie faculty in January. There was going to be a faculty basketball team and volunteers were invited to join. The team would not be in a league but would play some college intramural teams, the local YMCA, some church teams and possibly some industrial teams. It sounded like a good idea and Jim needed the exercise. He looked up T. J. Hendrix the originator of the idea. Hendrix was in physical science. He was a somewhat flabby man who stated his reason for starting the team was to get in shape and do some "running."

Jim was in the presence of T.J. on many occasions and he liked the guy. One of T.J.'s stories involved the Dean of Sciences. About twenty years earlier T. J. had recommended to the dean that the college start an "environmental sciences" major. It would be an interdisciplinary study involving courses from all the sciences. Since T. J. was well grounded in meteorology, earth science, geology and astronomy he thought that he could be the director of such a program. He would incorporate the biologists and earth scientists.

The dean didn't think it was a good idea and sent a letter to T. J. explaining his reasoning. According to T.J. he was in down town Punxie going to his car in the grocery parking lot when a man came up to him and asked directions to the college. T. J. gave him the directions and told the man that he T.J. was a member of the faculty. The man introduced himself as Dr. McClure and told T.J. that he had just been hired as the Director of Environmental Studies. T.J. said he was "livid with rage" but managed to keep his cool with McClure and the dean.

T.J. never mentioned this to the dean but circulated the dean's letter to select members of the physical sciences. He keeps the letter in his desk to remind him of the deception rampant at Punxie. McClure turned out to be unorganized and he was put into another administrative position and Knute Rowlands of biology was now heading the program.

Practice nights were set. Martha agreed whole heartedly that Jim should join the team. Jim never had any exercise. He was thin by nature and had no trouble with weight. His only exercise was occasionally wrestling with Jimmy. By joining the team Jim would get to meet other faculty members and get some counter balance to his sedentary ways.

It was obvious at the first practice the team was not going to win many games. There were two excellent players who would make up the deficiency in the others. Link was an outstanding player at Bloomsburg and Hank excelled at Lock Haven. They were middle-aged now but could still cut it.

Another player that showed promise was Tyrus Cobb Schmidt, named after a famous baseball player. He was a medium built fellow who could jump to the net. Someone told Jim that Schmidt played minor league basketball at one time and had a shot at the pros. Schmidt spoke with authority about basketball and carried on a running conversation about the professional basketball teams. He had a paperback book written by a pro basketball player which he loaned to Hank. Jim didn't think Ty Cobb Schmidt looked that good.

Schmidt was not married but had a girlfriend who stuck pretty close to him and attended many of the practice sessions. She was tall and thin. She was outstanding in that she wore strange makeup. Her lips were often painted silver as was her fingernails and she wore much eye liner. She would come to the practice sessions and sit, not in the bleachers, but on one end of the floor. A smile adorned her silver lips and a vacant stare was her usual expression.

At the third practice session there was some argument about a foul. Each player acted as referee from time to time and some were better at the job than others. In this instance one of the disputants was Ty Cobb Schmidt. He took the ball and went to the center of the court and sat on it. He was challenging anyone to come and take it away from him. Some of the players looked at each other in disbelief. Hank shrugged his shoulders at Jim. As if on cue, everyone sat on the sidelines and conversed as if they welcomed the break. Schmidt eventually threw the ball at a basket and retired to the locker room.

Jim thought Schmidt's bizarre behavior indicated some other problem. This was supposed to be a friendly team, full of companionship and comaradie. Instead it seemed as if Schmidt was using the team as a forum for some personal problem. He was making some sort of statement but no one was sure what it was.

The episode of the ball sent Jim's mind racing. Where had he seen Schmidt before? Then it dawned on him. It was payday and he was behind Schmidt in a line at the local bank. When Schmidt presented his check to the clerk, it was rolled tightly into a tube. He was grinning as he unrolled the tube and kept flattening it out on the counter. Schmidt looked around to see if anyone noticed he had violated the prime rule of not folding, spindling or mutilating. At that time, Jim just assumed that every professor was nutty in his own way. He was beginning to think that Schmidt was some special kind of nut.

The team went on to play the YMCA and the local high school team. They won both games on the strength of Link and Hank. An industrial team which was part of a league was more experienced and beat them. A team from the Christian Missionary Alliance Church was out for blood. They used every trick in the book to win. They beat the faculty physically as well as statistically. They were all elbows and body blocks. Jim thought their behavior odd for a church group.

There was an admission fee to the games with the money going to each teams favorite charity. The faculty spent a lot of their share on beer and pizza after the games. As T.J. Hendrix said, "This is my favorite charity." However, they did donate a considerable amount to the town's "get a hospital" fund.

There were several complaints against the managing

122

skills of T.J. Players were upset that he hated to lose and so he kept Link and Hank in all the time and rotated the other three spots. Both stalwarts were willing to sit down from time to time since they were not fanatic about playing even though they were good at it. Since it was a friendly game and the team was informal, several of the players felt free to offer constructive criticism to T. J. He did not take kindly to this.

Hank was the organizer of schedules for the games and he took it upon himself to send messages out to each team member through campus mail. It consisted of reminders of upcoming games and messages from the custodians about the condition of the locker room and shower stalls. On the bottom of one of the messages he put LET THE MANAGER DO THE MANAGING. He thought it might help alleviate complaints.

At the next practice, Hank was approached by Ty Cobb Schmidt who said "Did you send me this message?"

Hank was taken aback. "Yes, I sent this message to everyone on the team."

Schmidt bristled "The next time you send me a message like that I'm going to come looking for you." Hank didn't know how to handle the situation. After all, he had borrowed Schmidt's book about basketball and thought he and Ty were friends.

Hank tried to apologize and assure Schmidt that he didn't have any one person in mind but Schmidt wouldn't hear of it. He stepped up to Hank and stared into his face. There was obvious anger there and something had to be done to defuse the situation.

Jim thought he could ease the tension by saying "We all got the message. It wasn't meant for just one person. Let's play ball."

Schmidt rushed over to Jim and squared off. "I've had enough of you and your smart remarks too, you little runt."

Jim didn't know what to do. He looked around for some club or device that could be used for protection in case Schmidt started swinging at him. He thought perhaps he made a mistake signing up for a friendly round of basketball.

Link said "Let's play ball."

Schmidt's mouth tightened. "You're another one, a hotshot player who hogs the ball all the time. Anyone can score points playing like that. You think you're something special because you come from a basketball family."

Link had had enough. He went over to Schmidt. "Okay, asshole, start swinging any time you want. I'm giving you the first shot."

Schmidt realized he had overstepped his abilities this time. His body language indicated wilting. He tried to make a stern face but it wasn't in his eyes. Link pressed the issue, his expression was one of calm serious mayhem. He itched for a chance to blast Schmidt. Everyone would have liked to blast Schmidt but for most it would have been a losing battle.

Hendrix went over to them. "Ease up Link. Come on let's play ball."

Everyone lined up to make practice layups. The tension remained and the events of that evening colored the team's relationships for the rest of the season. Players began dropping off the team until only seven remained at the end of April when the team disbanded.

There was another incident involving Schmidt and the administration. During the first semester of the previous year he had been suspended for the entire semester for some infraction that wasn't made public. The administration wanted to fire him but the union assured them that there would be a court battle. Whatever the infraction, Schmidt accepted the discipline without going to court.

Schmidt often wrote letters to the editor of the college newspaper. These consisted of diatribes about students not studying and faculty shortcomings. The faculty advisor and the editor of the newspaper didn't know how to handle these. They didn't want them in the paper but yet he didn't know how to refuse to print them.

There were duties to perform. Jim had become an official member of the Dean's Council and he made his way to the meeting. He had to be on some committee and he figured this would be as good as any so he didn't try to weasel out of the appointment. Besides, the Council never met that often and it was a stepping stone to promotion.

Dean Pratt held his meetings in a room reserved for that purpose. It was next to his office and was furnished with coffee and donuts. His secretary often came into the meeting and handed him some paper. He would assume a concerned expression, depart and return minutes later and resume the meeting. The assembled parties had to cool their heels and wait. As one member bluntly stated "Can't he just tell the secretary that he'll call them back."

The nickname "fuzz-nuts" seemed appropriate and Jim still didn't know why. Jerry had a knack for cutting through to the essence of a person with his nicknames. Many faculty used the name. Jim vowed never to use the nickname for fear he would mention it to the wrong person.

There was nothing spectacular about the dean's meetings. He brought up the usual problems of transferring some classes from one building to another. He would draw diagrams on a chalkboard and explain them. He carried an unlit pipe which he put between his teeth, much in the manner of a British colonel. He would hold the pipe and point to his diagrams with the stem.

Pratt was a budding artist and his preference for the arts became obvious and Jim feared social studies would suffer for it. Other members also feared for their turf.

When the discussion got around to hiring new personnel, Pratt stated that what they really needed on campus was a potter. It was widely known that Pratt threw his own pots and had a wild assortment of crockery he created at his house. He had a small kiln in his backyard. He attended crockery meetings in Ohio and it was rumored that he sold some of his own crock pots at these meetings.

Jim asked for recognition and was granted permission to speak. He rose. "Why do you say we need a potter? We don't even have an art major on campus. The only people required to take an art course are elementary education majors and they take only six hours of the most appreciative nature."

Pratt smiled. "We only have two art professors on campus and they are busy teaching theory and showing slides of famous works of art. We need something hands on, something practical. Besides the art classes are jammed with at least thirty students per class."

A thin gaunt looking professor rose to his feet. "I beg to differ with you on that. The average art class has seventeen students. Might I point out that our language classes have an average of thirty seven students. If any area of study should get a new professor, it should be foreign languages."

Pratt countered. "Your classes have so many students because you're all giving away grades. Once word gets around that the lowest grade is a B then the classes are filled."

The professor hardened. "That's a reckless statement. I'll match our grades with any other discipline on campus. You better check your statistics. In case you don't have them, I'll be glad to let you have a copy of mine."

Pratt puffed harder on his unlit pipe. "Well, when we decide to make some additions to the faculty we'll take this matter up again. Right now we should take care of the urgent problems at hand."

No one was sure what these urgent problems were. Pratt never alluded to them. They appeared to have something to do with space and moving department classes around in buildings. When he suggested putting the language people in a small area the lean professor said that he himself, had nine filing cabinets full of material and the small area couldn't even house him.

Days later, when the Social Studies Department had a meeting, chairman Gregory reported of a meeting he had with

President Curry. Gregory approached the president with statistics indicating his department was overloaded with students and the dean's practice of stuffing students into overloaded classes was becoming critical. He wanted to feel Curry out on the possibility of hiring someone to replace retirees.

With an air of much disgust Gregory stated that Curry was not giving him much support. Bruce Evans was on a temporary contract and it looked like he wasn't going to be rehired or replaced with a permanent appointment. So far, Gregory hadn't heard any statements from Curry to support those made by Pratt at the Swartz party.

Gregory told the department that he would be resigning as department chairman at the end of the academic year. He said the final decision came when Curry said "What we really need at this college is a potter." Everyone figured that Dean Pratt had gotten to Curry. Everyone also decided that Pratt had too much influence on Curry.

Most department members told Gregory that they had confidence in him and that he should remain as chairman. He answered that he had done as much for the department as he could and perhaps a new chairman could have more influence with the administration. Gregory said that he already had forwarded a letter to Curry and Pratt to let them know of his intentions. There was no backing down now.

It was Gregory's letter which prompted Dean Pratt to request a meeting with Jim. It was a formal letter sent to Jim through campus mail. Pratt's request to see Jim at his earliest convenience created uneasiness in Jim.

When Jim arrived at Pratt's office he had to wait while the dean finished a phone call. Jim shuffled in a chair and tried to make trivial conversation with the secretary but she seemed preoccupied. Pratt called from his inner office "Come in Jim."

Jim wondered if Pratt wanted to see him about Jim's attentions to Hellie. Perhaps Hazel Short had followed up on her impulse to tell Pratt about Hellie. Or was it that Jim was just too

127

friendly with students in general. Students liked Jim and he liked them. This was all he could think of.

Pratt extended his hand to Jim and motioned for him to sit down. He said "I'll get right to the point Jim. You're going to get your doctorate soon. Right?"

"I sure hope so. It's just a matter of touching up the dissertation and I should have it done by this summer and get the degree shortly after that."

Jim lied. It was more than a touching up. The dissertation was in disarray and needed major surgery but he wouldn't let anyone know that.

"Well Jim, the social studies chairman, Dr. Gregory, said he was resigning as chairman and we think you would be ideal for the job."

Jim thought "we?" He offered "The department members elect the chairman and I don't think I could win such an election. I haven't been here long enough."

"We know you could win the election Jim, especially if the department knew that you could work closely with me."

Jim looked dismayed. "Oh, I think they would prefer Jerry Swartz over me. Everybody likes Jerry."

"That might be true but this is privileged information. Jerry is being considered for my assistant. All deans will be getting an assistant dean next year or the year after and Jerry is assured of the job. So, he will be leaving the department and you as chairman will be given the opportunity to replace him with a new member."

"Oh," reflected Jim "Jerry is a competent and likable person. He should do well. He does well in everything he undertakes."

The dean became serious. "I know you think I'm asleep at the switch but I assure you I'm not. I know what's going on in your department and despite your opinion of me I think we can get along just fine. I'm not even going to bring up your getting people to cover your classes while you go off on some tree hugging expedition." He chuckled.

All Jim could think of was "That back-stabbing Jerry. He was the one Jim used the expression "asleep at the switch" to. So Jerry was sucking up to the dean, supplying him with information of the most trivial kind. Jim fought off the urge to mention that Jerry gave the dean the nickname "fuzz-nuts."

Jim had to salvage what he could. He countered "Actually I think you're the most competent administrator we have at the college. Just the other day I mentioned this to Clyde and he concurred. No other person could have shaken the classrooms around the way you did and have everyone's approval. That was a move that could have led to chaos and rebellion but you pulled it off.."

Pratt beamed. "You and Clyde really think so. That took a lot of doing and many sleepless nights but I got it done." After this, the dean would act very warm and friendly toward Clyde.

Jim thought he might as well go all the way. "We were all wondering why you didn't apply for the Provost job since you know the ins and outs of the college so well."

Jim knew he had scored with Pratt's ego. He would have mentioned hiring a potter but he didn't want to make himself puke. He wondered how he could ease himself out of the office. He wondered how he would react the next time he saw his good buddy Jerry. He really didn't want to hold anything against Jerry, he liked the guy and considered Jerry his best friend on campus. Jim wondered why Jerry would screw him like that.

Pratt ended the meeting with a flourish and a handshake. "Well Jim, can I count on you being a member of the team."

"You sure can Dr. Pratt and thanks for having so much confidence in me."

Jim left the office and wandered around campus for a while. The meeting left a bad taste in his mouth, a very bad taste, and there seemed to be no way to get over it. He decided he would keep the meeting to himself and not mention it to anyone, except perhaps to Martha.

13. AN ANNUAL MEETING OF THE MINDS

Homer was nominated for History Teacher of the Year by the Northeast Region of the American Historical Society for Higher Education. The membership in the society was so large it was divided into six regional sections. Each section operated independently and the Northeast had the largest membership.

The Northeast selection committee visited the Punxie campus several times to interview students, colleagues and administration concerning Homer. Several members of the Social Studies Department laughed at the idea of Homer's nomination. Homer was a fuddy-duddy, a closet personality. He taught morality along with history. He was a throw-back to the days when Punxie was a Methodist Seminary. How could he win such an award when he was competing against teachers from big universities from Maryland to Maine?

Homer was selected "History Teacher of the Year." The award was presented to him at the regional meeting held at Haverford College in Massachusetts. Chairman Gregory and Henry Felderberg attended the meeting. Homer was on sabbatical and working at the Library of Congress. Naturally, he and his wife attended. There was also a contingent of six former students of Homers. One of them had traveled all the way from Missouri for the event. It was a fitting tribute to a really dedicated teacher.

At the next meeting of the department, Chairman Gregory praised Homer who was not there and placed congratulations in the minutes. He said "When one member of our department is honored, it honors us all."

It didn't take some other members of the department long to start back-biting Homer. There are some people who simply cannot applaud someone else's success. Earl Gratis spoke of the time Homer's grading system was challenged by a student. It was his opinion that Homer was vindicated because the administration didn't want to go against a faculty member.

Even Jerry was not able to be generous. He said to Jim "Imagine a guy like Homer getting an award like that."

Elwood Liston seemed glad to see Homer succeed. He said "Man, that is a prestigious award. Homer really put Punxie on the map. I would like to get something like that before I pass on these mortal shackles."

When Jim reflected on the reaction to Homer's award he was most surprised at Jerry. Perhaps he didn't understand the mind of an Ivy League sociologist. Jerry was one of the friendliest people Jim had ever met. Everyone liked Jerry. Yet, Jim had never heard Jerry utter a complimentary word about anyone they both knew. He was an expert at getting in little digs about people. He was not a vicious person yet he just couldn't bring himself to give anyone credit.

One of the highlights of each academic year was the annual meeting of the Pennsylvania Association for Social Studies (PASS). It's purpose was to elevate the teaching of social studies in the elementary and secondary school systems of the state. It's membership consisted of college, elementary and high school teachers. It was dominated by social studies faculty from West Chester, California, Kutztown, Indiana, Shippensburg and Millersville. The other state related universities had little if any interest in associating themselves with public school teaching.

After several years of membership, Punxie faculty members were beginning to infiltrate the administrative ranks of the organization. Penn State faculty were often asked to deliver programs for the meetings so they would participate loosely in the affairs of PASS. They were more interested in making a show than in doing the actual work of running PASS. Faculty members at Pitt, Penn and Temple considered themselves above the workings of the organization and refused to participate. They had more important things to do than hobknob with common school teachers.

The program for each meeting was conducted by the

Vice President of PASS and this officer would become the new president as each officer moved up one notch at the annual election. This year's program was hosted by the Social Studies Department of West Chester University. Since Cheyney University was near by there was a joint effort between them to work together on the affair. . Every year the program consisted of a Friday dinner, all day Saturday presentations and dinner in the evening.

It seemed inevitable that Cheyney and West Chester would become one university and they cooperated on projects such as this. This move of unification would make the combined university the largest of the fourteen state owned institutions.

Four members of the Punxie staff asked for Friday off as well as funds for transportation and registration reimbursement. The request for reimbursement was denied and the leave was contingent on each member securing other members to cover their classes. Other members resented taking over the classes but did so with the idea that they would be repaid in kind some day.

The Social Studies Club at Punxie used some of its funds and chartered a bus for the event. So Jim, Elwood, Clyde and Agatha joined nineteen students in the bus heading for the Valley Forge Plaza and the Holiday Inn where the meetings were to be held.

Agatha and Elwood each requested a single room. Clyde and Jim would share a double room. The male students would be four to a room while the three female students would share a room. This was an arrangement that had been going on for the last fifteen years. Jim breathed easier when he learned that Hellie had to practice for a music recital. Benji didn't want to go because, as he put it, he wasn't into drinking and carousing all night. He would be glad to attend the meetings if he could get a good night's sleep.

The Punxie group arrived at Valley Forge about two o'clock in the afternoon and spent the next two hours getting settled. There was some difficulty with room assignments but

Clyde was able to straighten it all out. Clyde was the unofficial leader of the group. He had attended all the meetings since the creation of PASS.

After checking in, Jim and Clyde walked around the plaza for a while. They got a yogurt cone from a booth on the concourse. Jim picked up some patriotic toys for Susan and Jimmy and a George Washington mug for Martha.

While on the walkway Jim met up with Oliver Hazzard, a fellow graduate of Bloomsburg, now assistant professor at Millersville University of Pennsylvania. Oliver was a good student at Bloomsburg and was well liked by everyone. Jim had gone directly into high school teaching after graduation while Oliver went directly to graduate school

Oliver had a fellow prof, George Bunyan, with him and there were four-way introductions. It was one of those occasions where everyone knew the other person was a "good guy." If George was a friend of Oliver's then Jim knew he could trust the man completely. Oliver told Jim about other classmates who would be at the meeting. He flattered Clyde by referring to a book review Clyde did for the *Journal of Modern History.* Perhaps some people did read the journals.

Friday's dinner was roast beef, mashed potatoes and a tossed salad. There was apple pie for desert. Jim and Clyde sat with students from Punxie. It was a good opportunity to get on a personal basis. The professors were able to show a human side to their academic personalities.

After the meal, there was a slide presentation on the Middle East by a Biblical scholar from Moravian College of Bethlehem, Pennsylvania. It was a good program and the audience applauded enthusiastically at its conclusion. This was followed by a short business meeting and election of the one officer who would be at the bottom of the list. The others moved up one notch on the totem pole.

After the meeting, most of the faculty and students headed for the bar and the dance music. Jim and Clyde went to the quiet lounge, that is the lounge without a band, where they met with faculty from other colleges. It was as crowded as the music lounge. Clyde renewed old friendships and introduced Jim around. Agatha occupied a corner of the lounge along with some of her friends. Elwood Liston was nowhere to be seen. No one remembered seeing him at dinner.

Oliver Hazzard came forward with two drinks in hand. "Jim, old buddy, I do believe you drink martini's when you can afford them." He handed one to Jim. "Remember when all we could afford was beer."

Jim laughed. "That's still all I can afford right now. I'm only an instructor."

There was a pleasant reunion. Clyde came over to Jim and suggested they look in on some of the student rooms. The hotel had eight floors and the Punxie students were all on the fifth. The four rooms with Punxie males were empty. The room with the girls was packed with students, beer and snacks. A group of clothed bodies were stacked on one bed. A hand reached out from the stack and inserted a quarter into a slot on a machine. It was a bed vibrator and the bed went into spasms and the group of bodies yelled approval.

Clyde pulled on Jim's arm. "It's fine. They'll be goofing around all night. No harm in that." They headed back to the quiet lounge. On the way, they met the hotel security officer who was also checking on the students.

Jim found Oliver and George again and participated in telling jokes. There were discussions about conditions at Millersville as opposed to those at Punxie. Millersville had a slight edge in the category of desirable places to teach. Two profs from Elizabethtown College said they envied the salaries and low teaching loads of the state professors. Their salaries, which they freely admitted, was about six thousand dollars lower than those of Punxie at the same level. Teaching a summer course at Elizabethtown brought in one thousand dollars less than doing the same thing at Punxie.

134

In the midst of the discussions a young black man approached the group. He went over to Oliver and asked "Dr. Hazzard, can I talk to you?"

Oliver went off to the side with the young man and they were nodding to each other. The student was serious while the teacher was grinning. Oliver gave the lad an A-OK sign and they parted. He then returned to the group.

"Boy that was something" said Oliver. "You won't believe this."

Naturally everyone was interested. Oliver said the man was a student of his and they had a good relationship, one of confidence. The student met a "white" woman in the bar who said she would like to have him come to her room. The understanding was that there would be a sexual event. Oliver's advice was - if the student felt like it, to go with her.

The student was worried that it might be some kind of set-up. The woman was quite attractive and the student thought there might be someone in the room who would beat him up. Oliver advised him to take a quick look everywhere then lock the door.

When Oliver asked the student if he was afraid of getting AIDS or some other disease the young man answered that he wasn't afraid of that. Oliver said the idea of AIDS was a huge detriment to his own sex life.

The evening continued with drinking and telling stories. There was some philosophy about government. After all, many of these professors taught political courses and problems associated with democracy. When George made a comment about the resignation of Nixon a prof from Kutztown said "Yeah, what about LBJ?" This took everyone by surprise. His colleague assured everyone that the prof was a dyed-in-the-wool Republican and took his politics seriously.

The next morning Clyde and Jim met Agatha for breakfast. In the midst of toast and cereal Elwood appeared. He seemed happy. Jim looked at him "You look in pretty good shape. I thought the cat might be dragging you in this morning." "What gave you that idea. I visited an old friend from my alma mater last night. It was a very satisfying evening. Yes sir, a very satisfying evening." He never identified the friend or the gender of the friend.

The forthcoming events of the day were discussed. Jim took out his program and circled a couple of meetings he would attend. Clyde looked at Jim's list and said he would join Jim for a few of them but he had other things to attend to so he couldn't make all of them. Agatha said "Would you believe I saw some of the boys leaving the girl's room about four A.M. this morning."

Elwood looked serious "Hell, I thought they were going to make a night of it."

Near the end of breakfast they were joined by Oliver Hazzard and George Bunyan. Jim introduced them to Agatha and Elwood who nodded to George and asked "Are you related to Paul Bunyan?"

George in a straight face said "No, I don't have any relatives named Paul. My dad's name is Christopher and I have a brother Andrew. Paul teaches at Mansfield but he's no relative of mine." It was obvious that George had heard the question many times and had a lifetime to prepare some response.

Saturday progressed slowly with academic presentations, lunch and then more presentations. The presentations were good but not well attended. Many students from West Chester and Cheyney were assigned to attend these presentations.

Everybody eventually retired to the respective rooms to get ready for dinner. Jim ran into Elwood who was proud of the fact that he hadn't attended one meeting all day. He smelled of booze and cigaret smoke.

The after-dinner speaker was an East Stroudsburg professor who discussed his latest book on George Washington's visit to Fort LeBoeuf, Braddocks Defeat and the construction of Fort Necessity. He illustrated the lecture with slides made from

136

the pictures in his book. Most of those in attendance approved of the presentation. Actually, the entire academic nature of the program was excellent.

Then it was back to old friends and new acquaintances. The West Chester students had rented a suite and invited all students to join them for snacks and drinks. They were an aggressive group. Their invitation stated that they would call the police on anyone using drugs or smoking pot. It didn't mention underage drinking. The suite was visited by hotel security throughout the evening.

Many of the Punxie students spent the evening goofing around in the Punxie girl's room. Students from other institutions joined them from time to time. Some of the Punxie students went to the West Chester room to swipe some of their drinks and snacks. There were several West Chester profs in the student suite and they participated in the event. Students made them welcome and seemed to appreciate their presence.

In the Punxie girl's room, hard booze replaced the beer of the night before. Jim and Clyde visited the room and warned the students to confine their drinking to the room and to make certain no underage drinking occurred. Clyde laughed to Jim that he hoped that statement would get them off the hook in case something adverse happened. Both were well aware that underage drinking was going on.

For all practical purposes the meeting was over. There was the night to spend, breakfast the next day and the bus ride back to Punxie. The bar was crowded with students and professors. A professor from Kutztown challenged Elwood to a fight in the bar but Elwood ignored him and moved to another part of the room.

Clyde, Jim, the Millersville profs and the Elizabethtown fellows all drank too much as they enjoyed the deep philosophical discussions of teaching and academia. They would all be nursing hangovers in the morning.

The morning seemed to come early. The Punxie girls

reported to Clyde that their purses had been stolen sometime in the night. Clyde wondered how that could be. It was obvious how it happened. There were too many students coming and going in the room and some of them were from other colleges or were not even connected with a college. Clyde and the girls filled out a report with the hotel security and the local police. The bus driver waited patiently for Clyde.

The Punxie faculty took seats on the bus as students filed in. Everyone looked disheveled. One male student stopped to vomit before he got on the bus. Most of the students collapsed into a seat.

Jim and Clyde sat together. Jim closed his eyes. They were burning from cigaret smoke and the effects of martinis. Clyde nudged Jim and pointed out the window. "See that guy out there."

Jim looked out to see a ragged man passing by. He was bent over and pushing a shopping cart loaded with empty aluminum soft drink and beer cans.

"Yeah," said Jim " I can see him with my one good eye."

Clyde mumbled "I feel just like he looks." With that, Clyde went to the rear of the bus to lie on the long back seat. Jim was joined by a very weary student, Sarah Rice. Sarah and Jim talked for a while. The bus lumbered on. Most students were asleep in their seats. A few looked out the windows. Sarah leaned against him and went to sleep. Jim put his head against hers and nodded off. They were friends and it was a comfortable feeling.

Elwood came up to where Jim and Sarah were sitting and sleeping. He took out a camera and snapped them. Later, he would keep the picture handy to badger Jim with it. It was an excellent picture and probably could have won an award. However, it was a joke that upset Jim and caused him considerable stress.

14. THE SUMMER OF SOME DISCONTENT

Jim's work on the doctorate had progressed to the point where he needed four more hours of residency toward his degree. Through some maneuvering his advisor Jonesey had managed to get some of his dissertation hours to qualify as residency hours. Thus he scheduled six hours of dissertation credits from mid-June through July and applied for a dormitory room. He would work on the dissertation even though Jonesey would be away most of the summer doing "research" for his book on the economic theories of presidents during the "forgotten" years. Jonesey's book would really be a compilation of the work of his doctoral students. They would receive a citation in the preface of the work. If all went well, the dissertation would be complete except for touching up at the end of summer. Jim would let Benji have a look at it before he submitted the final draft to Jonesey.

Martha had objected to Jim staying at State College which is the town where Penn State was located. It had been renamed University Park but the old name still hung in there. The university insisted on the name in order to get its own zip code. Jim promised to come home for weekends and this was a satisfactory arrangement. Martha realized that Jim was under pressure and getting the degree was an important step for both of them.

Jim car pooled with Link who was also working on a degree at Penn State. They would have access to Link's car since he had a two car family. Expenses for the car were to be shared equally between them. Martha would have the family car at her disposal. One of the problems with car pooling is coordination of time. Since Link and Jim were easy going individuals there would be no trouble on that score.

On one Wednesday afternoon in June, Jim was surprised to see Martha and the kids walking up to his dormitory. They had decided to drive down for the day. Jim had a lot of work to do. He had just discovered a book on the economic situation of the United States before the Mexican War. It was a large book but he felt he had to read it in case there was something vital or something he could use to pad the dissertation. It was possible to put the book aside but it worked on his mind. However, he didn't want to give Martha the impression that she wasn't welcome so he spent the day with the family. They enjoyed supper before the three drove back to Clearfield. This surprise visit upset Jim since it was an omen that he would not be able to make plans with certainty.

Jim made a point to let Martha know there should be no more surprise visits. She definitely should call before she came down. Her retort was that if he was busy he should say so and they would understand. However, it was not a point of understanding and Jim was used to giving up his time to do family things. He did enjoy their company and perhaps he did need the break from the dull routine.

What was upsetting was the fact that Hellie had taken to writing somewhat mushy letters to Jim with traces of perfume on them. What if Martha should discover these letters? What if she smelled the perfume while visiting his room? He decided to keep the family from his room by telling them that his room mate Mark Stradlatter kept a messy side of the room and would be embarrassed. Mark was about the same age as Jim, in his middle thirties. He was working on a masters degree in meteorology, one of Penn State's specialties.

Jim didn't want Hellie to write to him but he was too taken with the letters to throw them away. She put a little heart instead of the dot over the i in Hellie. Jim answered some of the letters but was careful not to say anything that would lead Hellie on or be truly embarrassing should they fall into the wrong hands. Just by writing to her he was sending a message that she was more than a casual acquaintance in his life, she was important to him, at least to his ego.

The room mate Mark Stradlatter was a congenial fellow.

Jim never saw much of him. He was a medium sized fellow who was on the edge of becoming portly. He did push-ups and other exercises on the floor when he was there. More often than not he did not sleep in his bed and he informed Jim that he was sleeping a lot in the women's dorm. Jim assumed Mark had a woman friend there. What else could he think? They were all adults and nobody seemed to care. Jim wondered if sex was the entire driving force behind every facet of people's lives.

Stradlatter had a large bottle of hair tonic on his dresser which he used liberally on his straight black hair. He would douse the hair with the lavender smelling liquid and take a couple of swigs of it. Mark often drank from the hair tonic bottle when he was not grooming his hair. Once when Mark was out of the room Jim checked the label on the tonic to find it was forty percent alcohol. That's eighty proof.

It was Friday morning, the week after Independence Day when Hellie appeared at the social studies and political science library of the Penn State campus. She approached Jim as he sat at one of the computers.

"Hi, love of my life."

"Hellie, what are you doing here?"

"What do you think? I'm here to stay with you and share a moment of history."

"What do mean stay with me?"

"Just that, I figure we could get a motel room in Niagara Falls or the Poconos and well, shack up. No commitment, just stay together. You could take a few days off."

"I couldn't do that Hellie. I go home every weekend."

"Call your wife, tell her you've got a lot of work to do and that you can't make it home this weekend. The weather is lovely this time of year and so am I, and so are you."

Jim thought about it as he looked at the beautiful creature beside him. Her summer clothes emphasized her clear somewhat reddish skin and the delicate looking cleavage between her breasts. They were inviting his kiss.

After much deliberation and soul searching Jim said that he would call Martha and tell her that he had a lot of work to do and that he wouldn't be home until sometime Saturday afternoon. He did have a lot of work to do but the fact was, he was lying. He would catch a bus to Clearfield. But in his twisted system of honor he told Hellie that she would have to leave in the evening and they wouldn't be spending the night in a motel, not at Niagara Falls or anywhere.

Hellie agreed to this and Jim abandoned his work for the day and the two planned an afternoon of parks and recreation. Hellie had driven down in her parent's car and they could use that. There were a lot of interesting sites around the area. First, Jim had to find Link and tell him he wouldn't be going back with him that evening.

It was a fun day and the time flew by. A dressy supper at Sullivan's Sea Food House was expensive but enjoyable. Hellie ordered lobster which was the most expensive item on the menu. She objected when Jim ordered roast duck because she thought duck to be an endangered species. Jim had to pay with a credit card and made a mental note to be sure to get the credit card statement before Martha or have a good excuse lined up. He was a novice at the game of deceit and too clumsy and inept to even consider it.

When evening rolled around and Hellie drove Jim back to the dorm she insisted on coming in. Stradlatter was obviously gone and Hellie grasped the opportunity to lie on his bed. She invited Jim to join her but Jim refused. Tears came to Hellie's eyes. Why would a red blooded thirty-five year old man refuse to join her on a bed. She could have just about any man she wanted and she knew it. Did she have some sort of psychological problem? Jim was too young to be a father figure. She followed this with several other thoughts and ruled them all out. No, the problem was with Jim and not her.

Hellie stated that she had drunk too much wine and was afraid to drive. She would stay the night on Stradlatter's bed. It

142

was after midnight and Jim was too exhausted to resist and so agreed to the arrangement.

Jim was tired and on his bed but he slept very little. He would look over at the beautiful Helga who seemed to be sleeping contentedly in her bra and panties. She was indeed lovely. It was like looking at a painting. How could he have let himself get into this mess. Tears formed in his eyes and through the blur he watched Hellie. It wasn't the mess of the situation that bothered him, it was the mess in his mind.

As they dressed and left the dorm in the morning they passed Stadlatter on the dorm steps. There was a brief exchange of pleasantries and Jim passed up the opportunity to introduce Hellie to Stradlatter. Hellie asked Jim if he was ashamed of her. Jim admitted he was very proud to be seen with her.

Jim agreed to let Hellie drive him back to Clearfield. He was in a state of shock most of the way. What if she wrecked the car and his name and hers appeared in the newspaper or on TV. His fears were groundless as usual. The drive was pleasant and all went smoothly. Jim told Martha he got a ride back to Clearfield with another faculty member from Punxie, he made up a name. This was believable since all faculty members from Punxie were either working on a degree at Penn State or Pitt.

Hellie's visit was the event of the summer for Jim. Stradlatter said that he smelled the same odor on his bed that he noticed on letters sent to Jim. When Jim stated that "the visitor" had laid on his bed briefly, Stradlatter beamed "I'll never take the bed seriously again, to think that beautiful woman, that beautiful body, had laid on this bed. I will never change the sheets this entire semester."

July came to an end and the first day of August was the end of the academic summer for Jim. He packed all of his things into the family car which he had driven down for the last week. That way he would not have to wait for Link and could adjust his own time. Martha and the kids were grounded for the week.

Jim decided to take the scenic route back to Clearfield

which meant driving up over the mountain. Penn State was nestled among the hills called Nitanny Mountains and every road out of town led to a vista. He would drive slowly back to Clearfield since he needed a come-down from the highly charged emotions connected with study and academic things. Jim pulled off on a flat area of a high ridge overlooking the Nitanny Valley and reread Hellie's letters one last time. He smelled them repeatedly.

It was time to dispose of the letters. He looked for a trash can but there was none available. He thought he would drop them in the first trash can he found. Then he thought, NO they have my name and address on them and could easily be traced to me.

He decided to burn the letters but since he wasn't a smoker he had no reason to carry matches. He searched the various car compartments and there were no matches. Just tearing the letters up would not solve the disposal problem.

Luckily, this back road was so deserted there was little traffic. He made a pile of the letters on the side of the road. By using the car cigaret lighter he was able to get the pile burning.

The paper burned brightly. The letters were almost consumed with flames when a slight breeze caught the pile and scattered it into the brush. In a matter of seconds, the dry summer grass and low brush started to burn. Jim tried to put it out but the flames were too high for him to stomp on them.

He took the easy way out. He got into his car and drove slowly away. About five miles up the road he pulled over as a fire truck raced by. Some alert driver had called the 9-1-1 number and the fire department. Probably someone with a cellular phone. Jim hoped the damage would not be great. His conscience was beginning to catalog and record more disagreeable information about him that would probably come back to haunt him in later life.

15. BACK TO THE OLD GRIND

When Jim got back to Punxie there was a letter from President Horace Ignatious Curry waiting for him. It informed him that he had been promoted to assistant professor. Jim wondered about it since he didn't recall applying for the promotion. Perhaps it was an automatic promotion. When Jim asked Ms. Needs, the department secretary, about it, she replied that she had typed up the application which was submitted by Harold Gregory, the department chairman. Gregory also approached the campus-wide promotion committee. Jim scrawled out a note of thanks to Harold and put it in his mail slot.

There were still three days to go before classes began. The various offices were busy registering students and handling last minute appeals by students on probation. Most students had pre-registered in the previous semester and were not caught up in the mess of bureaucracy. Jim had pre-registered all of his twelve advisees.

A quick check of his E-mail produced the usual run of academic news items. Much of President Curry's newsletter was now distributed by E-mail. Perhaps he was worried that people were throwing the newsletter away without reading it and he knew that faculty members were hooked on the electronic system.

A note about an article in *Higher Education & National Affairs* stated that some employers are expressing dissatisfaction with the training and skill levels of recent college graduates, citing deficiencies in such areas as thinking abstractly, establishing priorities and setting goals, interpersonal skills and writing. Jim thought "What else is new?"

Another missive quoting the *Council for Aid to Education* said that in the next 20 years the rising cost of college tuition will eliminate college opportunities for approximately seven million Americans. Jim was lucky, if he taught at Punxie

145

for ten years, his wife and children could attend tuition free at Punxie and tuition at half price at the other 14 state owned universities.

There were several announcements of faculty papers presented over the summer. One was in Japan and another in England. Jim thought that he would have to get in on these trips and the subsequent tax write-off they afforded.

Bertha Crenshaw, Coordinator of Elementary Education and Student Teachers was reassigned to the post of Director of the Institute for Research, Foundation Relations and Community Services. Jim thought "Just what we need, less teachers and more administrators."

Thanks to a gift from the local gas company the college scholarship fund now had a total of $41,067 to disburse to needy applicants. The disbursement of the fund last year raised some eyebrows when two students from Pakistan, whose parents were quite wealthy, were given a free ride at Punxie. One of them had rung up a widely publicized string of speeding violations.

In Jim's mailbox there were three requests for generic letters of recommendation from seniors who would be graduating this year. These went into a central administrative file and were ready in case anyone wanted a genuine generic recommendation.

Jim couldn't remember two of the requesters but did remember Josh Murdock who had begged him for a C because a D would put him on academic probation. Even at Punxie, failing students were put on probation. What could he possibly say about Josh. Surely, if he was a graduating senior he must have done better in someone else's class. The second year prof would have to think about that one.

Jim wandered over to the faculty clubhouse to get a hot sausage sandwich and see if anyone of interest was around. He didn't expect to see anyone since it seemed to be the habit of professors to only show up on the first day of classes. Clyde and Bill Barr were there along with Link and Justin Appeal of the

English Department. They were busy discussing a document that each of them seemed to possess.

Jim soon found out that it was the union newsletter which listed the promotions as well as those who were granted tenure and sabbatical leave. There was also a seniority list for the entire faculty. Jim paid dues into the union through payroll deduction but for some reason he had not received the newsletter.

Justin was outraged that he did not get promoted to associate professor. It was his fourth shot at the position. He had met all the criteria and went beyond it in many categories. He had been a member of the faculty for nine years and held a doctorate from the University of Pittsburgh.

Justin pointed to Ms Hazel Short who had been promoted to associate professor. She didn't have a doctorate and had only been at Punxie for three years. How could they possibly pass him up and promote her. He said that he considered filing a grievance against the promotions committee and the president. Hazel Short couldn't possibly have presented as many papers at conferences as he. She couldn't possibly have any better student evaluations, peer evaluations and dean's evaluation than Justin. In his nine years at Punxie Justin had run his string of publications to sixteen. After all, he was an English prof and knew how to write and which publications would accept his work. For all anyone knew, Hazel Short had never published anything.

It was true that Hazel had a colleague, one of her department members, on the promotion committee but it still wasn't enough to evaluate her over Justin. There were no English profs on the promotion committee but Justin knew two of the members personally. He didn't know them well enough to badger them into telling him why Hazel was promoted over him. He asked the assembled coffee drinkers what they thought.

Bill Barr said that Hazel was very active in bringing high school students to the college and that might have been weighted more than most activities in the scheme of the promotion criteria. Justin countered that there was a contract and that the promotion committee was obligated to follow the contract and they couldn't substitute points of that magnitude. The contract clearly stated that one of the criteria for promotion was service to the college or the department. It didn't say to the college "and" the department.

Justin was also irritated by the fact that he was fourteenth on the promotion list and Hazel was fourth. He accepted the fact that the wife of the dean of education, a member of the Education Department, was promoted over him. She was twenty-seventh on the list and it was obviously a political appointment since the president had the option of his own promotion list.

Perhaps it was because she was a woman. The group of five didn't rule that out. How could you equate sexism into the equation. They all agreed that Justin had been screwed again. Jim tried to make light of the subject by saying that Hazel never had a permanent office and perhaps this was some sort of reward. There were no signs of appreciation of Jim's humor, especially not from Justin.

Justin mentioned the case of Ina Braden when he was a student at the University of Pittsburgh. Ina had sued the university for sex discrimination. If she won her lawsuit the university would have to reimburse female employees to the tune of thirteen million dollars. The day before the case went to court Ina Braden died of a "heart" problem. She was cremated before nightfall and the next day the university lawyers asked for a dismissal and got it. He reasoned that today most colleges and universities were apprehensive about offending women and minorities.

Bill Barr said he didn't like the idea of special treatment for women. How can they say women are a minority when they make up over fifty percent of the population? Not that he had anything against women, he liked women. He just didn't like

148

them getting special treatment. Even though he liked women, Bill Barr had a few remarks concerning female thought processes as opposed to male thought processes. He assured everyone that females didn't do as well as males in his classes.

The promotion discussion was never resolved to anyone's satisfaction. Justin would have to accept it and apply again this year. All agreed that Jim's promotion was justified in that he had been hired at the instructor level when he had previous teaching experience, even if it wasn't at the college level. He was at the dissertation stage and had forty-five hours beyond the masters degree. An applicant with those credentials should have been brought in at the associate professor level. But, this was Punxie and what could you expect.

Bill Barr said that if he were Jim he would never have accepted the position at the instructor level. Jim countered that he wouldn't have the job. There were thirty-eight applicants for the opening and he was lucky to be the finalist. Barr said that he heard Jim was an outstanding teacher. Jim said the college didn't know that until he was put to the test. Anyway, the dean told Jim that if he didn't take the job on such short notice he, the dean, would simply put other department members on overload schedule and pay. If there was one thing that most faculty members liked, it was overload pay.

Barr admitted that most college faculty were so desperate for money they would bump their grandmothers to get more of it. He finally said that now that he had some of the facts, Jim was justified in accepting the instructor position. He reasoned that Jim would move along the promotion ladder rapidly. Justin assured Barr that it was not that easy for some people. All agreed that Justin should have been promoted. Hazel was the sixth person without tenure to be promoted over Justin. No one blamed Hazel.

The day before the semester start there was a department meeting which consisted of committee assignments, some scheduling discussions, new courses to be created and deadlines

149

for various reports. Jim volunteered to be the department representative to the Dean's Council for another year. Jerry told Jim that since this group only met once a month it was better to get on the council than on most committees. He said that all you do is sit back and listen and the blowhards would do the talking. Meetings lasted about an hour and the dean did whatever he wanted to anyway. The group was an advisory group and the dean didn't have to take their advice and usually did not. Jim reminded Jerry that he served on the Council last term. To himself he wondered why Jerry didn't remember that.

Clyde was elected to the Curriculum Committee and there was much talk about his obligations to get the new department courses and name changes approved. The Curriculum Committee consisted of a belligerent group of individuals who made departments beg for favors. They often held up programs that should have easily been accepted. Some of the programs had prior approval from Harrisburg. Like some congressional fatcat committee they could hold up progress for years simply by being obstinate. The department was still stuck with the course title History of the Commonwealth of Independent States even though the organization had little identity. They wanted the name changed to History of Russia or History of the Former Soviet Union but the curriculum committee would have none of that. They also wanted to start their proposed one credit course in "democracy." This course would allow them to assign majors needing one credit to fill it. The instructor for this course would meet three different classes in five week sessions and thereby fulfill his obligation for twelve contact hours. It was Clyde's mandate to get some of this settled.

Clyde said that he would work diligently on the department's problems with the curriculum committee and he would "get back" at some of the department's which held up "our" progress. He hated to be vindictive but there were certain events in the past that he was not prepared to forget. He would also keep working on the masters degree in social studies and history. After all, if Punxie was ever going to get university status it had to start offering more masters degrees. There were eighteen departments on campus and only six of them offered work toward a masters degree.

When the first meeting of the curriculum committee took place a discussion of the masters degree took up much time. It would have taken up less time if the chairman hadn't insisted on tracing the history of the state system of higher education and its universities. He was a graduate of Indiana University of Pennsylvania which he referred to as I-U-P. He pointed out that Indiana was the cream of the crop when it came to state owned universities and lowly Punxie. He went to great lengths to point out that IUP was the first of the state universities to offer a doctorate in education and how their connections with the state legislature has paid off over the years. Jerry broke the hypnotic spell by asking the chairman to get on with the meeting, time was getting short.

One member thought that there should be a tightening up of requirements for the masters degree. After all, if we were going to offer the degree, it should have some merit. Clyde said "why don't we all put our masters thesis on file and then students could check them out and review our standards. This sent panic through the committee and Clyde's proposal was defeated. The idea of standards would be put on hold.

All faculty members with less than six years of service would have to be evaluated again this year. Evaluation consisted of two peer evaluations, student evaluations in all classes and the chairman's evaluation. These were sent to the dean and he would add his evaluation before sending it on to the president. Agatha Aggasis and Henry Felderberg agreed to work together on the evaluations.

Jim was given the task of writing a letter to the college president to notify him that congress had declared the second week of November as History Awareness Week. The department will plan some activities and would the president plan on giving some short remarks to the many high school students that the department would bring in for a conference. If the department members were going to share in the promotions they had better get some activity such as this and bring in high school students. Jim outlined his letter while the meeting was going on and presented it for comment.

Jim began to read " To: Dr. Horace Curry From: Department of Social Studies. He was cut short by the chairman.

"Jim, I thought you were a high school teacher at one time. Didn't you have to take education courses. You can't begin a letter to the president like that."

Jim didn't know what Harold was driving at. "What's wrong? I see letters like this all the time."

Harold laughed. "It's not Horace Curry, it's Horace Ignatious Curry. You can't leave out the Ignatious."

The rest of the department muttered to themselves and to those around them. What did he mean? Has Harold Gregory finally flipped out?

The chairman continued. "If you want to make it in academia you have to have a middle name and use a middle name, like Thomas Hart Benton, William Rainey Harper. A college president wouldn't be caught dead just using two of his names. If he didn't have a middle name he would have to invent one."

Jim said he would remember that and thanked the chairman for pointing that out to him. His letter was acceptable and he passed it on to Ms. Needs for typing. She would give him a copy for proof reading and let the chairman get a look at it and then send it on to president Horace Ignatious Curry. Elwood Liston pointed out that Harold Gregory didn't use a middle name. Gregory laughed "Ha, and I didn't make it in academia either."

What a day of necessary nonsense. The department members retired to their individual offices, there to plan for the upcoming semester. Jim had a mountain of duplicating to do and he hoped the duplicator in the dean's annex wasn't too busy. Since Jim was now well known to the dean's staff they let him have privileges with their equipment.

On the way to the duplicator he was stopped by a student and asked if he was Mr. Tailor. Jim wished he could deny that but he said he was. The student said he was a transfer student from The University of Pittsburgh at Titusville and Jim was his advisor. He had a letter from the admissions office and it listed Jim Tailor as advisor. Would Jim help him to make out a schedule?

Jim made out a schedule and punched it out on the computer. Most of the classes were closed and new student Elias Gregory came back to Jim often until Jim told him to take whatever classes were open that he thought he could handle. Jim signed Elias to two of his classes and filled out an overload form. Elias had to take the overload form to the department chairman and the dean for their approval. Jim asked Elias if he was related to the department chairman. He said he wasn't but he would say so if it helped him academically. "Ah," said Jim to himself " a student with a sense of humor. Perhaps Elias would be worth watching."

Hellie dropped by to thank Jim for the wonderful night they spent together at Penn State. He felt that an apology was necessary and wanted to apologize but he didn't know how. They made some small talk about Helga's schedule and she blew him a kiss and departed.

Jim would soon learn that boring tasks were all part of the job. Mundane bookkeeping chores and time spent in trivia were all in a day's work. Department meetings, committee meetings and sometimes an emergency meeting of the entire faculty were obligations of the faculty. Jim would spend as much time at these kinds of activities as he would teaching.

16. CARD CARRYING CURMUDGEONS

It was a slow day and Jim was at the clubhouse. Doctor Thomas Chauncy, professor of geology was holding court. Five other professors were in attendance. Jim was thinking about the next class and had tuned them out. Chauncy caught Jim's attention when Ripkin of Physical Sciences referred to himself as a chemist. Chauncy berated him saying "You're not a chemist, you're a teacher. You don't make your living at chemistry, you make it by teaching. Your occupation is college teacher."

Ripkin was put out. He liked to think of himself as a chemist. He held teachers and education majors in contempt and would refer to poor students as "education majors" regardless of their actual major field. Somewhere in his career he had learned to sneer at education and teachers in general. He used the phrase "Those who can, do and those who can't teach."

Chauncy said that he was always in conflict with members of his department who claimed to be geologists. Yet, the only thing they ever did was take geology courses in college and do a thesis mapping some surface deposits. Some of them received grants to do a summer project but basically they were teachers or to make it more prestigious, college professors. He said he made himself an omelet every morning but that didn't make him a chef. Bill Barr said he referred to himself as a mathematician.

Chauncy believed that the mission of Punxie was to teach and any research grant money should be directed to improving teaching and not in tracing some obscure rock outcrop. It even said so on the Punxie paychecks. It said "Our mission is teaching."

Ripkin argued that the obscure rock outcrop might have valuable economic minerals or be an important aquifer. Chauncy said that might be true but our mission was to teach. He said that Ripkin was not doing chemistry or investigating obscure rock outcrops, Ripkin was teaching students at Punxie. Again he referred to the paycheck motto. It was the business of the Pennsylvania Geological Survey to evaluate the rocks. Chauncy did concede that doing field work enhanced teaching and it had value from that angle. He just didn't like teachers referring to themselves as geologists, chemists, artists and so on. He didn't like anyone belittling teaching. Our greatest inspiration has come from teachers.

There were many discussions at the "clubhouse" about teaching and the role of the college in society. Jim enjoyed them immensely. Most professors were glad to be at Punxie and getting the good salaries. They were the affluent class in the town of Punxsutawney. He liked Chauncy's explanation of why he went into teaching.

Chauncy related that he never wanted to do anything but teach at the college level. He went from undergraduate directly into a masters program with a teaching emphasis. He paid his own way and worked five different jobs during his undergraduate days. He liked the wilds of the earth and so he chose earth science education as his field. He was proud of his master of education and doctor of education degrees. He was insulted when some promotion committee member rated him low because according to him Chauncy didn't have a terminal degree in his field. He emphasized "my field is college teaching."

"You can't beat this job" said Chauncy. "You get to read books, deal with interesting subject matter and the cream of society, our intelligent young people."

Ripkin challenged the "intelligent young people." He was supported by Bill Barr in that enterprise. Chancy said that Ripkin held that attitude because he never had a job where he dealt with the average citizen. He had always associated with college students as one of them and as their teacher. What Ripkin needed was to spend some time in the military to become aware of what the average citizen is really like. Ripkin said he worked in a shoe store two summers while he was in college and thought the average citizen was more intelligent than the students at

155

Punxie.

The geoscientist mused "You chemists have little human compassion. Nobody measures up to your standards."

Ripkin beamed "Thanks for calling me a chemist." He got Chauncy on that one.

Chauncy said it was easier to pay people off with titles than to give them money. In mockery he said he was not a teacher but an astrogeophysicist. He said he liked certain titles such as forensic archeologist and paleobiologist. He said there should be a contest to see who can come up with the best description of some obscure endeavor. "We got lunar geologists on campus but we don't have teachers."

From time to time the college published a synopsis of doctoral and masters work by Punxie students and faculty. They also accepted material not related to degree programs. Chauncy said he wrote an article offering a prize for the best academic job title. The adminstrators in charge of the publication considered his material too trivial for their publication.

Chauncy had another observation concerning professors. The college was always hiring ABD (all but the dissertation) professors. They have no education experience. They know nothing about testing and evaluation, the reliability and validity of their tests. They know nothing about classroom management. The first two years of their appointments are educational disasters. He agreed that most hirelings were enthusiastic and this helped. According to him it took three years for a new professor to get some handle on his occupation. "Too much emphasis on chemistry" he said "and too little follow-up on absorption and effectiveness. You have guys like Bill Barr in math who think flunking students is teaching them something."

"So" thought Jim to himself "someone else has caught up with the mindset of Bill Barr." Jim wanted to interject the premise of "tough teacher" but he would reserve that for another time. Also, he didn't want to aggravate Bill Barr, not yet anyway. Chauncy said that the college should hire more people like Jim who had endured the battle ground of high school teaching.

The clubhouse was the center for the gossip of the day. A male English prof had been arrested for soliciting sex from a male undercover state trooper at a rest stop on Interstate 80. It was always suspected that the prof was gay but never confirmed.

Jim didn't have much to say on that score. He knew a number of gay teachers and had a good relationship with most of them. Their sexual preferences were their own business. Elwood Liston said that there were a lot of "queers" teaching at Kutztown and he got in a fight with one over an incident at a conference. It was over some stupid thing like Elwood pushing the guy aside at the bar. It seems a lot of hard drinking went on at conferences attended by Elwood.

Another incident in Jim's first year at Punxie was the arrest of the chairman of the fine arts department on a shop lifting charge. Old professor Henning was getting senile and his pocketing merchandise was probably a mistake of some sort. He was fined and his position at Punxie was in jeopardy. The union backed him and the administration had plans to fire him but backed off.

The fine arts department consisted of lumping together teachers of art, music, philosophy and librarians. They were told to elect a new chairman but those defiant son-of-a-guns re-elected Henning, the felon. Provost Simmons didn't think it was worth the challenge and frustration. He antagonized them by not responding. He wasn't sure if he could take it to a higher level and didn't think it was worth a "grievance" hearing. Professor Tony Jamerson spent days writing defense positions and waiting for the challenge which never came. It would have been his finest hour, at least in the field of academics.

Another professor that made an impression on Jim was Peter Rankin, also of the English Department. He could best be described as nuts. Jim held the opinion that most professors were nutty in some way or another.

Rumors of Rankin's class conduct were fascinating. He would stand on his desk and lecture. He would jump into a waste basket. Once when he did this he fell to the floor and banged his head on the desk on the way down. Class was canceled as students helped him over to the college health facilities. Despite his goofiness, the students always spoke well of Rankin and several said he was their favorite teacher.

Rankin was well known downtown. He once walked into the Pizza Hut wearing his bathrobe and slippers. He said he was watching TV and had this urge for pizza after seeing an ad for it. His urge was so strong he didn't want to take time to dress. This was a story which received wide circulation in the town.

Jim decided to tell his story of Rankin to the clubhouse members. It was the first week of the new fall term. Jim was on his way to his office and saw this man talking to a shrub. He paused to listen. The man, who turned out to be Rankin, ignored Jim. A few students gathered around. The bush was confronted with many references such as "the burning bush", "all around the mulberry bush" and "when Burnam Bush doth move to Dunsinay."

Jim went to his office and called Provost Simmons who asked Jim "What do you want me to do about it?" Jim said the campus police should be notified, something should be done. The provost said "You call them then, I have a meeting in two minutes." The ball was now in Jim's court. He did call the campus police who came out of their burrow to see what was going on.

When Jim got there, Rankin was sitting under the bush, still ranting, something about "protecting God's creatures." Two campus security men convinced Rankin to get into their van and they took him to a local physician. The show was over and everyone went back to his station.

The physician had Rankin admitted to the hospital in Indiana from which he was transferred to one near Pittsburgh. He was out of teaching for about six weeks and his classes were

158

covered by other profs who received overtime pay for their efforts.

Rankin came back to finish the semester. However, before New Years Day he married the female director of the ROTC program at Indiana University of Pennsylvania and they left for England. Where they were presently was the center of much speculation. Rankin had skipped town leaving behind a lot of unpaid bills. Merchants tried to collect from the college. This effort was without success.

Another facet of the Punxie profs was their penchant for moon lighting. One of the fine-artists ran a florist shop in town. He spent more time at this than teaching. Another painted replicas of peoples homes. If you would give him a picture of your house he would paint it in whatever setting you requested. He was well respected for his "oils" and received many awards. His excellent reputation as an art teacher was well deserved.

Football coach Phillips ran an insurance agency on the side. He sold accident policies to most of the parents of his players and recruited some of his more mature players into selling insurance. He and his staff operated from a building in the town. The agency provided the coach with more money than he made coaching and teaching phys-ed.

A geography prof operated a small publishing company. He printed his own books as well as others. The books were well received by the general public. There was some question of ethics when he used his own books in his classes but he defended this by saying he never used his own books unless they were used at other institutions. His company did publish quality books. Besides, when you write your own book, you tailor it to your needs and can give the students a quality product at a lower price. He eased his conscience by presenting a cash award to a graduating senior and a cash award to the sophomore with the highest academic average in geography.

The real professional entrepreneurs of Punxie were the slum landlords. These were profs who bought up old houses in

159

town, renovated them, then rented them out to students. Housing space was short at Punxie just as it was on every campus in the Commonwealth of Pennsylvania. There was always a down-side to this renting venture. Many students held wild parties on the premises, even when there was a forbidden party clause in the contract.

Faculty landlords were always confronted by the legal system concerning underage drinking, noise and illegal drug use. They were badgered by the town for safety violations, fire escapes, too many students to a room, smoke alarms and parking. The town demanded that the landlords buy a license if they were renting to students. Other landlords that did not rent to students were exempt from the license. Often the rented property was trashed by the students who gladly surrendered their security deposits.

The big real estate magnate was Anthony Koski of education who through some maneuvering was able to buy a sixty unit housing complex in Indiana from the government for six thousand dollars down. He made payments with the rent money as well as reimbursement from HUD for low income housing and urban development. He confided to Jerry that he cleared over a quarter million dollars the first year and that most of it was tax free. Jerry was impressed but didn't want to get into the landlord business himself. He was afraid of confrontations. He also figured he wouldn't be at Punxie much longer. The Assistant to the Dean position should propel him into a bigger and better setting.

Koski also bought houses at sheriff sales. In one unfortunate encounter, after such a sale, the former owner shot him with a 22 caliber handgun. The bullet entered his upper arm and lodged against the bone. It was easily removed and recovery was complete. Police would not prosecute the shooter, saying the old man didn't mean to shoot Koski. It was an accident. The victim insisted on booking and prosecution. The shooter was sentenced to two years probation.

Then there was Jim's friend Clyde who ran a real estate business. Clyde's wife worked the business and Clyde acted in an advisory capacity. The real estate profits matched Clyde's salary.

Besides gossip, the clubhouse was also the distribution point for an anonymous short-lived publication called *The Faculty Forum.* Mostly it complained about the dictatorial policies of the administration. Jerry told Jim he knew who was writing it. When Jim inquired as to whom, Jerry said that it was privileged information and he was afraid it would get back to the wrong people. After three issues, the rebellious publication disappeared from the tables of the clubhouse. Jim put the privileged information in his mental file along with the price of the Lincoln.

It was difficult to be an efficient chairman or a dean at an institution the likes of Punxie. The union contract and tenure made it impossible to discipline staff. If an instructor didn't meet his classes there wasn't much that could be done about it. Usually these transgressions were widely known in the campus community. These problems were often discussed at union meetings but nothing ever came of it. The administration chose to ignore it but let the violators know that they knew.

John Freemont of the English Department told his class they wouldn't meet for three weeks. This would give the bookstore a chance to get the textbooks he had ordered but were not yet available. Apparently, in his mind, it was a battle between him and the bookstore. He would "show them" by dismissing classes for three weeks.

There were no sanctions put on Freemont. He was considered a poor teacher who insulted students as well as the administration. Freemont was given a quarter load reduction in teaching in exchange for editing and publishing an English Department newsletter which was circulated at other institutions in the State System of Higher Education. It contained creative writing from the department staff and students of the SSHE. It was probably a ploy to cut down on Freemont's teaching time.

The administration probably would have liked to get him out of teaching completely.

He didn't publish the newsletter on a regular basis although many manuscripts were submitted. He said that they weren't of good enough quality to merit publication. He skipped one semester completely. This was brought to the attention of Provost Simmons who had the payroll deduct one quarter of Freemont's salary.

Freemont was not a member of the union but he still asked for their help. They advised him to accept the reduction in salary in order to avoid a charge of incompetence, a charge, if proved, could lead to dismissal. After all, the understanding was that a newsletter would be published each semester. It's tough to have high standards and maintain one's integrity.

Another faculty member deserving recognition was Henry Blackenshep of the math department. At the end of one semester he had been given the wrong set of grade sheets. He never recognized the fact that they were not his. He dutifully filled out grades for each of the students. When another member discovered the switch the chairman had to retrieve the graded set from student records before they were scanned by the computer. The chairman said there were some errors on some of the sheets and it was easier to correct the entire sheet than to send in correction forms. The department embarrassment was thwarted but eventually the story leaked out.

Each semester the faculty members at Punxie were required to list their work hours. A typical weekly work hour list might be - meet classes 12, office hours 6, advise students 3, preparation for classes 10, research 6, committee meetings 2 - total 40 hours.

Most faculty went along with the requirements since these were forwarded to the chancellor of the state system of higher education and he used them to justify state monies. However, some members considered filling out the forms beneath their dignity.

Provost Simmons called a special session of the entire faculty where he went into some of the problems he faced and this was one of them. He said that several faculty put down as many as 80 hours, one put down 168 hours. He said that this was ridiculous and staff members had better take these mundane assignments seriously in the future. After that meeting, chairmen were asked to reject any forms that had less than 30 or more than 60 hours. John Freemont still turned in 86 hours on his form but the chairman of the department simply changed the numbers and sent it to the Provost.

When Bruce Evans was hired, Jim wondered how Bruce could get the position without advertising. Didn't federal law require advertising with the guidelines of equal opportunity and affirmative action? Was there some sneaky deal that kept Bruce on the payroll. He certainly didn't want Bruce to lose his competitive edge but he was curious about it. This information might come in handy sometime.

Chairman Gregory assured Jim that the jobs were always advertised but in such a way and in obscure newspapers that Bruce always qualified. However, when Bruce wasn't available they put out serious notices. Besides, everyone knew that Bruce was an excellent teacher and it wasn't patronage or anything of that sort.

It was not possible to give Bruce a permanent position because he refused to work toward a doctorate which was one of Curry's requirements for a tenure-track position. No one in the department was able to figure out why Bruce never went on for the doctorate. He had the talent. Perhaps he never wanted a permanent job in the first place. Like some migrating falcon he winged from place to place.

Gregory considered affirmative action a hindrance to progress. He said they had Agatha and a couple of years ago they had a black professor named Charles who was working on a doctorate at Pitt. Gregory said that regardless of the course assignment, Charlie would only talk about problems of the inner

163

city. It seemed to be his mission in life.

Black students hated Charles. He had some philosophy about treating them tougher than whites. Complaints against him were many. The department was saved when Charles was awarded the doctorate and immediately bolted for Michigan State.

After that, Gregory said he wanted no more surprises. He hired Jim because he had worked on many projects with Dr. Jones, Jim's advisor. Jones had invited Gregory to apply for a vacancy at Penn State. Gregory rejected the invitation. He often wondered how his life would be different had he accepted it.

Gregory told Jim that it was time for him to retire. There was no longer any conflict in his academic life. In the old days, there were decisions to be made. Each decision affected everyone. Should the department emphasize history as opposed to social philosophy or government or economics. It seemed like trivia but it did have some bearing on the future enrollment in department courses. It was important to the future of the department and the staff and hiring new staff.

Gregory said "There was a move on in the sixties to hire more sociologists and expand into social programs. President Lyndon Johnson and the Great Society had opened the doors to more intense treatment of the subject once sneered at as socialism."

Gregory followed this with the statement that many department members actually hated him and referred to him as Chairman Mao and worse yet as a communist, a very hated label in those days. He said that this was good because it gave him vigor and an intellectual challenge. One had to be well read in order to win arguments. Those who relied on being loud without substance lost out.

"It wasn't simply knowing your subject that mattered. It was fighting for turf. Take today's general education requirements for the college. Every department has something stewing in the pot. It's like the definition of a camel which is a

164

horse designed by a committee."

Gregory kept going down the path of nostalgia. "At one time geography was part of the department. It was an integral part of the high school and junior high school programs. Then the history consultants to the Pennsylvania Department of Education decided to put in economics and eliminate geography."

"Geography professors at Pitt and Penn State could have saved geography in the high schools but they were involved with spacial analysis and not concerned with lesser education. You know what happened. Geography lost out in our state."

"The Pitt geographers were so dumb they didn't realize that without the subject in the local schools there would be no one coming up to take up their study. Eventually, Pitt had to shut down its Department of Geography."

"Penn State was able to survive the demise of geography since they had integrated it into the required core courses of other majors. They had state funding and departmaent members could get grants from the state legislature. Pennsylvania slips more money to Penn State than to all the state schools combined. Penn State keeps expanding and has more than twenty branch campuses. They take state money but don't have to account for it."

"You know what happened. Geographers became earth scientists and became members of Geoscience Departments. Chauncy and I were in the same department at one time. We fought that fight. We lost some valuable territory there."

"Well we don't have the intellectual fights anymore. Our problems are with the administration. They are budget people, not educators. How many students can you squeeze into a class and a classroom? Hire instructors instead of associate professors. Retire seasoned professors and hire greenhorns. I better stop drinking in mid-day, it's catching up with me."

17. PERSONAL STORIES

Blackie's Tale

Autumn had come to the backwoods and the annual picnic at the president's farm was in order. Even though living quarters were provided for the college president he wanted a place to call his own, a place in the country. Most of the faculty considered Punxsutawney as being in the middle of country, but there was still room further out.

President H. I. Curry raised a couple of cows, two horses, two sheep and a bunch of chickens on the farm. Actually, he supervised the farm and a middle aged couple lived there free of charge and maintained the place.

Curry had 83 acres of land, most of it wooded. He had a large section set aside as a picnic area and he held a picnic for the faculty and their families every autumn. Jim had heard about these picnics and he had mentioned them to Martha. She was not interested in attending and neither were the children so Jim decided it would be in his best interest to pop in, say hello to Hick and pop out again.

Fortunately it was a warm day and everyone was in shirt sleeves when Jim arrived at the grounds. He had brought along a light jacket, just in case, so he left it in the car and walked about a hundred yards up the hill from the parking lot to where the action seemed to be taking place.

There were family groups playing volleyball. A father was throwing a baseball with what appeared to be his son. There were horse shoes. A long table with tablecloth was groaning from the weight of food as people came, picked up a few morsels then disappeared. A CD player playing standard tunes was hidden somewhere but the speakers were in a shelter.

There was no one in sight that Jim knew. He felt as if he was in an alien environment. Didn't any of the social studies people attend these things. He went to the table and looked over the menu. The main items were barbecued ribs that were getting cold, fat hot dogs, hamburgers, baked beans and cole slaw. Soft drinks and watermelon were at the end of the table. Jim picked up a soft drink and a chunk of watermelon and made his way to an isolated bench under a small oak tree.

Curry was no where in sight and Jim wondered how long it would be before he could authenticate his presence and depart. The sun was warm and priss that he was, Jim wondered about the bacteria content of the food left exposed.

Off to his left Jim noticed a solitary figure wending his way slowly toward him. The man was dressed in a long coat, a duster, like those worn by cowboys of the old west. His hat which was not quite western matched his outfit.

It turned out to be Henry Blackenshep of the math department. He limped up and sat beside Jim.

"Howdy Jim, I saw you come in."

"Dr. Blackenshep, how are you?

"Jim boy, my friends call me Blackie and I count you among my friends so you can call me Blackie. At least in these informal situations. I wouldn't want you to call me Blackie in front of students."

Blackie had the smell of alcohol about him. " It will be difficult for me to call you Blackie since you are one of our esteemed distinguished professors."

"Well, try it anyway Jim boy."

Blackie reached into the inner pocket of his duster and pulled out a paper bag containing a flask. He unscrewed the lid of the flask and took a swig of whatever was in it.

"Want a drink Jim boy?"

"No, but thank you anyway, I'll stick to my lemon-lime." He held out the can.

"Well Jim boy, let me put a little something into your can, it will spice up the lemon-lime. It'll be a home made gin-ricky."

"No thanks" Jim thought and added "Blackie."

"Okay, old buddy, but this is good stuff, forty six bucks

a bottle, direct from Scotland." He took another long pull on the neck sticking out of the paper bag.

"Great. Have you seen Curry around?"

"You won't see the president for a while, he's drunker than I am. He's probably sleeping it off in the house and will make his semi-sober appearance about five o'clock. You staying for the fireworks Jim?"

"No, I don't think so."

"You should stay for the fireworks. Curry really puts on a display, spends about five hundred dollars on fireworks. His are better than the Punxie fire departments on fourth of July."

"I have a long way to go tonight and I don't want to drink and drive that far and so I can't stay for fireworks." Jim made that up.

"Too bad, it will really be a blast."

There was silence for a few moments as each man breathed deeply, stretched out his legs and relaxed. Henry turned to Jim.

"Jim boy, my friend, I know I can trust you."

Oh,oh, thought Jim to himself. He definitely did not want to be trusted with any secrets. He had had enough of that as a high school teacher. His mind raced back to those days when Jack Martin confided in him.

Jack Martin was a speech teacher at the high school. Besides remedial reading and speech, he also had a master's degree in psychology and sometimes acted in the capacity of guidance counselor to high school students.

Jim had split a few beers with Marty after a couple of basketball games and Marty assumed that Jim was trustworthy and could keep a confidence. Marty told Jim that he had been having sex with Yolunda, a high school senior. He had been "dating" her since she was in the eleventh grade.

When Marty confided in him, Jim said "What if I'm called in to testify against you?"

Marty said "Well, I expect you to lie and deny any

168

knowledge of the affair."

Jim assured Marty he would keep the confidence but begged him not to tell him any more about it and if there were other students Marty was banging to keep it to himself. Marty said there had been two others in the past but Yolunda was cream of the crop. He called her Yoyo because as he put it she had this swinging hip movement during the height of the act. There was nothing better than sex with a seventeen year old girl.

Jim did keep the confidence. He didn't even tell Martha. When he would pass Yolunda in the school hallways he felt ashamed or perhaps it was some other emotion he didn't understand.

The situation came to a head when another teacher, Shep, told Jim that the principal of the high school was going to fire some male teacher because he was screwing high school girls. Shep believed it was the regular male guidance teacher and he had giggled this information to Jim.

Jim realized it must be Marty and called him that evening to warn him about the situation that Shep had described. The next day Marty was called into the principal's office and to avoid exposure of the entire situation submitted his resignation. Rather than thank Jim when they met at the grocery store Marty was very bitter and treated Jim rudely. The principal had gotten wind of Marty's activities when he attended an unchaperoned birthday party for a high school girl. At the party, he and Yolunda foolishly disappeared into a bedroom for over an hour.

Well, here was Blackie, Dr. Henry Blackenshep, about to confide in Jim. There seemed to be no way to avoid it.

"Did you hear any rumors about me Jim, from anybody?"

"No Blackie, I did not. I don't get around much and nobody really tells me anything."

"Well Jim, my career almost ended when I was thirty nine years old and a professor at West Chester. I was a lot friendlier with students then than I am now.

Jim thought it would be another sex story and Blackie

wanted to get it off his chest. There is something about having an illicit good time and not being able to tell anyone about it.
" This male student was in my office and we were having this discussion about nothing in particular. We were both standing and my back was by a wall when he pulled out this switchblade knife and sprung it open. I had a split second to decide what to do so I kicked him as hard as I could in the knee which sent him flying backwards and screaming."

"Wow, you could have been killed."

"That was my exact thoughts as I called campus security and the ambulance to take him away."

Blackie took another sip of the Scottish nectar from the brown paper bag. "When the dust settled I and the college were being sued by the kid's parents. West Chester was a college at that time and not a university. The administration considered terminating my contract."

Jim emptied his can of lemon-lime. "Seems to me the kid should have been sent to prison or something like that."

"That's just it, the kid said he was just showing me the knife. We were having a friendly conversation, which we were, and he had just purchased the knife and wanted to show it off.'

"Do you believe that."

"After thinking about it these many years, I think that was what happened. He just wanted to show me his knife. But, with all the nuttiness going on, my back was up to the wall, he pulls out this knife and clicks it open, what was I to think. If I wasn't back to the wall I could have jumped back or to the side but it was a decision I had to make and make it quickly."

"Seems to me you acted properly. You could have been gutted. What happened to the kid."

"He wasn't exactly a kid. He was twenty six years old and had spent five years in the marines. I had him banned from my class since I didn't want to see him and I would see him walking around on crutches with his leg in a cast. I didn't break his leg but messed it up pretty good and he would limp for a

170

very long time. He was charged with possession of an illegal weapon but nothing every came of it. They must have figured he suffered enough."

"What about you, what happened to the lawsuit?"

"Everything was dropped. I could have had a counter-suit, but we all decided to get over the situation as soon as possible."

"Is this why you're at Punxie now?"

"Pretty much so. The West Chester administration always had this on the back of their mind. When I became chairman of the department they never gave me any cooperation and I was just spinning my wheels so when the position opened at Punxie I took it. To think, at one time I passed up a chance to teach at Rutgers but decided to stay at West Chester and then this happened and I ended up at Punxie."

"I think Punxie is a pretty good place. We can do just about whatever we want and we have a wholesome academic atmosphere.'

"Naw, Jim boy, Punxie is for losers, and I'm one of them."

"Blackie, old buddy, you're not a loser, you are a respected member of the faculty. Colleagues, administration and students all love you and think highly of you."

"Really Jim, you're not just saying that?"

"Believe me Blackie, you are at the pinnacle of our profession. I just wish I had your reputation."

"Really Jim, you're not just saying that?"

Jim really did have a high regard for Blackie. "Really, Blackie, and if you don't mind, I'll have a swig of your Scottish import, I would like to see what forty six dollars a bottle tastes like. I'm heading out right now."

Blackie handed Jim the bag and Jim unscrewed the lid and took a healthy swig, swished the liquid around in his mouth and swallowed. "Wow, that's good stuff."

A Leather Stalking Tale

Earl Gratis was a pleasant member of the department. Unmarried, he seemed to be a loner and kept to the shadows of society and the department. He was friendly enough and had a keen mind for statistics as they related to his specialty of refugees, immigration and population patterns. He could estimate the population of a country or a state with remarkable accuracy. He was working on a doctorate at Penn State but his progress was slow and plodding. By taking one course and sometimes two a semester there was little light at the end of his academic tunnel.

Earl was subject to mood swings but they were surficial and never deep. On rare occasions he did take some mild medication for depression. Most everyone liked Earl but they did not invite him to functions or to their homes as an individual. He was not the kind of individual you would spend an evening with, one on one. He did attend parties which included the entire department. At these functions he would usually talk shop or come up with some statistics on football.

About mid-semester Earl approached Jim and asked Jim if he would write a paper for him. The paper involved the history of Punxsutawney State College and Earl had all the information but was having trouble putting it together. He said that Jim was such a free flowing talker and with his writing ability he should be able to do the paper for Earl in about an hour, two at the most. There was no mention of payment of any kind.

Jim reluctantly agreed to the project and accepted a bundle of material from Earl. It didn't seem to matter to Earl that Jim was deep in his own quest for a doctorate. Jim figured that this would create goodwill and he would be able to call on Earl in the future. Perhaps he singled out Jim because of his newcomer status and reminded Jim that he had voted to employ him, thus hinting that Jim owed him a favor.

The paper ended up at thirty two pages and took Jim

nine hours to write and type. Earl received an A plus on the paper and since this was the only outside requirement would receive an A for the course. His thanks to Jim was minimal and treated the affair as if Jim should have done the paper since he, Earl, was in no mood to write it himself. It was as though Jim had an obligation to help out since Earl's mental state was such that writing the paper would have been a burden.

Later, in a discussion, Earl was telling Jim how he was progressing toward the degree. He told Jim how he, Earl, wrote this paper on the history of the college and how Provost Simmons said that he would publish it for alumni consumption. It was a feather in his cap and the department should be proud of him. Jim wondered, "Was he so dumb or uncaring that he didn't realize that I wrote the paper."

When Earl had a doctor or dentist appointment he would ask Jim to take over his classes. This task usually fell to Bruce Evans when he was substituting for sabbatical leave recipients. Most everyone took advantage of the friendly attitude of Bruce and the fact that his future employment depended, to some extent, on their vote. When Bruce wasn't around, Jim was next in line.

Earl had a fondness for leather and had a suit made of black leather which he wore to special dinners. Naturally, all eyes were on the leather suit. He had a black leather hat and black leather boots which he often wore to work at the college. This prompted Jerry to give him the nickname of "Tex".

After the paper episode, Earl felt free to tell Jim some episodes of his personal life. He had dated the secretary Ms. Needs but it didn't work out. In her private life, she was a free flowing, swinging personality and Earl's cautious approach to life didn't fit in. Since Earl didn't socialize much he confined his amorous advances to women in his circle of employment. He tried dating some of the women in the education training school but they rejected him. That is why he approached Ms. Agatha Aggasis, the lone female member of the department.

He told Jim that he had taken Agatha to a concert at St. Marys, a town not too far from Punxsutawney. He went into great detail on how they shared a love of music. They had a nice dinner and it was a very pleasant evening. They were able to discuss subjects other than social studies. Earl felt it necessary to tell Jim that Agatha was a very unique person and contrary to appearances was very much in touch with the modern world. Jim thought "if Agatha is in touch with the modern world, what is she doing with Earl?

Over the weeks, he would talk about his fondness for Agatha and his brief encounters with her. She was divorced from an alcoholic husband who still had some influence on her and Earl wanted to free her from the association. The husband would borrow money from her from time to time which disturbed Agatha.

Earl had taken this situation as some sort of holy quest. Jim never commented on Earl's statements since he didn't know what to say under the circumstances.

Agatha was an attractive pleasant blonde, friendly with most people but never familiar. She was an accepted part of the department and everyone felt comfortable in her presence. Her divorce and the bitterness of it caused department members to treat her with extra care. Jim came on the scene after the divorce and was not privy to the details.

It was almost two years since Agatha's divorce and she must have figured it was about time to get on with her life. A start on this new life would be a few dates with Earl who was unattached. She was also ready for travel, dining, romance, sex - the entire package that people expect of life. Earl would be one station on the road to all this. Jim's first impression of Agatha was that she was a prudish old maid but he was wrong. He saw her in a new light after the meeting in West Chester.

The dates were getting more frequent and since Earl had no close friends he decided to tell Jim the innermost secrets of the affair. On about the fourth date he was bursting with jubilation. He was sitting in Jim's office waiting for him. He related the events of the Saturday date.

Earl had taken Agatha to dinner and a concert at Brookville. On their return they went to Earl's apartment where eventually they disrobed. Since Agatha always made a fuss about the leather outfit, Earl put down his jacket and they proceeded to lay on it. As fate sometimes interferes with the best of plans, Earl was unable to get an erection. Where most men would have been embarrassed to mention it, he had no trouble relating this to Jim. He also stated that this had happened before.

As he told the story to a wide-eyed Jim he assured Jim that this was no mental problem but some physical manifestation caused by excess alcohol. He said that he proceeded to kiss Agatha from head to toe and she loved it. Jim said that since he knew Agatha so well it was not in anyone's best interest for Earl to be telling him these intimate details of their relationship. Earl countered by saying that he knew he could trust Jim to be discreet. He said that Agatha was now in possession of his soul.

When word got out that Agatha was beginning to date again there were some other interested males. One of them was T. J. Hendrix of the Physical Science Department. He was the organizer of the basketball squad that ended in disarray. T.J. was a pleasant, serious fellow and he was more suited to Agatha than Earl. T.J. had standing in the academic community and Earl was hardly noticed. So it was that she started to date T.J. and put off Earl. Perhaps it was the impotence episode.

One day Jim noticed Agatha close to tears and asked her if there was something he could do for her. Tears welled in her eyes. It was as if Jim was the cavalry and had come to the rescue. She unloaded her burden on him.

Agatha told Jim that since she started dating T.J., Earl wouldn't leave her alone. He followed her everywhere and parked his car outside of her apartment. He even set a chair outside of her office and monitored her every move. Once she and her mother went to DuBois and Earl followed them in his car. When she parked her car, Earl came and threw himself over the hood of it and said he wouldn't move until she told him why she wasn't dating him anymore. She resisted the temptation to tell him he was boring. In his emotional state there was no telling what he would do. However, she did make a statement that she regretted.

Earl said that he loved her and his life was dedicated to her. If she didn't start returning his affection he would kill himself. To which Agatha replied that killing himself might be the best solution to his problems. This infuriated Earl. Agatha's mother hit Earl with her purse. They were able to get back in the car and drive slowly away with Earl on the hood. Agatha said she hit the brakes and Earl went flying and she backed up and out of there. She was frightened.

Jim said that there were stalking laws in Pennsylvania and Agatha should take advantage of them. She said that she didn't want to cause trouble and that she was partly to blame for Earl's condition since she had dated him and perhaps led-him-on. Jim refuted that by saying that adults should be able to accept the conditions of mature dating. In wife-beating cases, the woman usually feels that somehow she deserved it. Since Agatha had one divorce experience she felt that perhaps her problems were part of her personality. Jim said that this was ridiculous and an unmarried man Earl's age with no dating experience has to have something wrong with him.

The situation became intense with Earl coming to Jim's office and telling Jim how he loved Agatha and has dedicated his life to her and her dating T.J. was sacrilegious as Agatha now had his soul within her and T.J. was desecrating it. He said it drove him insane to think that T.J. might be shooting sperm all over his soul.

It was too much for Jim to handle and he went to chairman Harold Gregory and unloaded the entire story. Gregory said that he was aware of the situation and arranged for an emergency medical sabbatical for Earl. The chairman had contacted Bruce Evans who was tutoring high school subjects in a remedial school near Pittsburgh. The school would release Bruce since there was no firm contract and they could hire local high school teachers. The remedial school administrator was sorry to see Bruce leave but appreciated the emergency nature of the situation.

Earl agreed to take the leave and place himself under a doctor's care. He was from Lancaster, Pennsylvania and would go back home to live with his sister for a while. He was quite cheerful about the prospect of going back home.

By now, the entire department was aware of the obsession and sympathized with Agatha. Elwood Liston had offered to "beat up" Earl if the department thought that would get him off Agatha's back. Nobody was in favor of that solution

Earl took the sabbatical but didn't go to his hometown and stay with his sister. Instead he hung around Punxie and had more free time to harass Agatha. He came into the department every day. When Chairman Gregory approached him about his sabbatical, Earl assured him that he was under a doctor's care. There was nothing in the sabbatical that said he had to go to Lancaster. Gregory asked for proof that he was under a doctor's care. Earl showed him a prescription container of pills and emphasized the date.

This was not good enough, he was still a nuisance to the entire department. On one rainy day he went to the clubhouse and spotted Jim and Clyde there. He threw his wet umbrella over their heads, cursed them and walked out. Clyde reported this to the chairman and to Agatha who said that Earl was still calling her at odd hours of the night. She obtained an unlisted number but somehow he acquired it. She took to shutting off the ring mechanism on her phone in the evening.

Agatha stopped dating T.J. since she didn't want him to get involved with Earl. She decided to file a complaint against Earl who went to court to plead his innocence. The court did not take the complaint seriously and it became more of a nightmare for Agatha and the department. The judge looked on Agatha as the perpetrator rather than Earl.

Finally, Chairman Gregory went to Dean Pratt who went to Provost Simmons who went to President Curry. Now everyone was involved. President Curry contacted the college solicitor who contacted the state solicitor who contacted Earl to tell him that he should hire a lawyer to represent him at what would be a series of meetings.

Agatha, Chairman Gregory and Elwood Liston were called in to testify against Earl whose defense was that he was led on by Agatha and with whom he was deeply in love. His demeanor suggested a very disturbed individual. After this experience Agatha would also be a very disturbed individual.

Jim thanked his stars that he was not called in to testify. He tried to be friendly with Earl when they met in the department office but Earl was in another world.

The outcome of all the proceedings was that the state would give Earl an early retirement package resembling workman's compensation. In return Earl agreed that he would not live in Punxsutawney or ever return to the college.

When Earl returned to his office to retrieve his possessions he gave Clyde a key to his apartment. He said that Clyde could have whatever was there. Jim dropped by to wish Earl luck and bid him good-bye. Earl said that he trusted Jim with the innermost secrets of his life and Jim let him down. Earl said that he would never forgive Jim for his part in the affair and that he would get square with Jim someday. It would take Jim years to try to sort out all of this but he would never be able to sort it out and make sense of the events.

Clyde asked Jim to accompany him to Earl's apartment. When they got there, they found the apartment bare except for a full length painting of a nude woman and an etching of a cowboy in black leather. Clyde said that he would try to sell the artwork and donate the money to the Social Studies Club.

18. BENJI TAKES OVER

Hellie arrived at Jim's office early in the morning full of jubilation. She went over to him and kissed him on the cheek. Even though Jim had the same office he had last year, he at least had it to himself. This prompted Hellie to take advantage of the situation and become more brazen. Jim didn't mind being kissed on the cheek. There were no witnesses. In fact, he liked it very much.

Jim felt he could let his guard down a little more around Hellie since she would be graduating at the end of the year and he had no commitment to her despite the main event of last summer.

"Guess what sweetie?"

Jim was amused. "I couldn't venture a guess. Tell me right out."

"Do you want to read the letter?"

"Nah, just tell me straight out."

"I have been accepted into the masters program at McGill University."

"That's great Hellie. I think. That's in Montreal Canada isn't it?"

"That's right. And I have a full scholarship as a teaching assistant. They're even going to pay me a thousand dollars a month, Canadian dollars."

"Wow, that really is great. Oh, how I'll miss you."

"Yeah, I'll bet."

Jim stiffened. "I do love you Hellie but I can't let my feelings for you get out of hand."

"Mr. Morality. You know I love you and would do anything for you and I'm being careful not to ruin your married life."

"What are you going to get the masters degree in? I know you're majoring in elementary education now."

"My parents insisted I get a practical degree. My first

179

love, after you of course, is music. Did you know that?"
"I could have guessed it. Funny we never discussed it."
"I'll be singing a solo in the Spring Choral Program. Why
don't you come and bring your wife?"
"I don't know Hellie."
"No really, bring her. I'm selecting a song just for you.
Of course they won't announce that I'm singing it just for you."
"I sure hope not."
"It's sort of an Easter program but we can't call it that.
We are listing it as a Spring Chorale in order not to offend a lot
of people who object to state sponsored Easter programs.
Jim laughed. "I know that, after all I taught high school
civics for six years."
"Well, I'll be leaving." She went over and kissed him
again.
"Be good Hellie."
"I'll try to remember that when I'm at the fraternity party
tonight."
"Whoa, back up. You're going to a frat party."
"Sure, do you object? This guy asked me and I thought it
might be fun. You never take me anywhere."
Jim looked upset. "I'm jealous."
"Don't worry" she laughed "I won't get into trouble. I'm
saving myself for you, at least til after graduation, then I'm up
for grabs."
She blew him a kiss and left the office. Jim sat in his chair
and put his feet on the desk. He retrieved a small book of poems
from the right side of his desk. *Where Sleeps My Love* was a
book that Hellie had given him. He read:
"The youthful blood, thinned by the southern breeze
Goes splashing over rocks to join the sea
Of life. I think about the days of ease
When that same warming wind blew over me
And I, with youthful head held high, ran on
To greet the turmoil of the sea at dawn.

180

Jim was upset. How dare Hellie go out on a date. She should be committed to him. If she really loved him she wouldn't even consider another man. Then he thought "What the hell am I thinking of? It's too much for me to decipher. Its' in my best interest for her to get involved with someone.

It was the following Monday. The weekend was over and Jim had just picked up his mail at the office. There were several notices of new books from publishers as well as the minutes of the last Dean's Council meeting. He ignored a personal message from Jerry concerning the meeting of the department sabbatical leave committee. It was being held at that moment but Jim figured there were already enough members there giving their input. Besides, sabbatical leave was a given at the department level. The department would take note of the applications, check them for errors and then send them on to the campus-wide sabbatical committee. They would be processed and sent on to the president.

Later in the day his class would be visited by Harold Gregory who would be making the chairman's evaluation for the semester. Each new faculty members had to be evaluated every semester for six years by two department members and the chairman. This was part of the contract. Unless a student was murdered in the classroom, the evaluations were generally favorable. However, Jim was aware that the person he replaced had been dismissed and it was possible to get the ax before achieving tenure. The dismissal was not related to teaching.

Brett Kelsey was the man Jim replaced. He had applied for a field study program in Costa Rica and it looked as if he wouldn't get it so he agreed to teach two sections of history in the summer. A week before the summer session was to start Kelsey received word that he had been awarded the grant and was expected to respond immediately. He assumed that this was a prestige item for the college and accepted readily. This left Chairman Gregory holding the bag. Gregory said there was no one around who could cover the classes and he didn't want to cancel the classes since the summer allotment of teaching for each department depended on the enrollment of the previous summer. He was forced to teach the two classes himself and cancel his plans to spend the summer with his daughter who lived in Oregon.

Kelsey had been a questionable personality from the beginning. He would attend frat parties with students and get roaring drunk and stories of this nature have a way of creeping into the limelight. He had also been abusive with several sexist remarks to the secretary Ms. Needs who reported them to Gregory. He made insulting remarks as a way of being friendly. For instance, he would often look at people and say "you have green teeth" or some such thing. Kelsey's teaching was acceptable but his personality left something to be desired.

So it was that Chairman Gregory seized upon this opportunity to get rid of Kelsey. He too had been the victim of the personal remarks. Others passed them off but Gregory, who was usually reticent, couldn't do that. It was no longer a seller's market in professoring, it was a buyer's market and every notice of an opening brought thirty or more applications. Gregory would look for more reserved applicants in the future.

Jim slowly made his way across campus to his office. He was really in a down mode. He realized this and tried to get at the root of the problem. He seemed well physically. Was it the discovery that Jerry couldn't be trusted with a confidence or perhaps he was down because Hellie had a date to a frat party. He accepted the fact that he didn't want intimacy with Hellie but he also didn't want anyone else to have it. Back up. He wanted intimacy with Hellie but didn't think it was in the best interests of everyone involved.

As he walked along muttering to himself he noticed Henry Broadcast of the English Department approaching. He was about to speak to Henry when Henry looked down at his watch and walked by as Jim had passed at the exact moment he had to look at his watch. This gave Jim a chuckle.

Members of the English Department were the kooks on campus. They all seemed to be certifiably crazy even though they could teach. Jim noticed that Henry looked at his watch when passing, thus avoiding having to say hello or something. Another member of the English Department who refused to speak was John Freemont who cocked his head to the right as he walked and seemed to be looking up at the clouds or the tops of trees. Sometimes Jim would startle him by walking in his lane and saying "Hi." Freemont would mumble a quick hello and step up his gait.

This avoidance of salutation didn't really bother Jim, it amused him and he understood it since he didn't like to communicate either. Jim hated it when he said his usual "Hi" and someone responded with "Hello, and how are you this morning?" This called for an answer and perhaps some dialogue. Jim would ignore the remark if he could but sometimes he responded with "Oh, I'm cold, wet and hungry." Sometimes he couldn't' t get away and had to explain that remark. He wanted to say "Look you dummy, I'm just making inane conversation, I don't want to talk to you, all I want to do is get beyond you and to where I'm going."

Benji was waiting for Jim in his office. This was an appointment concerning the dissertation research that Benji was doing and Jim's assessment on how the project was progressing. Jim felt it was a mess. The front of the material didn't match the back of it and the middle sometimes contradicted the front. His advisor Jonesey wasn't very complimentary with the rough draft and Jim confided this to Benji.

Benji thought for a moment. "Mr. Tailor, let me take the copy and look it over. I'll compare it with some of the other dissertations and see how it stacks up."

"What do you mean, other dissertations?'

Benji looked serious. "I've been down at Penn State reading history and social studies dissertations. I've read about a dozen of them, well actually fourteen. I've made a list of those

183

that are in the same area as yours in order for you to include them in your front material concerning research."

"You mean you actually went to Penn State and read dissertations."

"Yes I did. If we are going to get you through this we have to know what successful dissertations look like. I was surprised that some of them were actually accepted. I found errors in most of them, some of them jumped right out at me."

Benji used the term "we" and this upset Jim a little. Jim knew that Benji was more competent to write a dissertation than he was. Benji could organize material in logical order. His writing style was fluid. He felt bad about his dependence. Benji was a superior student and person, a true academic intellectual.

"You know Benji, you should be getting the doctorate and not me."

"No that's not true. Look at all the ground work you did, look at all the courses you took and papers you've written. You're feeling down for some reason or other but you've earned the doctorate, you paid your dues Mr. Tailor. Besides, I'll eventually get my doctorate. It's in the cards."

"Benji, we know each other well enough for you to call me Jim."

"No, you will always be Mr. Tailor to me until next summer when you become doctor Tailor. Even if I became president of the United States, you will always be doctor Tailor, my mentor, my inspiration."

Jim pushed the manuscript pages together. He placed them in a cardboard typing paper box and handed it to Benji. "Here, can you get this back to me in a week?"

Benji headed for the door. "I'll have it back to you by Thursday."

As Benji was leaving he almost ran into Hellie who was coming through the door.

"Hello, Benji" said Hellie. "It's good to see you. I want to talk to you. Can you meet me for lunch at Rudys?"

184

"Yeah, I guess so. I could make it for one o'clock. How's that with you."

"Fine, see you then. one o'clock. I got accepted at McGill University and I'll tell you all about it."

Hellie and Benji knew each other before Jim came to the campus but he was a catalyst for their new relationship. They were both into music but this was only a minor area of their discussions. Jim was their focus and the three of them were very comfortable with each other. They could count on each other in a pinch. Jim often wondered what kick he would get out of teaching once Benji and Hellie graduated at the end of the year. Will new students come to fill the void that will be left when this occurred? Certainly no one could take their places in his mind and in his heart.

Jim embraced Hellie and she kissed him on the cheek. In a whisper he said "Boy am I glad to see you."

She took a seat and put one hand to her head. "Oh, I'm still recovering from the frat party. I drank too much."

Jim was taken aback. "I didn't know you drank to excess."

"I don't but the party was really swinging and I simply overdid it. I passed out for a while and started drinking black coffee but that didn't help. I was hoping I would puke but that didn't happen."

Jim was shocked. He knew that stuff like that went on but he didn't think Hellie would be a part of it. He would have liked to have been a part of it but he didn't want Hellie to be a part of it.

Hellie went on. "Around four in the morning the police arrived and took a bunch of underage drinkers downtown. They arrested the frat president for serving booze to minors. When the smoke cleared there were only about eight of us left and we all found beds to sleep it off."

Jim tried to speak cautiously. "Did you sleep with your date?"

185

"Oh, you couldn't call it that. There were four of us piled on this one bed and believe me we were all zonked."

"Well " muttered Jim " I guess a good time was had by all. Didn't your date try to make out with you?"

"Oh Roger wanted to have sex all right but I told him I was saving myself for my favorite professor Mr. Tailor."

"You didn't really."

"No I didn't although he did run his hands over me pretty thoroughly and the massage felt good. But I am not having casual sex. I'll save that for McGill University and those French students of Quebec."

Jim was pleased that she didn't have sex with Roger, whoever that was. He didn't like the fact that she went to a frat party but that was a double-standard of his. After all , he was home having sex with Martha three nights in a row. He was still upset beyond all reason. He wished he was more like Abdul but then he thought that perhaps Abdul was not seriously involved with any of his consorts. He had convinced himself that Abdul could not possibly have an intimate relationship with anyone.

Hellie stretched her feet out on the floor. She had moved the chair to where Jim had a full view of her body. Perhaps this was intentional. As she stretched, the dress she was wearing outlined her legs. She spread her legs and moved her pelvis forward and backward.

Jim gulped. "Are you doing that on purpose?"

"Doing what?"

"You know what I mean, writhing and moving seductively."

"Oh, you recognize seductive movement, well that's a relief. I thought you were numb. Actually, I really am stretching and trying to get the kinks out of my body. Maybe I'll do some jogging before I meet Benji."

"What do you want to see Benji about anyway, not that its any of my business."

"Where Benji and I are concerned, it is your business.

The three of us are on this lifeboat in the midst of a stormy sea and you are our captain. Naw, I haven't talked to Benji for two weeks and want to catch up on what's going on. He has the inside dope on everything going on in the student body and besides he's funny. He can get me laughing for hours and God knows I could use some laughs right now."

Hellie went on "Did Benji ever tell you the story about attending his first football game at Punxie?"

"No, he didn't."

" Well it seems Benji and another student went to the football game. The other guy's name was George. Benji and George sat about five rows up from the bottom of the stands."

"About halfway through the first quarter a guy in the back hollered ' hey Billy ' and George shook and spilled a lot of the popcorn he was eating. Later on, about the end of the second quarter the same guy in the back hollered again 'hey Billy'. George spilled his soft drink in front of him."

"Everything was going well until the middle of the third quarter when the same guy in the back hollered again 'hey Billy.' George jumped to his feet and turned around and said 'listen buddy my name's not Billy."

Jim looked dismayed "I don't get it."

Hellie laughed "If you don't get it then I certainly can't explain it to you."

"Well, I could also use some laughs right now myself. I wish I could join you at Rudys but I have to do some extra preparation. The chairman is coming into my afternoon class to evaluate my teaching effectiveness."

"You don't have to worry. You're the best teacher on campus and everyone knows it. Your only weakness is that you want to lead a certain female student down the path of righteousness and she would rather take the other path with you."

"Oh boy " said Jim flinching "I can't take any more of this kind of talk."

Hellie rose, pulled her dress up above her knee and appeared to be adjusting some garment underneath. " I'll see you tomorrow. I need to cool off somewhere and get the cobwebs out of my mind. Can I have a kiss."

Jim pushed the door shut with his foot as he embraced Hellie and kissed her long and soft on the mouth. As she left he mumbled "Oh what a tangled web we weave." He mumbled that phrase a lot lately.

Even though Jim was used to evaluators in his classroom, he felt tense when Chairman Gregory came in and took a seat near the door. The student who was assigned the seat went to another which was unoccupied. Jim took out his seating chart and pretended to take attendance as several students came in late and passed in front of Jim.

One of the late arrivals started talking to his buddy in the seat across the aisle from him. Jim wasn't sure how to handle this and if he should handle it at all. Usually when he started talking the students who were inattentive would begin taking notes and everything would be normal.

Jim started talking but the student took a few more seconds to finish his comments to the friend. To Jim, the seconds seemed an eternity.

Jim felt his lecture and presentation were flat and needed some stirring. He tried to move around the room more, write on the chalk board more and change the tempo of his voice. Nothing worked for him. He was down and that was the bottom line. Some students helped out by asking questions that Jim could easily answer. Jim tried to get a discussion going but it was of no use.

Gregory left after twenty minutes. When Jim received the evaluation for his signature, he was amazed at the glowing nature of it. As Jim signed the form he uttered, "I only wish I was that good at teaching."

19. A NEW DEPARTMENT CHAIRMAN IS ELECTED

Jim finished blacking out the dots on the mid-semester grade sheets. These would be run through a scanner and students would receive a report on how they were doing after eight weeks. Each student and faculty advisor would receive a copy of the mid-term grade. What the advisor was supposed to do was never ascertained. Was it his duty to get on the backs of those students doing poorly.

Filling out the mid-semester grade sheets was done religiously. Most faculty looked on it as a meaningless chore since most students knew their approximate grade most of the time. After all, if a student flunks every exam he has the feeling he isn't doing too well in the course. It was a requirement of the teaching staff and they did it.

The grades were ready and Jim headed toward the department office to present them to Rosemary Needs who would forward them to the Office of Student Records. On his way he passed two male students. Their expressions were intense. One dressed in a trench coat was saying to one in a Punxie sweat shirt "Remember, they want it just as bad as you do." They looked like high school students to Jim. The guy in the trench coat held his next statement until Jim passed further up the walk. Then he started once again to dispense useful insights to his companion.

Jim handed the sheets to Ms. Needs who said she wished everyone was as punctual as Jim. After some prodding she confessed her disgust for Elwood Liston and his slowness to return required documents. She usually held the forms until she had them all but Elwood was always late and it made the department look bad. She pointed to Elwood's mail slot. It was so crammed with materials it would be impossible to get another slip of paper into it. The multicolored papers indicated a plethora of advertisements. Rosemary said when there was an important paper for Elwood she would sometimes throw away some of the book and magazine flyers addressed to him in order to make way for what she thought were important notices. If he didn't want his mail she would be glad to throw it away for him.

There was a copy of a peer evaluation in Jim's box. It was prepared by Agatha Aggasis, the chairman of the department evaluation committee. Like all evaluations, to be valid, the report had to be read and initialed by Jim. In so many words it stated that Jim had good rapport with students, he was efficient, easily understood, had great knowledge and conducted his class in a business-like manner. This was fine and Jim appreciated Agatha's insights.

However, under comments, it was suggested Jim use more visual aids, perhaps an overhead projector for maps and perhaps he could speak louder. This was not really critical but Jim felt it was not in his best interests to have negative comments on any of his credentials. He was not one who accepted criticism easily.

Didn't Agatha realize that these peer evaluations were just so much a formality for faculty? No one would be fired over them. They were merely documents which could be used for promotion, yearly evaluation reports and tenure. Each evaluator had an obligation to look for positive items and expand on them. How could Agatha even think of putting negative comments down on the sheet.

The negative part of the document was from the evaluation of Agusto Califfe, an immigrant from the city of Sukhumi in the country of Georgia. He had been displaced in the conflict between the minority Abkhazians and the government. The U.S. gave him refugee status. He was immediately hired by Punxie since he held a doctorate from Tbilisi University and another from Syracuse University where he had studied before returning to the country of Georgia. President Curry thought Califfe would look good in the college catalog. Neither of his degrees were in social studies but he was assigned to the department anyway. He taught the History of Europe and

History of the Former Soviet Union.

Although it was up to the departments to hire, Curry hired Califfe first as an administrator and then transferred him to the social studies department. This irritated the department since Califfe was granted tenure at the time he was hired. The social studies faculty didn't object to Califfe but resented the manner in which he was inherited.

The situation of Califfe was similar to that of other faculty who obtained teaching positions by default. Most of these occurred in the athletic program. Punxie would hire a person to coach some sport. The case of Herm Skanie is an excellent example. Skanie was hired to coach the women and men's swim team. As part of his duties he also had to teach two classes of something. His field was physical education but these jobs were taken so Skanie was assigned three two credit courses of health. He had a half-load reduction to compensate for his coaching duties.

Skanie kept his coaching position for six years at which time he obtained tenure. Then he resigned from the coaching job. Since he had tenure it posed a logistic problem for the administration. The college couldn't fire him and so he was put on the permanent staff as an assistant professor of health and phys-ed. Skanie had twelve credits above a master's degree. He wouldn't have the twelve extra credits but football coach Phillips advised him to get them in health studies before he began his teaching duties. He took twelve summer credits at Slippery Rock University, his alma mater.

The Department of Social Studies had a similar situation in Mark Waxman who was hired as an assistant football coach. He held a masters degree in education with a specialty in history. Like Skanie, once Waxman obtained tenure he resigned his coaching position and was transferred to social studies. He kept a low profile and Jim didn't realize Mark was a member of the department since he never came to meetings. When Jim read the back pages of the college catalog he noticed Mark was a member of the department. Mark received his mail at the athletic department office and didn't have a mail slot in the social studies office. When some important memo was distributed Ms. Needs sent it to Waxman by campus mail. He ignored any notices dealing with department meetings. Chairman Gregory was going to try to do something about the situation but the union advised him against it.

The union eventually addressed the topic and it was decided that extra-curricular people would not be on a tenure-track. If so written, the contracts could be terminated at any time. However, president Curry usually hand picked these people and he was loathe to admit an error in judgment. Once he hired a track coach who had a degree in biology. He gave the man administrative duties. When he tried to transfer the man to the biology department they rose up in arms. Eventually Curry backed off and promoted the man to Director of Student Affairs. His salary was several thousand dollars more than the highest paid member of the biology department.

Jim was upset about the evaluation and he went to Jerry for his opinion. Jerry said to let it pass, it had no real significance. Jim was too worried about it to do that. There had to be two peer evaluations and the one by Clyde was glowing. Jim was a good teacher and everyone knew it. Why the hell didn't Califfe play by the rules? What did it matter to him?

Jerry had another solution. He would type up an evaluation for Jim. He asked Jim about the time and day of one of his classes and a topic he might have covered. In about ten minutes Jerry had a proper evaluation ready for Jim. There was heavy emphasis on Jim's rapport with students and his warm personality.

Since a new faculty member needed two evaluations a semester and nobody kept track of them Jim could throw Califfe's evaluation away and substitute Jerry's. Califfe would never know. If he did find out, Jim could say he needed two. He had misplaced Califfe's evaluation and since he already had two

192

he didn't want to ask Califfe to give up more time and come into his classroom again.

So Jerry did Jim a favor. Perhaps this made up for the betrayal. Califfe never followed up on the evaluation. It was not really a bad evaluation. Probably, in his mind, he thought he had given Jim an excellent report and some negatives were required since there was a blank to be filled and given Califfe's foreign background maybe it was customary to fill in every blank.

There was another thing about Califfe that Jerry mentioned and which Jim already knew. Califfe sent for many many examination and complimentary copies of textbooks. Almost every day a book would arrive for him at the department. It would sit on the mail desk where everyone could see it. Jerry said Califfe's library must be bigger than Punxie's. There was no doubt it was more up-to-date than Punxie's, at least in social studies.

None of the staff were able to tell where Califfe kept the books he had acquired. He only had a small library in evidence on the shelves in his office. At the end of each semester a used textbook buyer would appear on campus to buy high demand used books. They had a list and prices they would pay. Perhaps Califfe sold books to them. Bruce Evans sold his books to them when he was out of the loop and about to be unemployed.

At the next department meeting Chairman Gregory said the department would have to elect a new chairman for the next three years. He would definitely not seek re-election. The union contract stated that there must be two candidates for the office and a secret ballot. Gregory spent much time in trying to line up candidates.

It seemed that no one wanted the job of chairman. Professors would have liked to put that on their resume but didn't want to do the mundane tasks associated with it. As Homer once remarked "one line on a resume was as good as another when you're just counting lines."

An election meeting was ordained and Jim had the floor.

He stated that they needed someone with knowledge of college administration so he was nominating Jerry. He said that Jerry had good rapport with administrators and he could bridge the gap that had recently grown between the department and the administration. Other members seemed to accept the nomination. Why not? Jerry was everyone's friend.

Jerry rose and declined the nomination for "very, very personal reasons." He then nominated Jim. Chairman Gregory laughed. "You pat my back and I'll pat yours." Jerry said that Jim was working diligently on his dissertation and he would have it finished by the beginning of the new term for chairman. He concluded with "We all know Jim would make a fine chairman."

Elwood Liston said that Jim's statement about having someone who knew the administration was correct. The department should have someone who is respected and has been here awhile and Jim has been here less than two years. He had no objection to Jim but thought it should be someone with more department experience. He nominated Henry Felderberg.

Jim thought that this was a ploy by Liston who had insulted Henry's wife at Jerry's party. Perhaps this was his way of making it up to Henry. Naw, he thought, Liston's too crude for that. However, Liston usually had some ulterior motive in mind when he made a move. What could it be?

Jerry took the floor. "I was talking to Dean Pratt yesterday about our need for a chairman when Harold resigns the post. The dean said he would like Dr. Tailor for chairman because he really could work with Jim. Dean Pratt said Jim had a lot of fresh ideas, stamina and would use his enthusiasm to the department's advantage. It was as if the dean said it would be in our best interests to have Jim as our chairman."

Clyde moved the nominations be closed and all agreed. Chairman Gregory asked Clyde and Jerry to count the ballots. A representative from the union was on hand to observe the fairness of the election. Gregory asked him to look in on the count. Ms. Needs distributed small squares of paper to the individuals. She had extra pens and pencils handy in case anyone needed one.

Gregory wrote HF and JT on the chalk board. "Vote for one, fold your paper and give it to Clyde when he comes around" Agatha said with a laugh "What if we wanted none of the above?" Gregory ignored her attempt at humor.

As Clyde gathered the papers Jerry winked at Jim. How could Jim lose to a nerd like Henry Felderberg? Jim recalled Henry's pathetic speech after the "incident." Henry wasn't a loser but he wasn't considered a winner either.

Clyde and Jerry went to a corner of the room. Clyde unfolded the squares and showed them to Jerry, one at a time. Jerry jotted down the votes. There were 14 members of the department present who could vote. Bruce Evans didn't vote because he was a temporary employee. Homer was still on sabbatical and ex-coach Waxman wasn't in attendance.

Jerry went to the chalk board where Harold had written HF and JT. Under HF he put the number eleven and under JT he put the number three. He said "We the committee to count the votes declare Henry Felderberg our next chairman."

Jim went over to Henry and shook his hand. "The best man won Henry, congratulations. You can count on me if things get tough."

Henry thanked the members for their confidence in him and said that when his term was finished perhaps Jim would have the experience and maturity to be chairman. He assumed Jim's ego was damaged and tried to soften the blow. Actually Jim breathed a sigh of relief. He wasn't ready to be chairman. He thought to himself "so much for the dean's blessing, it's a sure kiss of death."

Henry thought to himself "Wait until Edna hears about this." Every member of the department thought to him/herself "Wait until Edna hears about this."

Henry thought it was necessary to explain his qualifications to Jim. He said that he was chairman of his high

195

school social studies department and the voters probably took that into consideration. He had been a teacher at Stroudsburg after graduating from the university there. He was certain the department considered his experience at the high school when they voted. It probably never occurred to him that nobody else wanted the job.

Later in a discussion with Homer Jim remarked about the new chairman's high school experience and Homer said that it was news to him. He knew Henry was a volunteer fireman at Stroudsburg and his in-laws ran a sea food restuarant but that was the extent of his knowledge about the new chairman. It was important to Henry to think that other people were concerned about him and his welfare.

When the room cleared, Clyde approached Jim. "Don't take it too hard. We did you a favor. We all liked you too much to vote for you." He too thought Jim's ego was damaged. It was insulting to Jim to have people think his ego was so fragile. Jim figured his three votes came from himself, Gregory and Jerry.

Jim responded "Clyde, you'll never know how glad I am I wasn't elected."

Clyde smiled "Why do you think I closed the nominations. I was afraid some jerk would nominate me and with the way my luck has been running I would win and have to deal with Curry, Simmons and fuzz-nuts for the next two years. Henry is meticulous and will see that the details are fulfilled, he will cross the t's and dot the i's.

"Dealing with the administration would be hell" agreed Jim. "Henry was a good choice. He's used to being brow beaten and he will boldly go where no man has gone before in defense of the department. I don't want to be chairman. However, it bothers me to lose an election.

"I understand" laughed Clyde.

20. BENJI COMES THROUGH : HELLIE GETS A GIFT

Jim made an appointment with Benji since there was much more to do on the dissertation and Jim felt he needed Benji's input. Jim figured they needed at least two hours and this was important. Jonesey, the dissertation advisor, wanted the final draft as soon as possible.

Benji arrived in a jovial mood making small talk about the spring-like weather and what he considered a mild winter. Jim felt like he had an appointment for an appendectomy, or at least with the dentist.

"Well Benji, let's get right to it."

"Right Mr. T. There's a lot to discuss."

Jim didn't like the sound of that. "You didn't find anything needing major surgery did you?"

Benji got serious. "Remember, I'm just an undergraduate student majoring in history. I haven't been out in the real world and you have to take what I say for what it's worth. I don't pretend to be at the dissertation stage in my actions and thinking."

"Come on Benji, we both know you're an expert in history."

"Maybe so, but I'm just learning about the hoops you have to jump through in a dissertation. I hope all the aggravation is worth it to you."

Jim decided to get off that subject. "Well, what do you have for me?"

"To begin with Mr. T. You misuse the word data. You keep using it as singular when it is plural. Datum is singular."

"My advisor Jonesey didn't catch that."

"Most people don't. It's accepted practice to use data as singular but it is not correct." He repeated "Datum is singular."

"Okay, what about the text?"

Benji breathed deep. "I think you should use more historical references to back up your statements about economics. For instance, you remark that Polk raised taxes. Hell, every president raises taxes, it goes with the job. Remember he had to raise and supply a large army. You have to give some reasons for his raising taxes, what did he spend the money on? I made some notes on that."

"Sounds good to me. What are some of the historical references I should have used? I assume you wrote them down."

"Yes I did. The fact that Polk almost doubled the land area of the United States is significant. This increased his tax base as well as his spending. Remember he shifted government policy from a treasury department under the direct supervision of congress to an independent treasury department. You should mention that the independent treasury originated with Van Buren. When Polk had congress declare war against Mexico he had to come up with a lot of money and his independent treasury paid off. He could get around congress for most of his emergency spending. His circumventing the congress is still practiced today."

" I forgot about Van Buren. I was concentrating on the presidents that came after Polk because those were the presidents Jonesey was interested in. If I go back to the earlier presidents it would be like starting all over again."

"Well you have to go to the earlier presidents in order to explain Polk's economic evolution. After the Mexican War the United States took over Texas, the rest of the Southwest and annexed California. Not bad for an obscure president."

"He came up with the idea of manifest destiny, that the U.S. should expand from sea to shining sea. I did mention that he gave Vancouver Island to Canada and caved-in on the boundary of 54-40 or fight. By accepting the 49th parallel with Canada he avoided conflict with the British. After all, he didn't want the Brits to come back and burn D.C. again."

Benji went on "I think you should mention that Polk rejected the spoils system of giving political cronies good jobs and this was picked up by Zachary Taylor who followed him. You're not related to Zachary Taylor are you?" Jim started to think about the possibility. Anything would distract him in his present state of mind. "No, I'm joking. He spelled his name different than yours."

The discussion continued in this manner for a good hour and a half. Jim was trying to soak it all up. He made copius notes while Benji rattled on. Jim was getting depressed. Finally, the discussion came to a natural conclusion. Benji rose to leave.

"Benji" said Jim "When this is over I'm going to give you a thousand dollars."

"No don't do that Mr. T. I won't accept it. You gave me a job and I'm doing it. Seven dollars an hour is our agreement. When it's all over it will come out close to a thousand dollars anyway. You've already given me over four hundred dollars and I appreciate that. So fourteen hundred dollars will be my scholarship at Punxie. You know, it's like free money I just use my brains and get paid for it. Sort of like you, a college professor, you really don't do any obvious work. You use your brains, stand in front of a class, yak for a while and get a good salary for it."

"Yeah, I guess you're right. Sometimes I feel like a leech on society. When I see students go out of here with little prospects of employment and dubious knowledge I wonder what it is I'm doing or what it is I should be doing. Are we deceiving the public, letting them think we're preparing their children for some questionable future."

Benji laughed " Let's don't tell the public about it. I want to do it someday and maybe I can make a living at it before the public wises up. There is no doubt that I benefited from coming to college. I could have picked up most of my history information by myself but I would have ignored subjects like geology, mathematics, art and philosophy. I think a liberal education is much more beneficial to a person than one geared to employment. It's good to know that somewhere out there, our scientists are advancing technology, even if I'm not involved in it."

Jim spent the weekend getting the final draft of the dissertation ready for the final approval of Jonesey. The step after that would be the dissertation committee. This would occur sometime in April or May.

There was a wet snow on the first day of April . The ground was covered and it looked like the snow would last until the promised warming days melted it. John Freemont was the English Department representative for Groundhog Day. He had come to Jerry for information and was surprised when Jerry informed him that Groundhog Day was long gone. Freemont simply shrugged his shoulders and said he must have been hibernating. He didn't follow those things and he had just found the memo appointing him as the college representative.

Jim was busy correcting tests in his office when student Phil Brickard gave a few raps on his office door and walked in and stood before Jim.

"Could I talk to you for a few minutes doctor Tailor?"

Jim's first instinct was to tell the guy it was mister Tailor and not doctor Tailor but it was a trivial matter. Students simply called every instructor doctor and didn't take the time to differentiate. The only people who worried about the title were those that had it. Usually those who didn't hold the doctorate wanted to be called "professor." They too needed some sort of status.

Jim put aside his papers and looked at Phil. He wasn't sure who the student was. Was he in his class or just someone wandering in. "What can I do for you?"

"I'm Phil Brickard, I'm in your economics class."

"Yes, I know who you are. I just corrected your test. You didn't do very well as I recall."

Jim was able to remember names when he saw them on tests and in the college newspaper. He could discuss his tests accurately but he had a hard time when the actual person was in front of him. Unless the student did something to stand out from the crowd he just melted into obscurity in Jim's mind. He knew

200

that was happening to him and he hated himself for it.

Phil looked sullen. "Since I'm not doing too well in economics I was wondering if I could do some sort of extra credit project and bring up my grade."

Jim took out his grade book and ran his finger down to Brickard, Phillip. "You're not doing that bad Phil, you have a low C right now with this test but you still have a quiz and final test to go. You should be able to get good grades on those with a little extra effort. Instead of doing extra credit work, just put that time into studying."

"I do study, I study long hours but I just can't grasp things like supply side economy and stock and bond manipulations. It's the mathematics that gets me."

"There's very little math involved here."

"Maybe to you there's little math but to me its a mountain of math."

Jim shrugged and wondered how he could get rid of Phil and get back to his test papers. "Phil just concentrate on the next quiz and final test. Follow the study guide I passed out to the class."

Phil wasn't going down so easily. He settled in the chair in front of Jim's desk and opened his jacket. Jim breathed a sign of acceptance.

Phil opined "You know I play basketball and the season just ended and that was probably why I did so poorly." Many profs would cut jocks a break and Phil knew this.

"Well, Phil, I can't give you extra credit for basketball and I don't expect the coach to play some player just because he's a social studies major. Now that the season is over you will have more time for academics."

"I do pretty good usually. My Q-P-A is about three point two so naturally I'm concerned that I might sink to a D in this course. I'm doing okay in your U.S. History course."

Jim was taken back. He had this guy in two courses this term and barely recognized him. Wow, what did it mean? Was he really unconcerned about students? He didn't think so but having a student in two classes and not remembering him must be significant.

Phil became an advisor. "Doctor Tailor, you should give some sort of work sheets as assignments. That way students who flunk your hard tests can still get a passing grade."

This was a discussion Jim had with Homer and Mark on several occasions. Both of these men had work sheets and what Mark called "busy work." Mark said that today's students were poor compared to those of just five years ago. He had to come up with some system of outside work in order to give most students a passing grade. Mark readily admitted he gave the same tests or slight variations of them ever since he started teaching. He had the statistics and could show a dramatic decline in his test scores over the last several years. He sometimes blamed himself and said that maybe he wasn't as effective a teacher as he once was..

Mark once said to Jim "After all, history hasn't changed, except maybe our shift in certain aspects of it has. Like now, I bring in the contributions of black Americans and women more than I used to."

Jim did assign term papers but this wasn't what Phil had in mind. He wanted some sort of weekly sheets to hand in. Homer created ten work sheets for most of his classes. On some of them he would list people and have the students write an identifying paragraph about them.

Homer would also have questions pertaining to geography. as he put it "Geography is the stage and history is the performance." Jim had considered doing something like that but at this stage of the game he didn't have time. His mind was on the dissertation. He regretted assigning term papers since this would take valuable time away from his pursuit of the doctorate.

Jim looked at Phil and smiled. "Well Phil I'm glad you came in and talked to me. It's good to see a conscientious student once in a while. I'll tell you what. If you don't do well on the quiz, come in and see me before the final test and I'll go over some aspects of what and how to study for it with you."

Phil rose. "Thanks for your time doctor Tailor. I appreciate it."

As he left Jim wondered that perhaps this was Phil's way of letting Jim know who he was. Jim reached for his stack of cards he had the students fill out at the beginning of the term. He found Phillip Brickard's. Sure enough at the bottom of the card it had "varsity basketball." It also indicated that Phil was from Smethport and was majoring in graphic design. He was taking two courses in social studies to meet requirements in general education.

Jim gave his grade book one more check. This would cement Phil Brickard in his mind.

Many profs kept student records on their home or office computers. Since Jim didn't have a computer in his office he couldn't dabble in this. It was too much of a burden to put his records on a disk in the department office.

On one occasion when Jim was in Clyde's office he and Jim were discussing a student and her progress. Jim flipped open his grade book and said she was doing B work in his class. Clyde punched a few buttons on his computer and the menu appeared and Clyde pressed a few more keys and the desired class appeared. Clyde announced the female in question also had a B in his course. It took Clyde about two minutes to get the same information that Jim had retrieved in a matter of seconds.

Term papers were also due about this time and Jim had collected them in class. He was still in the office and about to wade into them when student Vincent Mackay walked in.

"Mister Tailor, I didn't turn in my paper to you in class because I wanted to put a cover on it and add a couple of things. I have it here."

"That's fine Vince, I'll take it, just put it on the desk."

Vince moved the chair in front of Jim's desk to the side of the desk where he would have closer contact with his professor. He held the term paper in his right hand and rested it on his knee.

Vince muttered "I put a lot of time into this. I must have read thirty two journal articles."

"I guess you have them in the bibliography Vince. That's a lot of reading. The paper was not to be that elaborate."

"It came out to sixty four pages, double spaced."

Vince edged the term paper toward Jim. When Jim reached for the paper Vince leaned back in his chair which withdrew the paper from Jim's reach.

Vince continued "I have excerpts from a couple of the books you have on reserve in the library. The one on Adam Smith was really interesting."

"Yes I reread that one myself every couple of years, just so I won't forget it." Jim figured that Vince was polishing the old apple but he wasn't sure. He held out his hand for the paper.

Again Vince looked like he hated to part with this valuable object. He leaned toward Jim with the term paper but withdrew it as he went into another aspect of the paper.

"Are we going to get these back. I put a lot of work into it."

"Yes, as I explained in class you can pick up the paper after you complete the final test on the last day of class. If I don't get to checking these pretty soon I won't have them ready for the last day of class."

It occurred to Jim that Vince was playing some sort of nutty cat-and-mouse game with the term paper. What Vince was saying was trivial. He was putting Jim on.

Jim looked at Vince. "I have to start checking these papers. Just put yours on the desk. If you don't mind."

Vince made one last stab at handing the paper but Jim had taken one of the term papers from the pile and stated reading it with his red ink pen poised as if to start grading and marking.

Vince stood up, put the paper on the desk and headed

for the door. He turned as he reached the door. "See you in class mister Tailor."

Jim mumbled "Sure Vince, have a nice day." Jim hated the phrase "have a nice day" so much he only used it for people he held in mild contempt. He bristled when people used it on him so he assumed other people didn't like it either.

After Vince departed Jim picked up the sixty four page prize term paper. As Jim suspected, most of it was copied directly out of the books Jim had put on reserve at the library.

*

Hellie came in to Jim's office during his usual Monday office hour. There were two full weeks of classes before spring break. The College Chorale Program was this Saturday. She wanted to know if Jim was coming for sure. Jim said he was and wouldn't miss it for the world. He also said he was bringing Martha.

Before they parted Jim said he had a present for Hellie. She glowed, it was as if light actually emanated from her face. Jim reached in his desk. He presented Hellie with a small gift wrapped box.

Hellie took the paper off slowly and folded it neatly before her. It was a small box and as the paper came off it was obviously a ring box. Inside was a gold ring with a jade band. She was choked with emotion.

Jim beamed. "The Chinese say if you give someone a piece of jade, you give them a piece of your soul."

Tears formed in Hellie's eyes. "Don't worry my love, I'll treasure this piece of your soul forever." With that she held him close and kissed him. She trembled and sat down.

The conversation after the ring presentation was inane. They both babbled on with nothing making sense although what they said sounded profound at the time.

Saturday was the day of the chorale offering and the Tailor's had Martha's mother over for baby sitting. Jim wished he could include Martha in more of the campus activities but they

205

lived so far away. They both vowed to look for a dwelling closer to Punxie. Their house in Clearfield consisted of a living room, kitchen, two baths and three bedrooms. Each child had a bedroom. They purchased the house when Jim got the teaching job at the local high school. Martha's mother loaned them ten thousand dollars for a down payment and the local bank added another thirty thousand on a twenty year mortgage. They made six years of payments so far and were slowly seeing a steady decrease in the total mortgage.

Martha and Jim liked Clearfield. It was an ideal place, a nice clean town with a good local government. They had many friends there since Jim started teaching at the high school. It would be tough to leave.

Jim had made the trip to Punxutawney so often he figured if he took his hands off the wheel the car would make the trip by itself. He was tired of that daily fifty mile drive.

Martha wore her finery to the chorale and Jim wore one of his teaching outfits. The auditorium was filling fast and the college string orchestra was warming up as they entered. They chose seats in the middle of the auditorium. By the time they sat down the auditorium appeared packed. Most of the audience seemed to be older than college-age. Perhaps these were parents of students. Maybe Hellie's parents were there and she would bring them around to meet Jim. He hoped this would not happen.

The concert was beautiful. The singers shone like fireflies on a summer night. The operator of the spotlights had a special knack for his occupation. The lights seemed to blend in with the figures on stage. Lights, music and slight body movements of the singers joined in a poetic harmony.

The choir had finished singing "You'll Never Walk Alone" and the conductor turned to the audience. " Our next selection features soloist Helga Anderson singing John Jacob Niles hymn "Go Way From My Window."

Hellie stepped from her place in the choir and approached a center stage microphone. A cello hummed mournfully and the chorus hummed along. Then Hellie's sharp clear voice rang out.

"Go way from my window - go way from my door - go way, way, way from my bedside- and bother me no more, and bother me no more."

Jim wondered, to himself of course. "Was this the song Hellie was going to sing just for me?"

The song continued "Go tell all your brothers - tell all your sisters too - that the reason why my heart is broke - is all because of you- is all because of you."

Jim's ears seem to close to the rest of it and the deafening applause which accompanied the conclusion of Hellie's number. Martha leaned over to him "That was great she whispered."

Jim had a lump in his throat and just nodded. He was sure if he tried to talk his voice would crack. He applauded slowly.

There were more sentimental songs and a few hymns with religious overtones. Their renditions of "Greensleeves" and "The Sweetheart of Sigma Chi" were outstanding. Martha noticed tears rolling down Jim's cheeks.

She nudged him "I didn't think you were so sentimental."

Jim could barely speak. "I guess this is what college teaching is all about. People in tune with each other's souls. It doesn't get any better than this."

The music director and producer of the chorale was presented a dozen red roses. Each member of the group received a white rose. There were several encores and finally the curtain fell and closed the program.

On the way back to Clearfield they barely spoke to each other. They were still experiencing a religious bonding. It was a beautiful evening and having shared it, they were traveling as one spiritual entity through space and time.

21. IN THE FELL CLUTCH OF CIRCUMSTANCE

The big day, May 2nd, had arrived, the day of the dissertation defense. The main event was to take place at Beaver Hall in the annex to the office of the Department of Economics. The designated hour was 4 p.m.

Jim started the day by sleeping to 9 a.m. The children were already in their respective schools and Martha had pancake batter waiting for him when he was up and about. It was a Wednesday and Jim had requested a personal day for the event. The Provost of Punxie, as usual, gave approval if the classes could be covered. Clyde and Bruce agreed to take the classes. Jim left video tapes for Bruce and a test for Clyde to administer.

Clyde tried to set Jim's mind at ease by going through some of the events of his dissertation defense. He said that a preliminary defense was given before all doctoral candidates in a seminar designed for that purpose. He was working as a graduate assistant, teaching three classes at the time. His dissertation was on the History of the Seminoles. This was over twenty years ago. Clyde shared an office with a man he referred to as Springer.

On the day of his presentation Clyde said he went over some of his salient points with his office mate Springer. He and Springer had developed a warm and friendly relationship in the two years they were office mates.

In closing the topic Clyde remarked to Springer that the only question someone might get him on was that Clyde's work never mentioned why the main population of Seminoles were never transferred west with the Cherokees on the "Trail of Tears." Why did the Cherokees give up their homeland and not the Seminoles?

When the presentation occurred, all went well. Everyone was pleased with the presentation. Clyde's advisor and chairman of the seminar asked if there were any final questions.

You guessed it. Springer asked about the Trail of Tears.

Clyde's advisor said "Yeah Clyde, maybe you better look into that."

Clyde said he was livid with rage. When he got back to the office he told Springer that they will make out a new office schedule and Springer better stick to it. If he, Clyde, ever came into the office and Springer was there he will start punching him.

Clyde said he never saw Springer again except in the seminar class. The new topic added about thirty pages and many hours of research to the dissertation.

It was a long time until four o' clock and Jim figured he would go over his notes in anticipation of the questions he would be asked. It was only an hours drive to Penn State but he would allow three hours for the trip in case something went wrong. There was snow on the highways from a storm two days previously. It can snow in central Pennsylvania into June. Jim figured the highway department would have the snow removed and the roads salted and cindered but he was going to allow two hours extra just in case. These late spring snowstorms usually melted around noon.

Jim spent a lot of time urinating. He realized it was a sign of nervousness. What did he have to be nervous about? Jonesey told him his dissertation was excellent and there should be no problem with the five man committee. Jonesey especially liked the tie-in of historic events and the economic moves generated by them. Then he thought "What if the rest of the committee had it in for Jonesey? He had heard war stories to that effect. Then he was sure he was becoming paranoid and it was not the right day for this.

A preliminary paper condensed from the dissertation was published in *American Economic History*. It listed Faubus H. Jones first and James Tailor as co-author. Later, the paper would be expanded and appear as a chapter in Jonesey's book on *Pre-Civil War Economics in the United States*. Jim's name would appear as a footnote in the chapter and in the bibliography at the end of the work. Faubus H. Jones would add another title to his illustrious list.

The day inched along. Jim settled for a salad at lunch. As the kitchen clock edged toward one he began packing his materials. Martha could feel the tenseness but there was nothing she could do about it. Jim would simply have to work it out somehow. She had confidence in Jim. After all, lesser men had gone through this same ordeal and survived. If that goof-ball Liston could get a doctorate surely so could Jim.

Jim arrived at the Penn State campus shortly after two and headed for a coffee shop. He began pouring over his notes and the copy of the dissertation. He made frequent trips to the rest room and worried about it. If he didn't stop drinking coffee he might be embarrassed. Besides the caffeine was already having an effect on his nervous system. He decided to quit drinking coffee and participated in some relaxation exercises. The main exercise was putting his head down on his folded arms which were on the table before him. He would have liked to doze off to sleep for about a half hour. He couldn't risk falling asleep.

He appeared at Beaver Hall fifteen minutes early and checked the situation with Mrs. Cameras the department secretary and receptionist. She was a fixture in the office and Jim had many dealings with her.They liked each other. She informed him that they would be a little late since Dr. Simms couldn't get there until four thirty.

Dr. Simms was the representative from the administrative staff. He was the finance officer in charge of student loans for the School of Humanities. He had a doctorate in history and Jonesey recommended him to Jim. Penn State policy stated that the candidate for a doctorate could choose the members of his committee but one of them had to be from a different department of the university.

The committee consisted of the advisor Jones, three members of the department and Simms. Originally Jim had chosen Dr. Prestly, also in administration, instead of Simms.

However, interviews with Prestly upset Jim. Prestly stated that he ate, slept and drank history. He wanted Jim to spend a year at the library in Princeton which had an outstanding history collection. He said that if Jim would spend a year of research at Princeton he would be more than ready to begin writing his dissertation. Jim didn't want academic greatness, he just wanted the degree. Academic greatness could be put on hold. He had a wife and two children to support.

Jim checked around and found that Prestly was unmarried and had a string of history publications that covered seven pages. This made Jim nervous. He would like someone on his committee who had a nagging spouse and who carried out the garbage every night, someone who didn't have idle time on his hands, someone who would consider Jim's dissertation as a minor duty, perhaps a nuisance, and definitely not as the heavyweight event of the year.

Mrs. Cameras told Jim that the last dissertation defense took a half hour and it was more of a formality than actual combat. She said that Jim's dissertation was approved by Jones and he would see that it went through without much difficulty. Jones had at least three dissertation students a year and none of them had failed yet.

For some unknown reason, Jim assumed she was just trying to set him at ease and the war stories he heard about dissertation defenses were more accurate. He wasn't going to take any chances by relaxing, he was going to keep alert and fight to the finish.

A red light appeared on the desk of Mrs. Cameras. She punched a button and the voice of Jones, the voice of doom, said "We're ready for Mr. Tailor." She turned to Jim and waved her hand toward the door.

There was a large table in the room with chairs around it. The committee members were seated at the sides of one end and the end chair was empty. Jones indicated that Jim was to sit in the chair at the head of the table.

Once introductions and salutations were out of the way Jim was asked to give a synopsis of his writings and findings. This went well, at least Jim thought so. After all, he had been preparing this presentation for the last six hours. Surely he could give a fifteen minute presentation without any hitches.

Dr. Simms got right to his point. "I liked what you wrote but I have some questions about it. If the rest of the committee agrees, you would only have to rewrite about a dozen pages."

Jim cringed. He could fill his stomach lurching. What the hell could Simms possibly say. Didn't Simms discuss the dissertation with Jonesey? He fought an urge to get up and leave the room.

Simms went on. " You have a lot of pages on the economic decisions of President Polk during and after the Mexican War. Did you consult any sources in Mexico to see what they thought of Polk and how his decisions affected them and their economy?"

Jim didn't know what to say to that. Of course he hadn't consulted any library in Mexico. Jim paused a while before answering. This was a technique he learned when he had to appear as a witness in a lawsuit.

"Well Dr. Simms. No I didn't consult Mexican documents except those listed in the bibliography." He assumed that the bibliography was territory that nobody bothered to read since he himself never consulted bibliographic references.

Jim went on. "I considered the Mexican reaction, especially since Polk took so much territory away from them, but then I thought that this was a treatise on American economics and the cause-and-effect of the Mexican War on the economic policies of the president. Besides, I can't read Spanish."

Once the words were out of his mouth, Jim regretted them. Why the hell did he have to say that he didn't read Spanish. One of the main rules of interrogation is to keep your answers brief and never bring up another topic. A new topic always opens up new avenues of questioning.

Simms looked askance. "You don't read Spanish. I don't see how you could do this dissertation without consulting sources in Spanish."

Jonesey sprang to Jim's defense. "Mr. Tailor satisfied the dissertation requirements by successfully passing the language requirements in statistics and computer science. If a candidate does that then we wave the foreign language requirement. What languages do you read Dr. Simms?"

Simms answered "I'm not defending a dissertation. It was just a point that I thought should have been covered. I still do. I don't see how you could dwell on the Mexican War without consulting original Mexican sources."

Jones knew that only three votes were needed and he had these in-the-bag since the other members of the committee owed him favors and they often exchanged these on dissertation committees. What Mrs. Cameras said about the completion of the dissertation was mostly true. But there could be some hitches.

Jones confronted Simms. "There are plenty of Mexican sources listed here, it's just that they have been translated into English. Jones thumbed through to the bibliography. Here is Gonzolus' work on the value of the peso and the economic depression of Mexico in 1850. It was originally published in Spanish. We can assume that the translator knew what he was doing and it was an accurate translation."

Simms tightened his mouth. "It's just a point that I thought should be discussed. We have discussed it and we may as well move on . My intent is to improve what appears to be an acceptable dissertation."

Each of the other committee members had some question about the dissertation. Professor Handratty discovered a few spelling errors as well as a few grammatical goofs. These could be repaired in the final form. Jim thanked him for pointing them out. Professor Henreaux complimented Jim's correct use of datum and data. Jim sent a mental thank-you note to Benji.

It was almost six o'clock when Jonesey looked at his watch. He rubbed his eyes and looked at the group. "I think we have discussed this enough. I'll ask Mr. Tailor to go back to the office and wait for me. We can discuss this further in his absence."

Jim thanked them all for their efforts and taking the time to help him in this important event in his life. He retreated to the office. Mrs. Cameras wanted to know what happened since these defenses usually took a half hour and this one had taken three times that amount.

Jim was too wiped out to speak. He sat in the chair by the desk, sank forward and closed his eyes. He mumbled "I think it's going to be okay but I won't get the degree until next year."

It wasn't over yet. Six o'clock passed. Mrs. Cameras put on her coat and headed for home. "Don't worry Mr. Tailor, Dr. Jones will take care of you."

Jim was alone in the office while the discussion continued in the annex. The clock on the wall reached six thirty. Jim felt hopeless. All was lost and he would have to go through it all again. He really felt down when the big hand hit twelve and the little hand was on seven.

Shortly after seven Jones emerged from the office. "Sorry it took so long Jim, we had a little problem that had to be ironed out."

Jim could barely squeak. "I figured as much."

Jonesey sat down beside him and opened the dissertation. " We will make those changes suggested by Henreaux and a few minor other changes but it was accepted and you'll be awarded the doctorate at the convocation at the end of May, one other thing."

Jim was too tired to get excited. "What's that?"

"This was the big discussion. Dr. Simms didn't want his name associated with the dissertation."

Jim looked puzzled. "Does this mean that we have to go
214

through this again?"

"No" said Jonesey " It's just he's a fussy person he's okay."

"I still don't know what you mean."

"Well, if you ever publish any of this, you're not to mention the members of the dissertation committee by name. Dr. Simms was offended by my shooting him down and he developed some distaste for the entire dissertation. However, he did agree to vote yes on it and so your work was accepted unanimously."

Jim thought to himself. I won't mention Simms and I won't even think about Penn State ever again. "That seems fair to me. If Simms doesn't want his name mentioned in connection with my dissertation I certainly won't do it." Jim was sure Jonesey wouldn't mention it when the dissertation appeared as a chapter in his book.

Jonesey led Jim to the door. He extended his hand. "Congratulations Dr. Tailor. I'll be in touch with you about commencement. Go to the bookstore and get yourself fitted for a cap and gown as soon as possible."

Jim wanted to embrace Jonesey but thought the better of it. He shook has hand vigorously. "I'm indebted to you forever. Thanks ever so much."

When Jim reached a telephone in the downstairs hall he called Martha and tried to relate some of the events to her. She was delighted. Jim said he hadn't had any supper and would get something to eat before coming home. Martha said according to the evening news the roads were bad and Jim should be extra careful driving home.

Jim went to Bracken's Steak House on the edge of town. He still couldn't believe he had the degree. He treated himself to a glass of champagne and ordered the finest cut of New York steak and a baked potato. He ate slowly and savored every minute and every bite of it.

22. THESE ARE GREAT TIMES

The semester was winding down. The second week of May arrived with a burst of flowers and a flood of migrating birds. The bluebirds were early this year. Bluebirds were contesting tree swallows for Jim's bird house. It was a promise of Nature's future bounty.

Jim was designated as one of two Punxie representatives for "college day" which was being held at the high school in St. Marys. This would involve colleges and universities throughout the state and give high school seniors a chance to talk to college personnel about their respective institutions. The other representative would be George Grecco best known for his oratory in the faculty senate.

There were too many things going on for Jim considering the dissertation and all so he tried to get out of the assignment. Chairman Gregory said that Jim was hand-picked by Dean Pratt because he was young, good looking and a smooth talker. Gregory said those were Pratt's exact words and he felt this is what was needed to impress high school students. Pratt said they always sent old fuddy-duddy faculty members and pedantic types to these affairs and it was a turn-off for high school students.

Gregory thought George Grecco was selected since he knew most everything about curriculum, graduation requirements, expenses, lodging arrangements et cetera about the college.

There was no getting out of it. There were "college nights" like this all over the state and Punxie covered most of them. President Curry thought the local meetings were more important than those in someone else's bailiwick so he asked his committee of deans to come up with the best possible representatives. Jim should have been flattered. Curry would at least see his name in a position of importance.

Jim had only seen George Grecco a couple of times and asked Clyde what he thought of Grecco. After all, they would ride together and be in each other's company for about six hours and it is possible they might have to stay overnight together at some future conference or meeting.

Clyde said that George was an agitator and he went off on tangents from time to time but he was pleasant company. "Let me tell you a story about Grecco."

"George and I were at a conference in Shippensburg about four years ago. It was one of those conferences on excellence in teaching kind of nonsense, you know, things that administrators take seriously. Anyway, the conference is over at noon and we were heading out to get on a four lane highway and get home as soon as possible."

"George says to me 'I really would like to get some Amish food while we're down this way. Let's take the blue highway to Lancaster. There's a lot of Amish restaurants around there."

"I wanted to get back but I went along with his request and we should eat since we had about a five hour drive ahead of us. We drove all over the place and finally found something called Reubens. It had a big Amish farmer statue outside. So in we go."

"I look over the menu and order sauerbraten. George puts his menu aside and says 'I'll have the hamburger platter.' That tells you all you need to know about George Grecco."

Jim wasn't sure about the gist of the story but it was funny, not a knee slapper, but intellectually funny. Must be a moral in there somewhere.

While Jim had Clyde's attention he asked him about Thomas Lindsey. "According to the list of graduating seniors he is graduating. I have been his advisor for more than a year and I don't know what he looks like. I have never seen him. Shouldn't he have been coming to me for scheduling and don't I have to check his record to see if he qualifies for graduation? How could he do that without me?"

Clyde chuckled. "He probably filled out his own schedules and signed your name or anybody's name for that matter. The registrar and people who work scheduling can't take time to match students and advisors so some students just sign their own forms. The chairman and dean go over the records to certify graduating seniors. Consider yourself lucky, you didn't have to put in the work on it."

"That's running a pretty loose ship isn't it?"

"Only if someone catches up with Tom. He probably has all bases covered. He's an interesting student. Funny you never met him. I can just see him sitting in a bar twenty years from now telling his buddies how he outwitted his advisor by signing all his own permission forms."

"That is pretty good" admitted Jim "however, just wait until I have to write a recommendation for him."

Clyde laughed "He'll probably write his own excellent recommendations and sign your name to them, or make up a name for some imaginary professor. Does anyone check up on the recommendations."

Jim thought then submitted "Well when we hire someone we call those people designated as referees. Doesn't the recommendations have to be on letterheads and in department envelopes?"

"If I know Tom he probably has a stack of letterheads and envelopes from about a dozen Punxie departments and he has the guts to use them."

Jim didn't know what to say and so he said "I don't know what to say."

*

Benji had applied for an assistantship at several large universities. He had been accepted with tuition waivers at the University of Pennsylvania. He had his hopes up for Ohio State and called the History Department there to see if there was any action on his application. He was put on hold by the secretary while the chairman finished whatever it was he was doing. After about ten minutes the chairman was on the line asking Benji what it was he wanted.

Benji explained his reason for calling. The chairman sniffed and said he didn't think Benji's application was very strong. Benji said he couldn't think of how it could be any stronger. He had a

218

three point eight average, had attended and presented papers at conventions and worked for the Social Studies Department at Punxie. Two of his papers were printed in *The Journal of American History.* These were the kinds of things of which academics was made. He had fulfilled the written and unwritten obligations.

The chairman made some remark about Punxie's reputation in the world of academia. They never had an application from a Punxie graduate. Benji said that the printing of his two papers was validation of his abilities. The chairman said that the committee for student aid and assistantships would finish its work in a day and they would get back to Benji next week.

In the meantime, Benji had been accepted at Clemson, Penn and finally Princeton. The deal at Princeton was the most attractive. Benji would work in the Humanities library the first year and receive all fee waivers. He would have his own office and be paid a stipend of five thousand dollars a semester. Ohio State wouldn't be considered. So it was Princeton for Benji and McGill for Hellie. Other graduating students were accepted into masters programs with and without assistantships. Some were not so fortunate and many were not accepted into any programs.

When Benji informed Jim of his choice, Jim suggested they celebrate over dinner with Hellie. It was a pleasant dinner in a sea food house north of Indiana. Each had reason to celebrate. On the way back to Punxie Hellie put her head on Jim's shoulder.

Jim said to his two friends "These are great times, aren't they? You guys have a great future ahead of you."

Hellie kissed Jim on the cheek. "So do you Jim, so do you." Then she turned to Benji and kissed him on the cheek. "We must all keep in touch."

About a week later Benji received a message to call the chairman of the history department at Ohio State. He was informed that a full tuition scholarship awaited him if he wanted to accept it. Benji told the chairman that he, the chairman, said that Benji's application was not very strong. The chairman said apparently the committee saw something in the application since they had Benji listed as number one on the list of applicants.

Benji told the chairman that he should be more human and less condescending to lowly undergraduates and he Benji would not consider going to Ohio State under any circumstances, it was not student friendly. The chairman appeared unfazed and said he would pass Benji's statement of refusal on to the committee. Benji thought an apology should have been offered.

When Benji told Jim and Hellie abut the Ohio State acceptance they were both amazed that mild mannered good natured Benji would speak up, especially to someone as important as the chairman of a department at Ohio State. Benji assured them that he was capable of forceful action when it was needed. He was considering writing a letter to the Dean of Graduate Studies at Ohio State.

When the two friends questioned that action he said that if no such action was taken then the abusive chairman would be home free. At least this way the dean would know a little more about the miserable guy.

Jim pointed out that the chairman did call Benji and offered him a full tuition scholarship plus expenses. Benji said "Can you imagine me working in that department considering the way I feel?'

"Sometimes we have to swallow our pride" said Jim with a chuckle.

"That's a lesson I learned a long time ago" said Benji "But this is one time when I don't have to swallow pride."

Jim was astonished that Benji had the nerve to engage the chairman in such a manner. Benji said he was insulted and a man of that position should have some humility. Jim told Benji he was proud of him and shook his hand vigorously.

Jim, Benji and Hellie had dinner together two more times before the end of the semester and there was a melancholy air about it the last time which was a week before finals and graduation.

Even though Jim was not assigned commencement duties he volunteered to be one of the department representatives. He wante to see his friends receive their degrees. The college field house where the commencements were held was small and could not hold the graduates, faculty and visiting guests. To compensate for the lack of space each department assigned two of its members to graduation. This was not an eagerly sought assignment.

The commencement included 520 baccalaureate and 24 masters recipients. Speaker for the event was a man from the National Gas Company who spoke about accepting responsibility and designating praise and blame. Jim wondered why this guy was invited and not the governor, a senator or some other Pennsylvania dignitary. Who in the world would invite a man from the local gas company to be the featured speaker at a college graduation.

The speaker said that during World War II you could blame Hitler, during the Cold War you could blame Stalin but who do you blame today? Everything is done by committee, in committee and no individual was responsible. It was like an executive in a corporation who has little legal responsibility for the corporation's deficits. He challenged the audience to identify the person responsible for defeating universal health care for all American citizens. They might say Democrats or Republicans but who were the individuals?

Jim was taken with the speech. He had to admit it was the best commencement speech he had every heard and he had heard speeches by famous people including George Bush and Bob Dole. Other commencement addresses would soon be forgotten but this one would live on in his memory and he would think about it from time to time.

Since there were three schools at Punxie, each of the deans performed at the ceremony. When Dean Pratt was announced, he tipped his mortar board toward President Curry who was there to hand out degrees. The degrees were not actually there but each graduate received a roll of paper with a ribbon which gave the audience the assumption of a degree.

After the ceremony Jim went to the reception center for cookies and conversation. The first person he met was John Freemont of the English Department. The ubiquitous Bill Barr soon appeared. Dean Pratt joined them.

John congratulated Jim on his successful doctoral defense and asked Jim if he wanted to sell his master's cap and gown. John had borrowed the one he was wearing. Dean Pratt said that John had his masters from Pitt and Jim's was from Penn State. John's degree was in English and Jim's was in economics. The colors would be wrong. John couldn't wear Penn State and history colors when it wasn't his degree.

John and Jim looked at each other with eyes of disbelief. They ignored the dean's comments, made some small talk, then split for the punch bowls. Bill Barr was left to engage the dean. Jim told John he would get back to him at the beginning of the next semester and he would definitely sell his masters gown. With a laugh he said that John could dye it the proper colors.

Benji found Jim who gave him a big hug. They were glad to be together. In a few minutes Hellie came along with her parents and introduced them. Her mother said that she wanted to meet Mr. Tailor who was so special in Helga's life and thank him for his help to her, especially in graduate school applications.

Jim said "I love your daughter. If I wasn't already married, I would have tried to marry her."

To which Mrs. Anderson replied "I think your relationship was close enough."

Jim was not about to ask for a clarification of that statement.

Hellie took Jim and Benji by the arms and stood between them. "Take our picture dad." Mr. Anderson raised his camera, the flash went off and the event was recorded for posterity. Hellie said she would send them each a copy of the picture.

As they parted Jim threw caution-to-the-wind and embrace Hellie. Benji also embraced her. It was his way of covering up the close relationship that Jim and Hellie shared. Jim wondered what h would do when they were no longer together. He had so much lov for both of them. Love he never imagined could be possible.

At the club house most professors emphasized the separation of student and professor. They decried intimacy and

222

close friendship in any manner. Jim thought that without people and intimacy life would be meaningless.

At this point in his career Jim began experiencing a strange phenomena. He started having nightmares which had variations on the same theme. In his dream he would look at his watch and find that his class was already starting. He couldn't remember how to get to the classroom or there was some impediment to getting to the classroom. In a variation he would dream that he picked up the fall schedule to find that he had a class that he hadn't covered and it was five weeks into the semester. Often he would dream that he was in the classroom and didn't know the subject he was supposed to be teaching. Or sometimes he couldn't get to the college because he left his car in the parking lot somewhere and couldn't find it. These are the nightmares of conscientious teachers.

It was soon Jim's turn to graduate and officially receive the doctorate and be consecrated into that holy society with all the rights, privileges and emoluments therein pertaining. Somehow it seemed anti-climactic.

Martha dressed the children in their finest garments with warnings not to get messed up and dirty. After all, they were representing the family. The family made their way to State College a.k.a. University Park. Martha drove since she thought Jim would be too nervous. Jim assured her he was nervous a month back and not now. It was Martha who was nervous. She admitted to this charge.

At the auditorium Jim ushered Martha and the children to a site in the rear section. There was an air of excitement and murmuring in the auditorium. He was directed to the front seating.

There were 47 doctoral recipients, 687 masters and 3,943 baccalaureates. Penn State was a large academic factory that spit out degrees at a fantastic rate.

The chancellor of the university did his usual routine of changing water into wine. He introduced a distinguished Penn State professor, a Pulitzer Prize winner, who gave the main address which was a lot of blather. Then he got to the main event.

Baccalaureate recipients rose as the chancellor waved a benediction toward them, thus anointing them with degrees. He went through the same metaphysical incantations for the master recipients. Graduation was an event in the finest medieval tradition.

The doctoral recipients were special. They were called to the stage one at a time and personally handed the degree by the chancellor. When Jim reached for his degree he could hear his daughter Susan scream out "Way to go Dad." The crowd roared approval. Jim waved his degree toward the back of the auditorium and took his place in the line of doctoral recipients.

Eventually all doctorates were dispensed. The chancellor gave a few closing remarks and the music started. "Pomp and Circumstance." An usher told Jim's row to follow the chancellor and the deans out of the building.

As Jim walked toward the rear his eye was attracted to two slightly waving figures seated at the aisle halfway up the auditorium. It was Benji and Hellie. He hadn't noticed them when he entered. His heart leaped with happiness.

Benji gave Jim a thumbs up. Jim paused momentarily and smiled. Hellie pursed her lips and blew Jim a kiss. He blew one back at her. It was the last time he would ever see Hellie but he would think of her for the rest of his life.